Acknowledgements

To say that this book has been an undertaking is an understatement. It has been a labor of love…and at times…filled with many frustrations. However, through it all, and even before it all, there have been people in my life that have helped me achieve the feat of writing those beautiful words…The End.

First, I would like to thank my wonderful husband, James; without your support and encouragement, this book would have just been another file on my computer. I am so thankful to have you in my corner, cheering me toward the goal of not only finishing but publishing this book.

In addition, this book wouldn't have been possible without the constant push from my two amazing children, Gabriel and Michael. Not only did you inspire me to lead by example: by following my dreams, your sardonic quips were the figurative whip I needed to get back to work on my own manuscripts all the many times I procrastinated with other projects.

During the writing of this book, I took a chance on submitting it for my post graduate certificate in creative writing. I will be eternally grateful to Humber College for accepting my application and for working with me on this manuscript. I will, forever, be indebted to the wonderful Helen Humphreys, my mentor, whose sharp eye and invaluable advice helped shape the final edits of this book. The Murders of Lillian Ross would never have reached this stage without your help and support.

Finally, I would like to thank everyone who has helped guide me along the road to become an author. Some people I would like to thank are: Heather Edwards for the words of encouragement whenever I was ready to throw in the towel. My beta readers through Stephanie Phillips. Colin McClelland, you will never understand how much I loved all of our conversations when we worked together. You taught me that there was a lot of good in the world and to trust in others when I often did the reverse. Annette Schoelier for being the ear that would listen when I would go off on a rant. And to Marilyn, a special teacher in my life, who pushed me into this wonderful world of words.

I appreciate all of you and thank you from the bottom of my being for the inspiration and support you have given me.

PROLOGUE

Recorded 11:17 A.M.

Operator (O): 911, state your emergency?

Caller (C): (inaudible)...I need help. (woman's voice)

O: Where are you?

C: (crying) I... (inaudible)

O: I can't hear you. Please calm down.

C: (crying)

(22 seconds pass)

O: Hello? Can you tell me where you are?

C: Oh, God! (crying) Oh God, why did they do this? Why?

O: Ma'am, I need you to tell me what happened. (inaudible...note: first responders are sent to traced address) I can send help.

C: Help? (inaudible)...No one can help. Oh, God, please no.

O: Did someone hurt you?

C: (crying)...They killed me. Oh, God! They killed me.

(Line goes dead.)

O: Hello? Hello? Are you there?

~911 Call Transcripts from the case "People vs. Lillian Ross"

●────────────────────────────●

It was a world of whispers.

The fluorescents buzzed quietly in the ceiling; the papers rustled as the small man in the gray tweed suit beside her, whose bald head gleamed with sweat, shuffled through his file...even the footsteps in the hall behind the heavy door where guards marched past whispered. Allison heard the footsteps fading down the corridor; listening for when they would finally stop in front of her door; opening it to reveal the prisoner.

The clock on the wall ticked silently, but Allison could hear each sweep of the hand as the seconds, then minutes, slid by. She hated waiting but, more so, hated the feel of this place.

It was a bright afternoon through the barred windows and Allison longed to be outside again. She could feel the stale oxygen in here, stifling, hot; the cloying mix of too many people crammed into the building and the artificial flowers from the air freshener. It was almost suffocating and made her head hurt.

Allison glanced at the man sitting beside her as he shifted again. *Ira shouldn`t be here,* she thought to herself, *but I need him this time.* It was hard for her to admit to needing anyone, and she felt a stab of guilt as she took in Ira`s features. He was only in his 60`s but every line crisscrossing his pudgy, red face added another year to his appearance. The only thing that remained youthful were his sharp, brown eyes scanning the paper in his craggy hands.

Ira had been her attorney ever since her father had passed away from cancer a few years before, and while he didn`t have to be at the meeting, Allison was thankful he'd come.

Ira had carefully buttoned up his suit jacket, straightened his tie and tucked the white handkerchief into his breast pocket before heading out today. Not once had Allison seen her attorney dress otherwise, either in the courtroom, or the grocers. Ira was a man of principles.

Currently, his handkerchief was clutched tightly between his fingers as he mopped away the sweat pooling on his brow. Ira placed the contract on the table, the fingers of his free hand slowly thumbed through the stack of papers as he tried to look calm.

I shouldn`t have brought him, she thought for the tenth time since picking him up. He hated prisons; his practice was in contract law and he rarely had to leave his office. But when she'd asked him, he'd come for her —and for her father—his best friend for over thirty years. He had spent the entire drive up to the state correctional reminding her that this wasn't in his job description and then the conversation had taken a worse turn when he lamented her choice of careers. Allison ground her teeth just thinking about the plea in Ira's voice.

"Why do you have to write *this*?" He had emphasized the last word.

Allison had given no answer. How could she when she didn`t know herself? She'd been writing since she was a child, but after college, she'd focused on true crime. She wasn't sure why the stories that actually destroyed lives were the ones she longed to put on paper. In the end, she supposed, it was unanswerable. That was her muse and she never felt settled unless she was pursuing a case.

Allison arched her back to remove the knot slowly building in her shoulders, before finding a more comfortable position in the metal chair. She knew who she was going to meet, who she was getting ready to interview, but she still didn't understand why she'd agreed.

That was the source of her stress. Not the fact that she was going face to face with a criminal. Since launching her true crime career a decade earlier, she had waited in similar rooms for sociopaths and murderers many times. It wasn't the criminal who made her nervous; it was the fact that this one had sought *her* out... had begged her to write the story behind her.

A loud click pulled Allison from her thoughts and the door swung open to reveal the guard and her prisoner.

Lillian Ross.

The name seemed ordinary enough; refined even. Yet this was a killer who had coldly murdered two men. Two men who had loved her. Allison wasn't naive. She was positive the two men had committed sins of their own, but there was nothing that could condone the way Lillian had butchered them.

To say that Lillian Ross was breathtaking was an understatement; even in the dingy orange prison-issued jumpsuit, Lillian was ethereal. Her long limbs filled the jumpsuit like she was on a model on the runway and her thick, chestnut hair, with deeper tones of mahogany, shone in the overhead lighting; cold fluorescents be damned. Her deep green eyes had more of an almond shape than Allison remembered from the photographs. Lillian was thin, but she looked far from fragile.

Allison searched the woman's face for resemblance to the photographs she'd seen, but the only features she recognized was the arch in her thin eyebrows and the plump, heart-shaped lips beneath a narrow, aristocratic nose. Gone was the blonde, blue-eyed beauty from the photographs. The real Lillian Ross was something much more breathtaking without the dyed hair and colored contacts. A shudder raced up Allison's spine as the green eyes locked with her own.

Swallowing her discomfort, Allison cleared her throat before standing up. "Miss Ross." She extended her hand, "I'm Allison McKinnon and this is my associate, Mr. Ira Novick."

Lillian inspected the outstretched hand hanging in front of her before she glanced at the guard and then extended her own. They stood there for a moment, each arm extended, fingers only inches apart, as though neither were sure what to do next before their fingers slid together. Lillian's skin was hot and dry.

Her heat lingered on Allison's skin after Lillian dropped her hand to her waist and murmured a greeting to Ira. "Pleased to meet you." Lillian's voice was low and husky, the tones barely audible as she slid gracefully into her chair. Lillian glanced quickly at the guard, a soft smile twisting the corner of her lips.

The guard shifted slightly at Lillian's glance and, for the first time since they'd entered the room, Allison really noticed her. The guard's deep ebony eyes matched her equally dark hair and her large build made Lillian seem almost childlike in front of her. Everything else blended into the gray of the prison—a silent, yet watchful presence in their meeting.

"Miss Ross..." Allison said after taking a deep breath.

"Lillian, please," Lillian's voice was cool, but rich.

"Miss Ross," Allison continued, "Because, you have requested that I work on a book about your story and before I actually agree to do so, I wanted to go over a few things. I thought it would be better to meet face to face to discuss this, and Mr. Novick is here with regards to any legal matters that may present themselves, specifically regarding the legal releases."

Allison winced. She wasn't usually this straight-forward. People had a tendency to close up when she was brusque, and she learned quickly that being so was the worst way to get a story. Lillian stared at her, unfazed by her manner, before she directed her gaze toward Ira, studying him intently. Ira's color rose from the soft flush to an angry red under her scrutiny.

"I know I contacted you, Miss McKinnon; I have no problem signing releases. I don't expect anything out of this except the opportunity to share my story." Her eyes remained focused on Ira.

"But why now?" The question slipped out and Allison cursed herself again for her unprofessionalism. She wasn't a novice, but something about Lillian made her feel like one.

"I never wanted to before," Lillian said softly, "but, as the years went by, I realized I owed an explanation for why I did those things."

The room echoed with her words and she was silent for a moment. "You know, there have been several books about the case," her tone shifted. "None of them had my side of the story; none had any insight into me. They were just fluff. Sensationalism that sold a few books before fading into obscurity. I used to be fine with that, but then I realized I wasn't anymore."

Lillian looked up, "I think it was the latest book about me, 'Deadly Debutant'. Have you read it?" Lillian fanned the air with her hand as though she was clearing away a bad smell. "It was very funny and completely fictional. The writer made me a spoiled debutante who wanted to experience the darker side of life; claiming I'd reacted violently whenever I was told 'no.' It was horrible...more horrible as I realized that I would be forever remembered as that debutante instead of who I really am."

Allison shifted slightly and looked up at the guard, who stood unmoving behind Lillian, her large hands resting comfortably at her waist. "But why did you choose me to write your story?"

Lillian looked out the barred window as she collected her thoughts, finally, she answered with a shrug, "I liked the way you wrote. It's respectful. You stay with the facts and you don't sensationalize things. You keep things interesting, even when you're citing the actual case. I liked that and realized I wanted your words to illuminate mine."

"You've read my work," the answer was obvious.

Lillian gave a slight nod.

"Then you understand I've always written from the side of the victims and their families. My books focus less on what made the criminal do what they did and more on the impact of their actions and how the survivors carried on. I don't think I could write the book the way you want it to be done."

There, she'd said it; her voice clearly implying that Lillian wouldn't get pity from her. If she wanted that, she would need to look for a new writer. No matter how awful Lillian's past could be, nothing condoned the slaughter of two people.

Lillian smiled slightly and her features were even more pronounced. Her beauty clashing with the ugliness inside her; the same one that led her to murder.

"I know how you write, Miss McKinnon. That's why I chose you. I want you to write about the victim—because, in the end, it is the victim who has to be remembered." The smile twisted as she said this, and Allison could sense that Lillian wasn't talking about the men she had murdered.

While those words still echoed through the room, Allison nodded to Ira. With an alacrity that surprised even Allison, he explained the release to Lillian, allowing Allison to withdraw into her thoughts, which had suddenly turned dark.

CHAPTER ONE

Detective Roger Modeure (DM): So what can you tell me about that night?

Lillian Ross (LR): (Silence)

DM: Look, I'm just trying to help you, and anything you tell me right now is going to do that.

LR: Hmm...

DM: Miss Ross, I know it's hard, but we need to know what happened in that apartment.

LR: Why?

DM: (pause)...To help you.

LR: You already know what happened, Detective... (Pause)...there really is no reason for me to give a statement.

DM: I'm going to be honest, Miss Ross. We have some idea of what went on, but we want to hear your side of the story.

LR: Well, detective, type up whatever you think happened and I'll agree with it because I have nothing to say.

~ Interview transcript between Miss Lillian Ross and Lead Investigating Detective Roger Modeure.

-- Time-stamp 3:45 P.M., location interrogation room   11B--

The gate to the prison buzzed with a loud hum before it slid open with a metallic clang making Allison jump slightly. She felt on edge today, and the hour drive up to the prison had done little to calm her nerves.

This was the first official interview with Lillian, and she hadn't seen the woman or heard from her since her visit with Ira. Even though all the legalities had gone smoothly, Allison had spent the entire week leading up to this interview with a quiet dread. Was she prepared enough? Had she done the research? Doubts invaded her hours as she waited for the hour to arrive.

Allison navigated down the lane toward the parking lot in front of the drab brown buildings of the state prison. The visitor's parking was mostly empty. Only a few cars were present and, outside of a shiny, black BMW, the cars were all dusty and dotted with rust marks. Probably families visiting a loved one.

The car's engine hummed lowly as it idled, and Allison stared at the small camera mounted on the wall across from her parking spot. She knew someone inside was watching her, taking note of the hesitation keeping her locked in her car, maybe even noticing the way her fists clenched the steering wheel as she deliberated whether it was all worth it. Would she gain anything from interviewing Lillian Ross?

She took in a deep breath and held it, counting out the seconds before she had to let it go. She always worried at the beginning. Always wondered about the razor's edge she walked when she interviewed the criminals. Would she recognize something in herself that was as dark and cold as the killer? Sometimes she felt the monster there worrying away the edges of her sanity.

Allison clenched the steering wheel and took another breath. She caught her eye in the rear-view mirror and steadied herself in it. She knew the panic attack was fading; gone within moments, and she no longer looked terrified. She climbed out of the car, pulled her brown bag from the passenger's seat and locked the door, following the signs to the visitor's gate. She was dressed less formally today, but she still presented the image of a professional.

Allison never had much attention from men. She wasn't tall or thin and her curves, while fitting snugly into a size ten, were considered chunky by most. Lillian Ross was her complete opposite, and Allison wanted to show her that she could present, if not a glamorous package, at least a professional one. "Shit," she muttered under her breath, realizing she was hesitating on the threshold of the prison. She smoothed her navy pencil skirt into place and stepped into the dark room before blinking away the glare from outside.

Across the small space, separated by a few feet of worn, white linoleum floor, a small glass cubicle housed a slightly overweight guard. She looked up, her lips tight, blue eyes dull as she performed a routine once-over of Allison, before returning to the paper she was reading. Obviously, the prim woman standing in the doorway was no threat.

To Allison, it reminded her of a large fishbowl instead of a workspace. Not for the first time, she wondered how the guards felt being trapped in the claustrophobic bubble only a few feet from freedom.

The guard ignored her approach and Allison waited patiently as she shifted her bag to her left hand. The guard continued to ignore her as she finished reading her paper and then she looked up at her. "I'm here for a visitation with Lillian Ross. My name is Allison McKinnon," she said before the guard, Officer Cronin from the name tag, could ask.

The guard took out a large ledger and flipped it open, her fingers slowly going down a list of visitors before reaching her name. She glanced back at Allison. "Identification."

Allison fished out the small, clear plastic picture wallet she used for visits to prisons and slipped it through the slot in the glass. Officer Cronin studied the photograph before she slid it out of the wallet and then had her sign the ledger.

"Step up to the door and I'll let you in," she directed, returning the identification.

Once past the door, Allison placed her bag on a table and waited as Officer Cronin's twin prepared to search her purse. The guard smiled at her slightly; a subtle, friendly look. "Can you open your bag, please?"

The bag was empty except for the essentials. In interviews, Allison always used a pencil and a simple pad of paper, preferring to jot down everything in point-form.

A metal clang shook the door as it opened up into the sally port allowing Allison to step in. The door slid closed behind her, and she waited for the second door to open.

Allison slowly walked into the waiting area and sat down. It was bittersweet to see the effort the prison officials had taken to make it homey. The walls were the same pink shade as the other room, but this room also offered a few magazines and a small play area for children visiting their mothers.

"Miss McKinnon," a masculine voice called out. Allison smiled at the tall, brown-haired guard—Officer Taylor, from the name tag—as he waved her over with his large hand. "The warden would like to speak with you for a few minutes."

The offices of Warden Careen Smith were simple and displayed an almost understated elegance. Allison could sense the woman who furnished the office in the simple things that adorned the room. It was there in the plush leather of the chairs, the abstract watercolor that hung over the large, mahogany desk, the neatness the files sitting in their appropriate folders.

Warden Smith gave Allison a warm smile as she looked up from the papers she was reading, her gray eyes cold and calculating.

"Miss McKinnon," she started, the southern drawl both thick and warm. "How's your mamma doing?"

The warden's voice was a perfect blend of southern hospitality and authority. She stood and stretched out her arm. Allison took the offered hand and didn't grimace at the firmness of the handshake.

"My mom's fine..." The word 'ma'am' hovered on her lips. She pressed them firmly together before saying, "Warden Smith."

"Oh, please. You know, by now, that Kai is fine," Warden Smith purred.

Allison nodded as she sank into the chair. She'd been here before, several times when she'd interviewed inmates for different projects, but a greeting on the first day wasn't usual for Kai. They both ignored the fact that Kai didn't know her mother; although she always asked about her. It was a fact that grated as much as Kai's insistence to be called by her nickname. It had been a few years since Allison had been to this prison, but it seemed as though old habits died hard.

As if reading her mind, Kai said, "I'm surprised to see you here again. I didn't think we had anyone here to pique your interest." Kai leaned back and folded her hands in her lap.

"I was surprised myself," Allison answered, focusing on the sparkling diamond wedding ring on Kai`s hand. "It's not my usual style to get involved in cases like this."

"I see," Kai said, her words clipped, the drawl gone.

If she wanted to, Warden Smith could lose the drawl as easily as she took off her coat.

The pause between them was fraught with an unexplained tension. Allison shifted in her seat as she watched Kai's hand smoothing away some invisible dust on the mahogany desk.

"Is there a reason why you wanted to see me, Kai?"

Kai smile lost all its warmth. "I always like to see ya, Allison. We talk about the most interesting things," the drawl was back, now even thicker than before. Allison's eyebrow cocked in answer, but she remained silent.

"I know ya follow the rules when you're here, but I wanted to remind ya of it before you went in to see…" The pause was accentuated by Kai rifling through a few papers. "Err. Before you went to see Lillian Ross," she finished.

Sighing, Allison nodded. "I know you didn't forget who I'm here to see, Kai," her voice was calm, and she forced it to remain neutral. "I know how well you run this place and how good you are about knowing everything that goes on in it."

Kai's eyes turned to steel at the challenge. She slammed her palm down on the papers with a loud bang making Allison's nerves hum. "You're right, Miss McKinnon," all civility gone from her tone, "I have never blocked a writer from coming in to interview my inmates, but I will if anything goes wrong with this one. Already, I've had a dozen calls about Lillian Ross. Someone heard that Lillian wanted to talk for the first time and concerned citizens are appearing out of the woodwork." Kai stood up and crossed to the barred windows, looking onto the prison grounds. "She seems to know the secrets of a lot of people, but I guess she would considering how many powerful men she slept with. At least, that's what I heard." Her voice faded away as though she'd lost the train of thought she had. "Normally, there isn't much fuss when a writer is working on a book about Lillian but, this time, it's different. She wants to talk and that has people worried that her clientele list will become public."

Allison watched Kai's back, the way her shoulders were tight as if she was holding the world at bay. She noticed the tightness in the warden's neck and the creases in her usually pristine suit.

"Have you been threatened?" Allison murmured.

Kai's shoulders sagged and she shook her head slightly, almost unnoticeable if Allison hadn't been watching her.

"No, not threatened," she said softly. "Advised. I've been advised that it is in the best interest for my career if I revoke your visitation rights."

Taking in a deep breath, Allison's heart hammered in her chest. "And are you?" she asked weakly.

Kai continued to stare out at the bleak prison grounds and shook her head.

"No," she hesitated before her voice gained confidence. "No, dammit. I don't really care what those bastards think. This is *my* prison and if you have visitation rights, then you get your visitation. But I want to make one thing clear, Allison…"

She pointed her first and second finger at Allison like she was cursing her. "If you upset my inmate in any way, or you make things harder for me than they already are, you will be out of my prison immediately. There will be *no* second chances. You will never be invited back here to interview *any* inmate. Do you understand me?"

They stared into each other's eyes, the clock slowly ticking as they took measure of the other. Allison finally nodded, "Yes, I understand you, Kai. Honestly, I'm not trying to cause any trouble for you."

A sharp laugh echoed through the room as Kai moved back to her desk. "That's always the problem, no one ever tries to cause trouble, but they do anyway," she said.

"Now, ya have an inmate to interview, so best be running along." Kai turned back to the papers on her desk.

And like that, the southern belle was back, and Allison was dismissed. She picked up her bag and slowly walked to the door before Kai said, "Oh, and Allison."

"Yes?" She stiffened as she stared at the door, praying Kai hadn't changed her mind.

"Ya have a good day."

Allison gritted her teeth, replying, "I will Kai, thank you." Allison closed the door behind her.

CHAPTER TWO

Jessica Hunt (JH): Oh sure, Lillian had plenty of admirers. She was the favorite of many guys. You know, they called up and asked for her personally.

Prosecutor Deveins (PD): Do you remember if any of the men called for her?

JH: No, I didn't take the calls. Adam had a few girls to take calls but when it came to Lillian's clients, it was usually him or Lillian who scheduled things. It was funny; he seemed to only trust her.

PD: What do you mean, 'only trust her'?

JH: You know, he would let her in on the business end of things. Tell her things he wouldn't tell the other girls, is what I mean.

PD: Did they have a sexual relationship?

JH: I think they did at one time, at least that's what I heard...but by the time I came around, they weren't fuc...uh... I mean banging as far as I knew. They were close, though. I think Adam loved her in his way. You know, just like she loved him.

PD: You think they were in love?

JH: (Laughs) Well, not head over heels, if you know what I mean— but they had something there. I mean, they did before everything happened.

PD: You mean before the attack?

JH: Oh no, I mean before everything happened...

~ Official Court Transcripts: People vs. Lillian Ross--

The door slid open and Allison swallowed the cold lump of panic rising in her throat. Kai had left her wondering about the "concerned citizens". Who were they? Why were they so concerned that Lillian was talking? From the background research she'd done, Lillian had worked as an escort for several years. Although nothing was brought to light—at least in the courtroom—there had been speculation she'd been hired by a number of powerful men.

Kai's disclosure made Allison spend the few minutes before the interview chewing on the information. She did not feel ready to interview Lillian anymore; all of her preparations had been burnt to ashes by the questions Kai had left her with.

Nothing had changed for Lillian, however. She looked the same as she walked into the room followed by the same guard who'd brought her in the week before. While she seemed unsure the last time, today Lillian walked in with her head high and her shoulders straight.

She looks like a woman who hasn't a worry in her life, Allison thought to herself.

Lillian slipped into the chair without an acknowledgement. The guard, Officer Jenkins, nodded as she removed the restraints around Lillian's wrists.

"I'll be outside the door," Officer Jenkins said. "If you need anything, just holler and I'll be right in."

She was looking directly at her, but Allison had the feeling she was talking to Lillian. *Strange*, she thought as the tall guard moved out of the room. Lillian took the moment to shift in the chair.

"Miss Ross," Allison began, "It's good to see you again."

"It's good to see you," Lillian replied softly, making Allison lean closer to hear.

Taking a steadying breath, Allison began. "Since this is our first official interview, I just want to outline a few things. First, I try to limit the notes I take when I'm here, but there will be some things I need to jot down. Don't feel you need to stop talking because I can always keep up. Second, I don't tape interviews. I write what I need to, and I focus on what you're saying. I find the tape just detracts from that. So, if you are wondering why I only have paper and pencils out, that would be the reason. Third, I let you lead the story, so I limit my questions to clarifying points. This is your chance to tell your story.

Lillian nodded and leaned back in her chair. "That's fine," she said slowly. "Whatever works."

"So, we can begin then?"

Silence filled the room again and Allison wondered how long they would sit there, the two of them face to face, the only sounds coming from the soft creaks of the chairs and the muffled noises of the prison.

"I suppose you want me to start with the murders."

Allison shook her head, "Not necessarily. We don't have to rush into things and, really, I want you to be comfortable with how the story is told. If you want to start with the crime, then we can, and we'll work back from there."

Allison risked a glance at Lillian and saw the relief filling the convict's face. Lillian leaned back in her chair, tension rolling out of her shoulders and her ivory mask softened into vulnerable lines that were even more feminine, if that was possible. Her hands spread out on the arms of her metal chair and the mahogany hair tumbled around her face, framing her deep green eyes.

She remained in that pose for minutes, the clock ticking away as Allison waited, resisting the urge to fidget with her pencils.

She was vaguely aware of what they looked like to anyone glancing in the room, but one thing she'd learned, the hard way, was to let the interviewee start the story. It didn't matter where they started, or how quickly they jumped into it, all that mattered was that she gave them time to collect their thoughts.

As if on cue, Lillian took a deep breath and let it out slowly. Allison raised her eyes at the exact moment Lillian did and their gazes locked. Lillian's eyes were swimming with some unknown emotion. *Insecurity, hesitation, fear?* Lillian said, "I suppose it's best to start at the beginning; at the point where I became me."

Allison nodded slightly as Lillian's voice picked up speed, gaining strength with every word she said.

"I guess you know the logistics of it all. Where I was born, who my parents are, the type of life I was destined for. It's been in all the books and there isn't much more I can add to that."

Allison nodded. "But you can start there." Doubt flashed in Lillian's eyes.

"I often find it is easier to tell a story if you start with little facts. The stuff that helps collect your thoughts together," Allison assured her.

Lillian shrugged her shoulders, took a deep breath, and then exhaled. "My parents were William and Irene Ross," Lillian paused, her lips twisting into a wry smile. "Of course, you know we were rich. Very rich; old money, new money, other people's money, yet it wasn't enough for my father. He wanted the power that went with it, so he bought and sold the careers of many politicians."

Allison's eyes widened slightly, and she turned a questioning gaze at Lillian.

"Shocking, isn't it. Most people knew he was in politics, but no one knew how many politicians were in his pocket. He didn't want the fame...just the power. It suited everyone else to keep my father's aspirations quiet during the trial. It was never a fair trial—I knew that the very moment I was charged."

Lillian grimaced before her face went carefully blank, as if she had trained it not to give anything away.

"They described him as a saint," she continued. Her words held no anger, but there was an icy edge to them, which was even scarier, especially when paired with the empty eyes that stared across the room at what Allison could only assume to be some speck on the wall.

"Who was I to remove that image? I mean, look at what I had done. I had stolen a saint from the world and people cried at the horror of it all."

Allison kept her face relaxed and pulled on all her experience to keep her emotions neutral. All the stories started this way, a revelation that life hadn't had a silver lining for the perpetrator. That either it was 'the system' or some other abuse

~ 21 ~

that led them down the dark path. It was always something, and usually it was just different tellings of the same story.

"When it came down to it," Lillian continued, her fingers pushing her long mane from her face, "it was easier to let them paint their own image of the crime and just agree with it. I mean, no matter what I said, they wouldn't believe me. Everyone who had secrets was terrified I would spill them, or that my father's business dealings would come to light. They were scared of all those secrets..." Her voice trailed away and her blunt fingernails bit into the edge of the table as she scratched at a mark on it.

"I was scared of those secrets, so I accepted the lie and ended up here." Tears brimmed in her eyes and she swiped at them before they could fall. "I guess I wanted my father to be what people said he was. Maybe I owed him that much for everything I did."

Allison looked down at her legal pad and realized that the only word on it was "secrets" underlined three times, but Lillian's words swirled in her head, branding themselves in her memory. There was something Lillian wasn't telling her. Some lie that she had gone along with, and as suddenly as the question formed, it began to click in place. Lillian had never fought for her innocence. The trial had been simple. Lillian had hired a defense attorney, but they hadn't had a defense. She had never testified; no appeals were filed...no evidence was disputed. It was as though she had gone through the motions, then just handed the prosecution their case. She had only pretended to fight.

"Are you saying that you didn't kill your father?" Allison asked.

Her mind thrilled with the possibilities before Lillian glared at her, eyes flashing with anger as she snapped, "No, I killed him, and I don't regret it. In fact, I would have killed the bastard twice if I could have."

CHAPTER THREE

Prosecutor Deveins (PD): Can you please state your name and maiden name for the record?

Hayley Forester (HF): Hayley Ann Forester, my maiden name was Hayley Ann Ross.

Prosecutor Deveins (PD): And what is your relationship to the deceased Mr. William Conrad Ross?

HF: I'm his...he was my father.

PD: You're Mr. William Ross's daughter. And Mrs. Forester, can you tell me about your father?

HF: He was a simple and good man who loved us very much... Lillian... (Sobbing)

PD: Mrs. Forester, can you answer the question?

(Pause)

HF: Yes. He was a very good father to Lillian and me; caring and protective. All he wanted was the best for us. He wanted what was best for everyone he cared for or even worked with.

PD: Did you have a good relationship with your father?

HF: (Long Pause) Yes, I had a good relationship with him.

PD: Did your sister, Lillian Ross?

HF: (Pause) Yes, before she ran away, she did, but we hadn't seen her for over fifteen years.

PD: Did you love your father Mrs. Forester?

HF: Yes...And Lillian loved him too. I don't understand how she could do what she did. After everything he did for us. After he loved us so much. How could you do it, Lillian? How could you?

~ Official Court Transcripts: People vs. Lillian Ross

●————————————————————————————●

The room seemed to echo with Lillian's words, or maybe they were simply echoing in Allison's mind, churning with a mix of emotions. She had come to the prison knowing that Lillian was guilty, but she never imagined the woman would admit to it so readily, and with such cold, unmasked fury. Lillian was *happy* she'd murdered him.

Lillian's harsh laugh broke the echoing silence and Allison studied her closely. Fine lines creased the corners of her eyes and she looked tired; as though she hadn't slept for years. Her one hand ran through her hair again while her other tapped the edge of the table.

"Don't get me wrong, Allison," she said. "I loved my father, but he wasn't an easy man to love. I mean, we had to love him. It was expected of us and, for the briefest of moments, as the blood was pouring out of him, all I felt was love. Then the horror of knowing that I had killed someone I loved."

She fidgeted in her coveralls and withdrew a small, white package, dented and creased. Lillian lifted it up for Allison to see the cigarettes, "Do you mind?"

Shaking her head, Allison watched as Lillian pulled out a cigarette, carefully lighting it. She sucked in a deep breath of smoke, then nestled the cigarette between her middle and index fingers before she exhaled; the musky scent of tobacco filled the room immediately.

"You know I didn't smoke until I went to prison." She laughed and took a second pull, her nostrils flaring as she exhaled a stream of thick smoke. "I mean, I did a lot of things, but drugs and cigarettes were not one of them. Once I got here though..."

She shrugged as though that explained it. She looked more relaxed with each inhalation of smoke. A black tattoo on her wrist flashed and Allison realized it was some type of writing.

"What does your tattoo say?" She asked.

Lillian glanced down at her wrist and pulled the sleeve of her shirt down to cover the tattoo. "Nothing...just some Hebrew word that looked pretty."

"So, you said that your father was hard to love. Why was that?" Allison asked the question to steer them back to the story.

"He was William Ross. How could he not be hard to love? He loved power. Loved to have power over people. It gave him a sense of purpose, a sense of the world being right, and it wasn't just in politics. Our lives were ruled by him. He chose what we wore, what we ate, how we acted. He wanted the perfect family with the perfect wife. My mother had to create the ideal balance of what a respectable woman was. Enough charitable work to prove that she was caring but not so much that she could be accused of being neglectful to her family. His daughters had to be delicate dolls," Lillian's face darkened. "Beautiful, refined, polite; wonderful to see but we were never to be heard, especially when people were in the house."

A soft twang tinged her words, but the bitterness was clear. Lillian had definitely chaffed at the restraints her father had placed on her as a child.

Was that what had driven her to kill him or was it more?

"I know that your family had Southern ties," Allison said quietly. "Your mother was from an old Southern family. She studied at Old Miss and your father was from old money with a lot of connections."

Lillian waved her hand to stop Allison. "I loved what they stood for; you know. I was proud of my mother and all her causes. I always thought we were normal, that children all over the country had a father like mine. I never thought of my father's..." Lillian's voice trailed off and she looked up at the ceiling, "...work. There was always someone at the house trying to get a favor or two from him. It was exciting in a way, but those deals were the only real things about my family and my house. Everything else was fake, or the truth was stretched so thin I was never sure what *was* real."

Lillian ran her finger over the metal armrest and slipped them underneath, following the line of steel. "My father was proud of his southern wife and his southern children, although he didn't want us *too* southern. We were supposed to be the storybook version of the South. The gentle breeze; the soft accent. Yes, the genteel women that was the very definition of refinement. He wanted that for his image, although, my mother was never truly allowed to be southern; truly herself. When we displeased him, which was often, he made sure we knew it."

Allison waited, longing to ask the question. She almost sighed in relief when Lillian answered it for her.

"He hit my mother," Lillian said to the table. "Made her regret everything about herself. Made her regret her life, made her blind to everything that was happening in her own house. The only time she was ever a mother, ever herself, was in her garden."

Her voice faded and she stared through the barred windows now, a far-away look in her eyes, "I suppose that's why I loved her garden."

"Her garden," Allison repeated, raising an eyebrow.

"Yes, Momma's garden." Lillian's voice turned dreamy as she remembered, "I loved her garden completely."

●━━━━━━━━━━━━━━━━━━━━━━━━━━━●

"Lillian! Quick, come here girl!" Momma's voice was calling to me and I quickly followed it across the green expanse of the carefully tended gardens.

The sight of my mother in her long white dress, a straw sun hat perched on her head and her long honey curls captured in a ponytail at her neck made me smile. She was beautiful in the sunshine; as if all her worries were erased from her face as she held out a long-fingered hand to me.

"Come on Lillian," she beamed. "I have something to show you."

"What is it Momma?" I asked, aware of how my long fingers fit perfectly into her hand.

"Look baby," she murmured, pointing up into a tree. "We have a visitor."

My gaze followed her finger to a small, white bird sitting on a low branch, the yellow on its head strikingly bright as the color shone in the noonday sun. The chestnut on its breast made the bird look even more exotic than the head did.

"What type of bird is it Momma?"

Momma smiled. "A Chestnut-Sided Warbler, sweetie. Isn't he beautiful? Just like my girls," Momma whispered, her eyes crinkling with delight.

For a moment, I was warmed by the look in her eyes instead of the sun as I glanced over at Hayley, my baby sister playing on her blanket in the sun. She looked more like Momma than I did with her honey curls and her big blue eyes, but I didn't mind. She was just a baby and she couldn't share special moments with Momma like I could. At least, not yet.

The bird chirped noisily from the tree before taking flight into the forest behind our garden. I sighed at the magic in its song, feeling Momma's hand gently squeeze mine.

"What do you think we should do now Lillian?"

"Can we play hide and seek?" I asked hopefully, biting my lip.

Momma's radiant smile was replaced by a sad, mournful one. She glanced at the glass doors leading into the sprawling house, then back at me. Her gaze locked on my teeth biting into my lips. "Don't bite your lip Lillian; you know that's a bad habit."

She paused a moment before slowly shaking her head. "No Lillian, you know we have guests today and you need to stay clean. If we play hide and seek, you'll get your dress dirty."

Worry replaced the light in Momma's eyes, and I fidgeted in my spot. I didn't want to make her worried...I didn't want to upset her, but it seemed like I always did. No matter how hard I tried, Momma would look sad about something I said.

"I know," Momma said quickly. "Why don't we pick flowers for the party?"

I tried to look excited as I nodded but I wanted to play hide and seek. Flowers were boring unless you were planting them. The rest of the work was better left to the gardener. Just as I started toward the roses, a dark shadow fell over me. I shivered and looked up into the green eyes of my father. His dark complexion and deep mahogany hair created a striking contrast to Momma's sunny looks.

"Lillian, get your sister and get in the house. Your mother and I need to talk."

Momma's back straightened and I gave her a worried glance. She caught my eye and nodded slowly, her voice trembling. "You go on and get your sister now. I'll be up in the house shortly."

I could feel the storm brewing in my father's gaze and wondered at his anger. What had we done to make him angry? We were dressed for the party; we weren't dirty. There was nothing for him to be angry about. Nothing. I fought the tears threatening to slide down my cheeks and scooped up Hayley, her feet kicking the air as I tried to get the toddler under control.

I could see my mother standing by the roses, her back stiff and her chin up in defiance but the tears pooling in her eyes gave the lie away. She wasn't strong and I wondered if she had ever been.

"Irene," my father's voice echoed across the grass as I tried to outrun the anger in his words. "I asked for the girls to be ready for our company, not out here playing in the dirt."

"They were just enjoying—"

A loud clap cut off her words like a knife. I glanced back as a sob sliced through the yard. My father stood above her, his hand clenched in a fist in her long hair, pulling her face toward his. An angry, red welt, the shape and size of his hand, burned on my momma's cheek. I stopped, tears running down my face, Hayley clutched to my chest.

"You will not answer back," Daddy said through gritted teeth. My momma's eyes darted around as she looked for an escape, any escape from the man in front of her.

"Yes, William," she breathed as tears ran down her cheeks, her finely applied makeup ruined.

My father stood, straightened his suit jacket and released her hair. "Clean yourself up for our guests. If you're not fit to be seen, I'll tell them you went to bed early with a headache." With this said, he calmly began to walk across the yard toward me. My heart leapt into my throat and Hayley squirmed in my grip.

"Lillian," he said, "Did I *not* tell you to get into the house?"

My gaze flicked to my momma, but her back was turned to us, her shoulders heaving under the sobs wracking her body. "Never mind your mother. She'll be along shortly but it's time for you and your sister to go in."

With that, his large hand, still warm from striking my mother, wrapped around my arm as he dragged me behind him into the dark house that felt cold compared to the warmth I had just left.

●————————————————————————————●

"Are you saying your father struck your mother?"

Lillian raised an eyebrow and lit a second cigarette off the end of the first.

"Yes, he hit her. That was the first time I had ever seen it. I was about five. Before I saw that, I thought he only hit me. It was the first time..."

The pause grew into a lengthy silence. *Is this it?* Allison wondered. *Is this all she wanted to tell the world, that her father hit them?* But she knew in her heart there was more.

There always was.

Lillian glanced up at Allison, her face slack, her eyes shining with unshed tears and she looked young, vulnerable and unsure of what to say. "It was the first time..." her voice cracked with emotion. "The first time I realized I wasn't the only one he hurt."

CHAPTER FOUR

Excerpt of opening argument from Prosecutor Harold Deveins:

Lillian Ross is not a victim. She plays the victim because it's easy for her to do so.

We all want to believe that a woman as beautiful and fragile as Miss Ross appears to be is pure and innocent.

During this trial, you will hear some shocking things from the defense. They will tell you about a girl born with all the privileges of wealth and status; a girl who didn't understand the harder side of life; the darker side. They'll tell you that Lillian Ross was confused and lured away from her home by Adam Laurent. Kidnapped, and abused until she couldn't think; couldn't do anything except give Adam Laurent what he wanted...

But she wasn't the victim doing what she was told. The defense will tell you that it was Adam who set everything up, Adam who lured Mr. William Conrad Ross to his apartment on that cold, winter day, Adam who had tried to blackmail him for money.

They will tell you that Adam Laurent became violent when William Conrad Ross refused the blackmail and demanded to know where Lillian was. They will tell you that Lillian watched helplessly as Adam stabbed William Conrad Ross. Not once, not twice...but eleven times before he cut his throat. They will tell you that Lillian reacted the only way a good daughter could. She raced over to protect her father, suffered horrible injuries in doing so, and ultimately killed Adam Laurent in self-defense.

But I ask you to consider this, members of the jury, why did she wait so long?

I wonder why a woman as fearful and abused as Lillian Ross would even think to stand up against her abuser?

The answer is simple. Lillian Ross wasn't the victim; she was the attacker. She wasn't happy at home; we know that. She ran away at the age of fifteen and had not been seen since. Before she left, she was a troublemaker keeping company with a bad crowd. She was failing school, combative with her parents and destructive to everyone including herself. She ran away. She wasn't kidnapped, and she became nothing more than a common prostitute.

Lillian thrived in that role; and you will hear throughout this trial how successful she was as a prostitute. You will also see the sad story of fading looks that were quickly making her less successful. You will hear how it was her plan to blackmail her father, William Ross, for exorbitant sums of money so he could hide the shame of a fallen child.

But William Ross tried to bring his eldest daughter back to the family, to save her from the hell she was living and so she retaliated. Lillian Ross enjoyed her life; loved the danger and the men that would pay to have sex with her. She didn't want her old life back...all she wanted was the money her old life offered her, something her father wasn't willing to give her.

The truth you will hear in this courtroom is that Lillian Ross planned the meeting at the apartment. She planned to take out all her anger on her father and it was her delicate hand that slashed his throat. Her delicate hand that turned on Adam Laurent.

Ladies and gentlemen of the jury, it was Lillian Ross, who sits before you with no remorse, and no explanation. It was Lillian Ross with blood-stained hands. Throughout this trial, it is my job to show you just how cold and calculating Lillian Ross truly is.

~ Official Court Transcript: People vs. Lillian Ross

Allison pushed open the door and stumbled into the front hall of her three-bedroom Victorian home. The quiet of the house was a welcome respite after the constant hum of the prison.

A large, gray cat came running down the stairs and curled around her legs, rubbing his oversized head against the back of her calves.

"Hello there Mercutio...did you miss me?" She bent down and gathered him into her arms. Her bag, filled with the notes from the prison, fell forgotten to the floor as she cuddled Mercutio and walked into the kitchen.

The knot in her shoulders, which had been throbbing constantly, eased up enough for her to ignore it as she set the cat on the counter. "Waiting for dinner, were you?"

Mercutio meowed in agreement.

Allison opened a can of cat food, the cat's green eyes watching her intensely as she worked. She tried to ignore the questions nagging at her since leaving the prison.

She wasn't sure why, but something about Lillian's story bothered her. Nothing screamed that her story was really any different from the many other convicts Allison had interviewed. They all had had a similar tale: abuse, lies, broken homes, despair. The proverbial why behind what they had done but it was always an excuse; the reason they did the horrible things was because they had wanted to.

That Lillian's story was the same wasn't surprising, yet, she told it with such clarity and without any hint of remorse. It was clear Lillian viewed it as a fact and wasn't looking to make any excuse for what she had done. The intensity in her eyes had blazed when she spoke of killing her father...the surety that she would have done it again was chilling. It hinted at the meat of the story.

Another loud and lamented meow from Mercutio drew her from her thoughts. He glared at her from his perch on the black granite counter and she sighed, "Sorry. I didn't mean to keep you waiting, you old grump."

She placed his dish on the counter in front of him and gently tapped him on the forehead. He continued to glare at her before he finally flicked his tail and turned to his dinner.

Allison noticed, for the first time, the flashing from the answering machine and she scowled at it before pulling out a long-stemmed wine glass, filling it with a red wine she'd left sitting on the counter from the night before. She took a long draw and continued to watch her cat. From the darkened hall table, the light continued to blink out of the corner of her eye like the name of a song that slipped the mind.

Lillian's father had been a great man by all accounts. This Allison knew. She'd spent the last year poring over witness statements and news articles outlining the good he'd done. William

Ross's entire life had been dedicated to helping others in need. There was never any indication of abuse toward either his wife or his daughters. In fact, the family had, by all outward appearances, been very close. The only thing that had marred their seemingly pristine life before the murder was when their eldest daughter had disappeared. The thread was there, Allison was sure of it, and she would have no choice but to access the newspapers around that event.

William Ross had given many interviews at that time, positive his daughter had been kidnapped. But after weeks that turned into months had gone by without any ransom note, Lillian was forgotten by the press and the family slipped back into obscurity.

William Ross had been active in his usual causes, one being the Center for Missing and Exploited Children. Still, the actual man was relatively unknown by the media until his death. From all the witness statements, he had been a good man; some had even dared to say great.

Lillian's story was contrary to everything published to date. Allison gritted her teeth. Turning to the window; she stared at nothing but the images flashing through her head of the earlier visit. Dusk was falling and her simple, often neglected, garden was cast in twilight. There was a melancholy glint to the light and Allison felt tears stinging her eyes.

"They always appear to be good men," she said to the room, the only listener being Mercutio, who was content, for the moment, with a full belly and he ignored such silly chatter from his human. "But that makes it all the worse."

A hard lump in her throat made it difficult to breathe as she tried to clear it with a deep cough...but it was lodged there, making the wine difficult to swallow as she drained her glass. The wine felt sour in her stomach. "What do you think Mercutio, should I believe her or not?" she asked, turning from the window.

The only answer was a reproachful glare from the cat before he licked his dinner from around his mouth, jumped off the counter with a loud thump and snaked his body around her ankles.

A shrill noise rang out through the room making Allison jump, her feet tangled around the cat, and she almost fell as she did so. The phone went off a second time and Allison sighed at the intrusion. Regardless of how dark her thoughts were, at least she'd caught a thread to work with.

The metallic click of the answering machine echoed through the house before her slightly muted voice rang out, '*You have reached Allison McKinnon. I'm either in my office, or not here, so leave a message.*'

"Allison," the familiar voice cut through Allison's nerves. She loved her mother, but she loved her more when they didn't talk.

"Allison. Pick up. I know you're there. I had Frank drive by on his way home so just pick up!"

The tone was a mixture of reproach and determination. Allison sighed. The last thing she wanted to do was talk to her mother.

"Look," her mother continued, "I've already left you three messages! I'm going to call you all night until I hear from you, young lady."

Young lady. Her mother reserved that endearment for times when she was really upset. Allison started over to the wall-mounted cordless. "Ira phoned me, young lady. He's worried about you and your latest project..."

Allison picked up the phone. "Hi Mom."

"I didn't expect you to pick up," Ruth said slowly after a short pause.

Allison closed her eyes and gritted her teeth. "What are you calling about?"

"As I already said, Ira phoned me today. He's worried about you since you took your latest job. I thought you were taking a break from your stories." Her mother's voice was filled with reproach.

Allison rolled her eyes and returned to her wine glass, filling it with more of the ruby liquid, "I was going to, Mom, but a really good story landed in my lap and I couldn't pass it up. It's just a regular book. Ira shouldn't have phoned you." *Especially since he's my lawyer,* she added silently.

"Don't get chippy with me," her mother snapped. "You know very well that Ira would never have phoned me if he didn't think you were pursuing the wrong story. He knows you can take care of yourself, dear... everyone knows you can take care of yourself. You've been proving that ever since your father died but, the truth is, there's going to be a time when you won't be able to handle everything that's thrown at you."

Taking another mouthful of her wine, Allison glared at her reflection in the window. "I know Mom—you have been telling me that for the last two years."

"But you haven't listened to me, Allison," Ruth McKinnon went on. To Allison, her mother was starting to sound like nails on a chalkboard. "It's like you never thought I could protect you. Never thought I would protect you and now you seem to think that I'm the one to blame for everything." Ruth's voice trailed away; a soft sob echoed through the phone line.

"Have you protected me Mom?" Allison couldn't keep the anger out of her voice. So many years, so many things between them and she *still* felt angry, "If you *had* protected me, Dad never would've had to step in. If you'd been there, maybe I would feel like I could turn to you when I needed help. The reality is, you aren't there—you never were!"

A hum filled the phone and Allison swiped at the tears burning her eyes. It didn't matter how much time had passed, they still circled around that same day; both of them afraid to say the things that really mattered.

"Allison..."

She held her breath; her mother's voice was so full of pain that, for a moment, Allison was ready to apologize for everything. *No!* The voice inside her urged, *everything was her fault, everything and she has* never *apologized to you!*

"Mom, I'm not getting into this with you, I took this story for my own reasons; I don't need to explain. I'm going to see it to the end, no matter what you or Ira say. I'd appreciate it if you stopped talking to my attorney about me, despite how long you two have been friends."

Her voice didn't waver at all, although her heart hammered in her chest.

Ruth remained silent on the other end, but Allison could hear her breathing; the pause stretched between them for so long that Allison said, "Mom?"

"That's fine Allison," Ruth sighed. "I was just concerned about you, but I guess I should have known not to bother you at all." Ruth's voice was crisp as she bit off each word. Allison had no doubt that her mother would prefer to dig deeper but these ground rules had been established long ago.

"Well, if you're decided..." the question hung on her mother's tone.

"I am," Allison murmured, glancing out the window again, as though that would offer her an escape from the guilt niggling at her.

"I can't apologize for things already said and done, Allison," her mother said in defeat. "I've tried to do right by you since everything happened, but you won't allow it."

"I know, Mom."

"I have a lot of work to do tonight, Mom. Why don't I call you in a few days when I am not so focused on this book?"

"A few days is too late, Allison," Ruth murmured, her words edged with tears, a perfect switch from the angry clip of a few moments ago.

Allison rolled her eyes as her mother continued. "From what Ira was saying, this... this criminal is the one that asked you to interview her and he's scared that it may bring up...things...for you."

Allison emptied the rest of the bottle into her wine glass; the red liquid splashed over her hands and trickled between her fingers like blood. She winced at the thought and carefully wiped away the wine with the dishcloth.

"Mom, I didn't tell you about this because I didn't want you to worry. This book is no different than the other ones and it's not going to bring anything back, okay? I've worked through this. I closed the lid on that part of my life, and you were there watching me do it."

Ruth began, "I know...but—"

Allison cut her off, "I really have to go Mom. Don't worry about this project and I'll call you in a few days."

With that, she stabbed the off button with her finger and tossed the cordless on the counter. She turned from the sink and saw Mercutio still watching her.

"And that is the reason why she doesn't have my cell number," she said to the cat before picking up her wine glass.

CHAPTER FIVE

I heard screams but I didn't think to call the police. I mean, I know what goes on behind those closed doors and that wasn't the first time I had heard screams from that apartment. Men came and went all the time, usually with the same woman. In fact, I don't think anyone really lived at the apartment. Not full time.

Lily was such a nice girl. Always asking to help carry my bags whenever she saw me, and it wasn't easy for me to cart bags up to my apartment. Lily would come for tea...she made me feel like a school girl again, it was like sharing secrets with a friend. (Fifteen second pause) I guess that's why she had all those gentlemen callers. She made them feel young. Some of those men were old enough to be her father, maybe even her grandfather. I know, I would watch them come to the apartment from my peephole. They were always all over her.

Still, when I heard the screams that night, I just figured one of the girls had a gentleman caller. I just turned up the volume to my television. I couldn't believe when the police came and took that poor Lily girl out of the apartment. I mean, I'm sure that she didn't hurt anyone. She was such a gentle soul; such a good girl...I couldn't see her doing anything wrong."

~ Witness Report of Mildred Schuntz; People vs. Lillian Ross

The fluorescent light over them buzzed an annoying song throughout the room. Allison fought the urge to fidget and focused on the same smudge on the table that had been there the day before.

The interview had started off the same as it had the day before, with Lillian being led into the room, then a few pleasantries exchanged as the guard left. Twenty minutes had passed, and they were still sitting together, quietly pondering the smudge.

Lillian's voice cut through the silence, "What's it like out there?"

Allison's eyes flicked to the windows and the gray skies beyond. She had woken up to the sounds of the storm after a restless night, but she couldn't remember what had kept her up all night. Was it the story Lillian was weaving for her? Or was it the demons of her own past that had come back to plague her... Whatever it was, the night had left her mood as gray as the dawn had been.

Allison answered her. "Wet and gray."

Lillian leaned forward. "Not the weather," she said, shaking her head slowly. "How is it out *there*?"

She emphasized her last word and Allison realized she wasn't interested in the local farmer's report. A longing flashed across Lillian's face before it became a blank slate again.

"The same as it always is," Allison answered. "Everyone is rushing around; no one really takes the time to connect with anyone. We barely notice the weather unless it's a hindrance. I don't think much of anything has changed, really."

Her voice trailed away but Allison was sure Lillian knew what she meant to say from the tightening of her jaw. The world hadn't changed in the five years that Lillian had been in prison.

Lillian turned her attention to the window as a flash of lightning lit up the dark sky. "What do you do when you are out there?"

"I work, clean the house, live." Allison shrugged her shoulders. Normally, she wouldn't answer these questions, but Lillian was not talking so she felt like someone should.

Thinking about her answer, Allison was reminded of how empty her life really was. If she thought about it, all she did was work. If she wasn't writing, she was researching. When she wasn't researching, she was interviewing. She rarely saw her mother, and she had a handful of friends, who were, more often than not, busy with their own families. Lovers had been limited and the last man in her life had been over two years before. Really, the only people she spent any amount of time with were Ira and her cat.

As if sensing her thoughts, Lillian asked, her eyes now boring into Allison's own. "And your husband? What does he do?"

Allison hesitated and bit her lower lip, "I'm not married," she said slowly, "and no boyfriend either." she added before Lillian could ask.

Lillian's eyebrow raised and she looked pensively at Allison, judging her perhaps. Allison fidgeted in her chair.

"Why not?"

Why not? If it was only as easy as a why or why not. Allison could think of a million reasons why not one guy or the next, but it always came back to her. Why hadn't she been good enough? Why not her? Rubbing her forehead, Allison put down the pencil that had been resting in her left hand, "Really, I've just been too busy." Her answer was firm, trying to end the conversation right there.

Lillian ignored her. "Have you ever been in love?"

"No," Allison snapped. "Have you?"

Lillian picked at her fingernails, which were as uneven and unpolished as Allison's and, for once, Allison found a flaw in Lillian's beauty. A small one but, at least, it was there.

"No," Lillian whispered. "No... I have never been in love."

Pain flashed across her face and Allison knew she was lying. "What about Adam?"

Lillian snorted in derision. "Adam? God no. I never loved Adam. I believed I did at one time, but I was just grateful to him for saving me. For taking me away from the hell I'd been living in. It was nothing more than a schoolgirl's crush. He capitalized on it."

Allison slowly picked up her pencil and watched as Lillian stood and moved to the window to watch the rain. In Lillian, a storm was brewing as well.

"When did you meet Adam?" Allison asked.

Lillian kept her back to the room. "I was fifteen. I'd been living on the street for about two months by that time. He was a small-time pimp with big aspirations and when he first picked me up; he figured he just had a new girl. He quickly realized he had found his meal ticket —the start of his 'great plan'."

"Why did you run away?"

Lillian turned from the window and leaned against it. Years of pain and anguish were etched across her face and, for the first time, Allison knew that this was the real Lillian; an emotional one instead of the calm creature that had been sitting here like a fragmented stone statue for the last two days.

"Why does any girl run away?" Lillian asked plainly.

Allison ignored the question and simply waited. After a few moments, "Because there were things in my life that were so unbearable I had nowhere else to go. Fine. There it is," Lillian said.

"How did you meet Adam?"

Lillian grimaced at the question and then her face softened into a sad smile. She moved back to the table. There was no threat in her movements, but Allison had to fight the urge to keep from shifting away from her.

"I had been living on the streets almost two months to the day when I met Adam." Lillian plopped down into her seat heedless of the loud groan that emanated from it. "It wasn't easy, and I was ready to go home, regardless of how awful it was; it couldn't be much worse than I was living. I was cold, hungry and I had never been as dirty as I was those few months. Days spent sleeping in alleys, begging for food...those things were starting to get to me, and I was sure that I would be better off dead."

Her soft smile made the words light, although it finally slipped. Her lips twisted into a wry grin. "Actually, I figured I was dead, and this was the hell I needed to live through to make it to heaven. I wasn't sure what I was going to do. The thought of going home was worse than the thought of freezing to death or starving."

She sighed deeply. "You have to understand how desperate I was to even consider going back home."

Allison paused in the notes she was taking and stared at her. There was no way for her to understand, because Lillian had only given her one kernel of information about her family life. The rest was clouded in mystery and, despite what the court case had brought to light, Allison was sure there were more depths to the complicated Ross family.

Lillian must have picked up on the question in Allison's eyes. "You don't understand right now," she said, "but you'll understand by the time this is all over."

She shrugged her shoulders and picked up the dented pack of cigarettes sitting on the table. She didn't ask this time before she slid out the long, white stick and lit it. The musky scent of the tobacco filled the room.

"All you need to know is that I was desperate. It was getting so cold. I would wake up some mornings, at least the nights when I slept, with a fine misting of snow on me. I didn't have the right clothing and what I *did* have was becoming thread-bare already. "

She exhaled her words on a cloud of gray smoke, flicking away the ash forming on the end of the cigarette as she composed her thoughts.

"Adam met me when I was at the end of my reserve. I had nothing left to fight with, nothing left to fight for. I was ready to give up. To go home where I could finally die and that was when I met Adam... at the end."

●————————————————————————————————●

The evening air was crisp and would have been refreshing to someone who wasn't forced to stay outside, but it chilled my bones, which were already numb from countless nights in the cold temperatures.

A cold wind nipped at the exposed flesh of my ears as a heavy drizzle of rain fell from the gray sky. It was a rain that soaked my clothing completely, eating away at my skin, as if it wanted to make me even more depressed than I already was.

Standing in the bus shelter, I looked like every other street kid begging for food. My hair was matted and hung down my back in thick cords from not being washed for weeks, my clothes were disheveled and caked with mud, and my skin itched from the dirt.

I stared at the people passing by with dull eyes filled with distrust and dismay as my dirt caked hand reached out for change. Most people looked the other way, huddled under their umbrellas as they ignored the rain-drenched girl at the bus station; shrugging her off as just one of the thousands of lost souls in America.

Rolling my eyes, I tucked myself into the corner of the shelter. It wasn't the best place to rest for the night, but I figured I would have a few hours before someone complained about me. The quarter in my pocket burned through my clothes and into my leg. I could feel its cold presence and what it meant. All I had to do was make one call and I could be warm, fed and home.

But you wouldn't be safe!

The thought kept me from reaching for it and stumbling to the nearest phone booth. I was safer in my bus shelter than I could ever be at home. Tears burned at my eyes as I tried to huddle around myself to escape the chill working through my clothes. I gave up watching the people passing by; simply resting my head in my arms, my knees propped against my chest and my hand hanging limply out towards the strangers passing by.

I knew the routine where panhandling came in. By now, I was an expert. The more hopeless I looked, the more likely someone would offer a few dollars for a hot meal. It sickened me how they would give me a look of pity before the coins dropped into my hand, the relieved look filling their faces at their charity. I never said thank you... I just put the coins into my pocket.

I knew these people. I knew the moment they walked away that they would feel good about themselves. They had helped someone who needed it and the invisible pat on their own back would bolster them for weeks, but they never did anything more than those coins. Not one asked why I was there, or how they could help me. It wasn't their problem and I was lucky to get the few handouts they sent my way.

My thoughts were as dark as the rain falling down around the bus shelter. I didn't notice the man shuffling up to me until I felt him sit down on the bench beside me. I glanced up, my eyes burning from unshed tears; my face streaked with dirt, making me barely recognizable as a person. He simply placed a large Starbucks cup beside him and inclined his head in invitation.

The earthy scent of chocolate drifted up from the cup and my mouth filled with saliva at the thought of sipping it. I glanced at the man...his square jaw, strong and shockingly masculine, was pointed towards the street, his eyes followed the line of traffic slowly winding its way home. He didn't look at me as I hesitantly reached for the drink, and with a final glance at the stranger, I took a long draw on the cup.

The chocolate was so hot it burned my tongue as I gulped it down, but the taste was better than any I had ever tasted. It burst on my taste buds and reminded me of the finest Belgian chocolates I had once in a long-ago memory shared with my mother. I sighed slightly at the warmth sliding down my throat and into my gut. For a minute, I forgot the painful throb of hunger that had plagued me for months.

As I swallowed my second gulp, I looked back at the man. He was still sitting in the same position, his hands loose in his lap and his back straight. He was dressed like the other businessmen I had seen passing by for the last hour, with his black dress slacks and tan trench coat, but his hair was slightly longer, the black curls falling over his collar in an unkempt manner.

Looking at him closely, I guessed him to be in his late twenties or early thirties. I had never been good at guessing the ages of anyone, so wasn't completely sure.

"I remember my first cup of hot chocolate," he offered before I could say thanks, his gaze still on the traffic. "I was just off the street and it tasted like heaven. It warmed parts of me I hadn't realized were cold."

I clutched the cup tighter, crushing it slightly in my grip. "You lived on the street?" I asked, not believing that someone dressed as good as he was could have lived in the hell I had lived.

He turned to me, his dark brown eyes taking in my appearance. "Yeah, for about a year when I was just a kid. Worst year of my life but when I finally got off the street, I really appreciated everything I had."

"Oh." I couldn't say anything else to this. My lips felt numb from the heat of the beverage. "Did you go home?" I don't know why I cared but there was something about the stranger that made me ask. If he went home, maybe he could help me get somewhere safe as well.

"Nope" he said, and then turned his eyes back to the street.

I sat there, sipping the hot chocolate, watching him watch the world go by. I could imagine how we looked to others; the older guy in a business suit sitting beside a frumpy and dirty girl drinking from a Starbucks cup. I drained the cup completely and then stared at it, wishing that more of the heavenly liquid would fall from it.

He asked nonchalantly, "Would you like to get something to eat?"

I jumped, not realizing that he was aware of my every movement. I gritted my teeth together at his invitation.

"Look mister, thanks for the hot chocolate but I don't sell myself for anything, even food. If you're looking for that, you should head over to the corners. There's lots of hookers over there...I'm not one of them."

He didn't turn to look at me, but I could see the wry smile spread to the side of his face. "I'm not looking for anything. I just saw someone who looked hungry and thought I would offer. If you want, I can take you to the restaurant, pay for your bill and then leave. You don't have to sit with me or talk. I'm just trying to help."

His words were smooth and comforting but I raised an eyebrow at them. I had heard this line from countless men since I'd run away from home. They all offered something; a place to stay, a piece of clothing, a few dollars or some food—but they all wanted the same thing, for me to sleep with them. I had been tempted more than once. I was already dead at this point, what was one more step into hell, but I kept telling them no. It didn't matter how bad things got; I wasn't going to do it. There was no way I would sleep with men to survive. I wasn't even sure I wanted to survive.

Still, I sat there chewing his words, ignoring the rumbling in my stomach that had become more pronounced once the hot chocolate had stopped flowing to it. I stared at his neutral features and realized that he was quite handsome, even though he was much older than I was. I could imagine the beautiful woman that was waiting for him at home. She was probably tall, with dark hair like his and sparkling eyes as she embraced him. He would tell her how he had met some poor street kid and gave her a meal... then they would feel good about their simple life and their effort to help.

Shaking myself from where my thoughts were going, I nodded slowly. He didn't seem to notice that I had agreed because he said, "Look, why don't I drop you off at that diner over there and you can get anything you need to eat."

The diner he was pointing to was just one of the many greasy spoons in the city. Nothing memorable but the smells that emanated from it made my mouth salivate more than the hot chocolate had. I nodded again. "Okay, but I don't do anything for food."

He nodded back, stood up, and opened his umbrella before stepping out into the rain. He didn't offer it to me, and gratitude washed over me for some reason. I liked him better for not trying to get close to me. Of course, I probably smelled awful, so he might only be trying to keep his distance.

When we stepped into the bright interior of the diner, I blinked at both the warmth and the light. A tired looking waitress, her red hair graying near the temples and her shoulders slumped as she leaned against the counter, swept her gaze over both of us, her lip curling into a sneer. She had obviously come to the same conclusion I had.

The man led me to a booth near the back of the diner, the table and faux leather greasy to the touch, and sat down on the bench. I stood there for a second, unsure what I should do before I slid into the seat opposite him.

"I'll just sit here until you order your food and then I'll go," he offered, but I was past caring if he was there.

The waitress dropped two menus down on the table and then walked away, not even asking if we wanted a drink. I glared at her before I looked at the menu. The stranger ignored his menu and continued to watch me, I could see the glint of his watch in the light, but I ignored the question in his eyes.

"So, I'm Adam," he said slowly, his voice filled with interest. "What is your name?"

I gave him an incredulous look and slunk down into the seat. "What do you want my name to be?" I asked, knowing that it sounded like a proposition instead of a defense.

He didn't say anything, just checked the time on his watch.

Go ahead, you did your good deed; go home to your beautiful girlfriend.

"Well," he shuffled slightly, "I'd better get going."

I nodded and didn't answer. As he stood up to leave, I felt panic. Needing to say something at least, I blurted out, "Thanks for the help mister."

"Adam," he corrected, "and you're welcome."

I watched him walk over to the waitress and slip her a fifty-dollar bill as he pointed to my table. He turned to the door and paused at it. His jaw tightening before he turned on his heel and marched back to my table with a look of determination on his face.

"I know you don't trust anyone," he said as soon as he reached me. "But I just wanted to help."

Doubt drew my eyebrows together and I nodded my head slightly. He continued, "I go by that bus stop every night at six, so if you would like something to eat tomorrow, just wait for me there. I'll get you a meal. No strings attached...just someone who's been where you are, just someone who wants to help."

With that, he turned away and strode away. I stared at the door, waiting for him to come back through it. The waitress cleared her throat and said, "That guy said you could order anything you wanted."

The rain beat a tempo on the windows of the prison like it had in the memory that Lillian had told to Allison.

"He was so kind to me for those first days," she finished. "I went back the next night and he was there sitting in the bus shelter waiting for me. I expected him to want sex, or something, when I went back, but he just took me to the diner, paid for my meal, and left. It went on like that for weeks and before I knew it, I was asking him to stay and we started talking about everything. I told him I had nowhere to go and I couldn't go home."

Lillian snorted, a bitter laugh that held no warmth. "He actually offered to get me back to my family. It was perfectly orchestrated. He built that trust before he asked if I had somewhere to go during the night and when I said no, he said he might be able to find something for me."

She stopped talking and glanced out the window, her eyes looking back to the world that had been so hostile to a fifteen-year-old, clueless girl. It was clear that Adam had been the white knight she'd been looking for.

"He was easy to love during those first few months. He seemed so concerned, as if he wanted to save me from my hell. I thought..."

Lillian leapt from her chair and started pacing behind the table, her fists clenching and unclenching.

"Did you suspect that he was a pimp?" Allison asked.

"No," Lillian shook her head, her hair falling into her face. "I thought that he was sent to me from God. A kindness after all the shit I'd been through. He was there to save me from everything. It wasn't until months later that I realized what he was. By then, it was too late, he had already created me into what he wanted, and I had forgotten how to be anyone else."

Glancing up at Allison under heavy eyelids, Lillian finished. "I never knew who I was. Not then, not when I was a child and not when I killed Adam. It was as though I was simply a half-formed person, drifting through life, at the mercy of whatever the world threw at me."

Her words died but Allison could see them echoing in those beautiful green eyes, and she wondered if she would ever be able to forget the haunted look on Lillian's face.

CHAPTER SIX

External Examination:

The autopsy began at 10:25am on January 13, 2010. The body is presented in a black body bag and when first viewed, he is wearing a pair of grey dress slacks, a white button up dress shirt with the top three buttons undone, two black dress shoes and one black dress jacket. The hands have been bagged to preserve any possible evidence and there is a gold ring on the fourth finger of his left hand along with a watch, Rolex, on the left wrist. No other jewelry was included.

The body is of a white male, measuring 73.2 inches, weighing 170 pounds and the male is 62 years of age.

The eyes are open, and the irises are green with cloudy corneas. The sclerae is clear. The hair is approximately two inches in length and is dark brown. The hair and clothes are encrusted with what appears to be blood. Both the upper and lower teeth are intact with no injury to gums, cheeks or lips.

There are no tattoos on the body. An old surgical scar is found on the side of the abdomen that indicates a possible appendix surgery.

The head, eyes, nose and mouth are not remarkable. The neck, front of chest and abdomen show significant injury. There are eleven stab wounds and one slash across his neck. The appearance of the injuries are deep and indicate extreme violence was used to inflict them. The genitalia are that of a circumcised adult male and show no evidence of injury.

Evidence of Injury:

1.   Stab Wound 1 of 11 located on the right side of the chest.

The stab wound is located eighteen inches from the top of the head and three inches from the side of the body. It is vertically oriented, and the wound is tapered. It measures an inch in length and shows a pathway through the skin, subcutaneous tissue, through the right rib. Length of wound is three inches and the direction of the cut is left to right.

Opinion: This is a fatal wound that is associated with the perforation of the right lung. The trauma around the wound site indicates excessive force...

~ Excerpt from William Conrad Ross's Coroner's Report, Dr. Amelio Rodriquez

Her hands rested flat against the table and Allison couldn't tear her eyes from them. Those long, delicate fingers had been stained red with blood and had grasped the chef's knife in fury as it flashed through the air into living flesh.

She repressed the shudder of revulsion as images of the crime scene flashed in her mind's eye. She had been up until the early hours poring over photos from the trial and of the crime.

The fingers flicked in agitation and Allison shook herself from her thoughts, "I'm sorry. I missed what you said."

Lillian grimaced at her. She had dark circles under her eyes and looked as though she'd had less sleep than Allison. "I asked how you would like to continue today," Lillian murmured.

"However, you would like," Allison had been over this several times already and it seemed as though it would be ongoing. Lillian didn't like to open up at the beginning of the interviews.

Allison leaned back in her chair and sighed, "This is your story Lillian. However, you want to tell it is okay with me. I am simply here to listen and record what you say. Nothing else."

Lillian's gaze bored into her own, an unknown emotion filling them. Allison waited, her body still, which was a complete contrast to the turmoil racing through her head.

"I loved my father you know."

Allison nodded slightly as Lillian stood up and moved towards the window. The sun was shining between the bars, but Allison felt none of its warmth.

"It was rather sick that I did but we wanted him to be proud of us. I was never good enough, never minded myself quick enough. Never got the grades that he wanted. It was never enough for him and he hated that about us. There were days when I just waited for him to hit me."

Her voice faded into a mumble, but her long fingers clutched at the jumper near her heart. She turned into the window and Allison could no longer see her face.

"It didn't make it easy when I decided to leave him. Decided to leave everyone that I had loved. I had promised myself I would never go back but, in the end, I did in a way."

"Why did you leave?" Allison set her pencil down on the yellow legal pad.

"Because I knew if I didn't, I would die. He was killing me." Lillian placed her head on the glass of the window. "I knew I would either kill myself or kill him. It's funny that I left and lived through everything just to wind up in the last place I'd wanted to go."

●————————————————————●

"Lillian, come here."

It was a command: clear, strong and tinged with displeasure —I knew I couldn't ignore it. I gave one last longing glance to the stairs and turned into my father's office.

He was sitting at his desk, his eyes fixed on a pile of papers on the mahogany surface. His usually pristine appearance was disheveled, his tie loosened and the first few buttons on his shirt were undone, his black hair slightly tussled as though he had run his hands through it. He glanced up at me and his eyes bore into my skin, making it feel as though it burned.

"Your mother gave me your report card today."

Hovering on the threshold, I nodded without replying. No matter how much I had begged her not to give it to him; I'd known she would.

"Close the door Lillian."

I turned to shut the door behind me, the safety of the hallway and my sister's wide eyes staring from the stairs were the last thing I saw as it clicked shut. I could feel him standing behind me and I tensed—his hands slid down my arm and I jerked, not realizing that he had moved up behind me.

"I'm very disappointed Lillian...so very disappointed," his voice purred in my ear forcing my eyes closed as I tried to block out the man, my father, behind me. "B's, you brought home B's."

"Just two, Daddy," I said, my lips quivering with fear. His fingers bit into my arms and I squealed in pain as they bit deeply into the flesh. He twirled me around, his eyes full of anger and...and something else that was even more terrifying. Something my young mind couldn't focus on.

"Two B's, Lillian, is extremely bad. You know what I expect of you and your sister. Hayley never displeases me the way you do. She makes sure her grades stay up."

My eyes stung as his hands slid to my hair. He buried his fingers in the long locks I had carefully curled that morning. "She's only in second grade," I screamed, "I'm in sixth grade, the work is harder, Daddy."

He just shook his head and, as though I was nothing but a rag doll, picked me up and threw me across the room. I screamed out in pain as I crashed against the heavy desk. With a growl, he was on me, his fists driving into me faster than I could catch my breath. He focused on my stomach, each blow knocking wind from my lungs.

I couldn't breathe, couldn't think, couldn't see as his fists rained down on me. Tears stung my eyes and terror scraped at my throat. This is it; he's going to kill me this time. I felt the pain blossoming inside of me as I gagged on the bile he forced up into my throat.

"Please Daddy...please," I was vaguely aware of the words spewing from my mouth between his blows, but he didn't stop. His eyes were wild and filled with hatred. "Daddy!" I screamed one last time before I curled up into a ball and allowed my sobs to fill the space.

His fist pummeled against me but there was no strength in this blow. He hit me a few more times, each strike weaker than the last as he lost the anger that had set him off. He straightened to his full six-foot-one height. I stared up at him through my tear streaked vision and watched as he straightened his tie and jacket. He looked at his fists and rubbed the soreness from them.

"Lillian," he said, his voice slightly breathless as he tried to catch his breath—he'd had quite the workout and my stomach and sides screamed in pain at the damage he'd done. "You will go to your room. You will remain there until Monday. I do not want to see you at all this weekend... I will have your momma bring up your meals and you will spend that time studying."

He ignored my sobs, which I swallowed back. I couldn't make him angry again. This time, he would kill me if I did. I nodded and said weakly, "Yes Daddy."

Moving to the door, he opened it and I saw my mother standing nervously on the threshold. "Irene, take Lillian upstairs. She seems to have fallen and hurt herself," he said as he moved to his bar. He filled a glass with whiskey and ice as my mother moved hesitantly towards me. Fresh tears slid down my cheeks as I silently begged her to do something...to stop the monster who was hurting her daughter. Irene's eyes slid away from mine and became vacant as if she didn't see me...didn't see the damage her husband had wrought on my body.

"Momma..." I groaned before he cut me off.

"Lillian, we do not want to hear any excuses from you. Stand up and go to your room." Daddy's voice brooked no argument. "Irene, Lillian is grounded to her room for the weekend. Make sure she didn't hurt herself and give her some Advil to manage any pain she has."

And with that, he dismissed the trembling girl on the floor and her mother. He sat down and took a long swallow of his whiskey. I watched my mother staring at his back and, for a second, I saw rage fill her eyes. She looked towards the large fireplace and her eyes fell on the fire poker resting beside it. *Do it Momma,* I pleaded silently with my eyes, *Stop him from hurting me...from hurting us.*

"Is there something you want to say, Irene?" he asked without even looking at us and I knew that he saw everything. He knew the murderous thoughts that we were sharing at that moment. Defeat washed over me, and I knew we would never escape him...he would always win.

As though she was thinking the same thing, Momma said quietly, "No William. I was just concerned about Lillian..."

"Lillian will be fine. She needs to learn what our expectations are, and I expect you to give your daughter a talking to when you get her to her room."

"Yes William," Momma said, and her voice was filled with defeat. Tears stung my eyes and I realized that I hated my mother more than I hated my father. He was a monster, but she was purposely blind to it.

She glanced at me and I saw the same hate filling her eyes. I knew what I was...I was the trap that kept her tied to William. If I was dead, she could flee with Hayley; her favorite daughter. "Lillian, let's go upstairs," she whispered.

I nodded and struggled to pull myself up. Fresh pain lanced through my stomach and I wondered if he had ruptured something important inside of me. I knew I wouldn't be that lucky...Daddy always made sure that the injuries hurt but he didn't break us. He played carefully with his things. By Monday, all that would be left was a few bruises as a reminder of what was expected of me.

Struggling to stand, I used the side of the desk to pull myself upright. I shook from the effort as I forced myself to remain silent. One cry of pain could set him off again and Momma would stand back...her eyes would go blank as she escaped into her own world. She wouldn't see what he did, wouldn't question the bruises that could only be caused by his fists. Taking a deep breath, I straightened as much as I could, wrapping my arms around my waist. Fresh tears made my vision swim, but I was triumphant, I didn't sob...didn't cry out.

I took a small step towards the door, my stomach screaming as fresh pain stabbed through me. I stopped, took a steadying breath as my vision cleared before I took another step forward. I focused on each individual step as I cried silently. Tears fell freely down my face, but I didn't make a sound.

I felt my mother following silently behind me, but she didn't reach for me...didn't try to keep me steady. When I finally passed through the door, she closed it behind us and then her hands touched my back. I winced from her touch, but she held me firmly as she helped me up the stairs. Every step was a torture and I was breathless by the time I made it to the top.

I collapsed against her and was half carried down the long hallway to my bedroom. Opening the door, she guided me to my bed, the pink comforter almost clown-like in its cheerfulness. My room was just an extension of what he expected a daughter to be like. Bright pink accessories accentuated the white furniture and four poster canopy bed. Not one thing in the room was truly mine...they were merely trinkets of Lillian Ross...the girl who pretended to love the palace she was trapped in.

It wasn't me living in this room. Even at twelve, I knew that the real me only existed inside my own head, but she was leaking out. That was why I was curled up in a ball on my bed as tears continued to fall silently. I wrapped my arms around my knees and felt, rather than heard, my mother fluttering around the room.

She left for a few minutes before she returned with Advil and water. "Here baby. This will help with the pain."

I shook my head and ignored the two, white pills, "I want to feel this...it's what I deserve." My voice sounded as dead as my soul felt. I wanted to die and a part of me regretted that he hadn't killed me.

Feeling the mattress dip as she sat down beside me, she ran her hand over my brown hair. God how I hated my hair...I looked too much like him. I was tall and thin like him...my eyes were the same green, my hair the same mahogany brown...the only way I resembled my mother was in our hands. Those same hands I didn't want on me right now. She knew...she saw but she was pretending that nothing bad was happening to us.

"Lillian..." her voice trailed off and I didn't reply. We sat like that as the minutes ticked by and my tears eventually stopped. I stared at the wall and wished she would leave me alone. "You have to stop making him so angry, baby. Just do what he wants, honey, and then he will be happy."

"You don't know that," I whispered, "No matter what I do, he will find a way to get angry...he'll always find a way to hurt me."

My mother's hands stilled in my hair, "You don't know what he does to me Momma..." the sob was wrenched from my throat.

Momma's hands tensed, and I could feel the defeat in her body. I knew that no matter what I said, she wouldn't listen because she was as scared of him as I was. "I don't want to hear that, do ya' hear?" she said, her voice filled with resignation. Her words were almost rote, "Your daddy is a good man who takes care of us and all he asks is for you to do your best. Your behavior is what caused this Lillian and you need to accept that."

Anger raged inside of me, but it was swallowed by the darkness flooding through me. I nodded slightly. "Answer me young lady," she snapped.

"Yes Momma," I whimpered. For some reason, her violence was even worse than Daddy's.

She released my hair and stood up. "That's a good girl," she said. "Now I will leave your Advil here. You make sure that you take it and spend the hours in your room studying. Your daddy hates bad grades."

"Yes Momma," I felt like gagging.

"I will bring up your dinner when it's ready," she said and then moved towards the door. I didn't turn over, but I knew she paused on the threshold. "Lillian..." her voice was filled with hesitation.

I squeezed my eyes shut on the pain I heard in her tone. I didn't want to worry about her, but I was a good daughter—I always worried about my momma. "Yes," I managed with a trembling voice.

"I love you sweetheart and I know your daddy loves you. He," her voice broke and I knew she was crying, "We...just want you to do your best so you can be successful later in life."

The tears started again but I didn't move to swipe them away. Instead, I kept my eyes closed. I felt every bruise he'd raised on my body and knew that these bruises weren't about love...they weren't about making sure I succeeded...they were about keeping the control he'd had on me since I was born. They were about keeping the control he'd had on my mother for even longer.

"I know, Momma," I lied and realized the lie was easier to say. Realized a part of me believed it and wanted nothing more than to please them both. I swallowed back the revulsion I felt. "I will try harder, Momma."

I knew it was a false promise, even if I did try harder, it wouldn't matter. Daddy would find a reason to be disappointed and, when he was disappointed, he let me know with his fists. Momma knew it for the lie it was, but she didn't say anything except, "That's a good girl Lillian. I will be up later with your supper."

And then I heard the door click shut and I turned my face to the pillow—finally allowing my sobs to flow unchecked.

CHAPTER SEVEN

Detective Modeure (DM): Mrs. Ross, I know this is a terrible time for you, but could you answer some questions for us?

Irene Ross (IR): Yes, I will try but I don't know how I can help. (Sobbing.)

DM: Yes, I understand but it is important for us to know what happened. Were you aware of where your husband was going the day of his murder?

IR: No. William had said nothing. I didn't even know that he'd finally found Lillian. As far as I knew, Lillian was dead. She died the day she ran away...I felt it in my body and a mother should know that...shouldn't she? Does that make me a bad mother for thinking that she was dead?

DM: No... no. You were just trying to carry on with your life, it must have been horrible for you.

IR: Oh, it was. William and I were devastated when Lillian disappeared. We thought she'd phone in a few days, but those days became months and then years. What could I think except that she'd died?

DM: So, you never heard from your daughter after she disappeared?

IR: No, she just vanished. We hired the best private detectives to try to find her, but all the tips led to dead ends. I found... (her voice cracks and sobbing is heard)...I found out that my daughter was alive within minutes of finding out that my husband was...was...was murdered.

(Sobbing for three minutes of the tape.)

DM: Mrs. Ross, would you like to continue, or would you like to speak with us at a later date?

IR: No... I want to do this now, it is just difficult.

DM: Did your husband mention anything to you about hearing from Lillian?

IR: No, he didn't. He said he had a meeting in town with Rupert and that he would be late getting home. He told me not to wait up for him. If Lillian had contacted him beforehand, he didn't tell me.

DM: Okay, thank you. What was your relationship with Lillian before she ran away?

IR: We were close, but we had some problems. She was getting into trouble...boys...drugs...drinking; you know what a teen girl can be like. William and I were trying so hard to get her on track and then she disappeared. When she was little, she would share everything with me but when she got older, she stopped.

DM: So, your relationship was strained before she ran away?

IR: I don't think it was strained but Lillian had a lot of lies she was hiding from us. When we weren't fighting about her behavior, the family was happy.

DM: What about her relationship with her father?

IR: She was closer to William than she was to me. They had an amazing relationship...like two peas in a pod. Always cooking something up between them and I was often on the outside looking in. Hayley was closer to me than Lillian; she was a daddy's girl. He was devastated when she ran away.

DM: I see. Do you think that there was something else that triggered the attack besides wanting money?

(Silence for two minutes.)

DM: Mrs. Ross?

IR: No. William was a wonderful father...he would have done anything for his little girl. Whoever that woman is that you have at the hospital, it's not Lillian...that woman is a monster.

~ Interview transcript between Mrs. Irene Ross and Lead Investigating Detective Roger Modeure.

-- Time-stamp 11:27 A.M., location interrogation room 6A--

The light filtered through the window weakly and Allison realized she'd been working all night. The words filled up her computer screen and were blurry as she tried to focus on what she'd written. She'd returned from the prison exhausted, but she couldn't give up on the thread that Lillian had created in her mind. She'd ignored the flashing message light on her phone when she'd gotten home...probably another call from her mother... snatched a fresh bottle of wine from the wine shelf and disappeared into her office with it and her notes from the case. Now her mouth was as fuzzy as her brain but there was no reason to even contemplate going to bed.

The cat had wandered into the room sometime after midnight and sprawled himself across several of the photos of the crime scene where he had slept the rest of the night. She gritted her teeth at the violence in the photos. It was messy...it was filled with hatred and if Lillian was telling the truth, there was a reason for that hatred. But the life that Lillian was painting for Allison did not fit to the life the reports showed.

None of the threads she'd thought she'd captured had panned out and Allison felt as lost now as she had at the start. William Ross was an upstanding citizen and didn't even have a speeding ticket before his death. There had been no calls to the police before Lillian disappeared or even after she disappeared. The only time the police had any dealings with the family was during charity events or when they were investigating the disappearance of their daughter.

Eye witness reports spoke of a close-knit family, who were loving and successful. People envied the family and there were enough witnesses that said the same things. There was often someone at the house and every one of them said things were well in Camelot. Surely, someone had seen evidence of abuse, Allison had thought before she had immersed herself in all the files she had. Unfortunately, everyone said the same thing; William Ross had been a good father and husband.

The scent of fresh coffee drifted into her office and Allison smiled to herself. She had stayed up past the automatic setting on her coffee machine and the scent was driving into her cortex; setting her program for the day ahead. She could never sleep through the smell of fresh coffee.

Stretching her arms like a tired cat, Allison stood up and stumbled toward the kitchen; the sky outside was still dark but hints of color streaked across the horizon. Red as deep as blood slashed across the clouds like a knife across flesh, reminding Allison of the photos she'd looked through over the night.

Shuddering at the cold racing down her spine, Allison pulled out a coffee mug with large pansies on it. She sloshed the hot coffee into the mug and gathered it into her hands, savoring the warmth through the thick ceramic.

Resting her hip on the edge of the dark granite countertop, Allison contemplated the flashing red number on the answering machine. Sixteen messages were waiting for her and even her mother wouldn't leave that many, although there was no doubt that the majority of the calls would be from her.

Sighing, Allison crossed the kitchen and jabbed her finger down on the button, the male, metallic voice filled the room giving her the date and time of each call before her mother's voice, growing more irate with each message, followed. Allison deleted each one before the message was finished, her finger hovering over the delete button.

"Ms. McKinnon," an unfamiliar voice filled the room, "This is Hayley Forester returning your call. I am available to meet with you, however, before I do, I wanted to let you know that another book is not in the best interest of the family. If I do agree to meet with you, I really need your assurance that you won't bother my mother. She doesn't need any more stress regarding Lillian. If you could contact me, my number is..."

Allison hit the rewind button and fumbled with the pen and paper she kept beside the phone. She jotted down the number and then hit rewind again, listening to the voice of Hayley Forester and comparing it to the husky timbre of Lillian's voice. If they were related in any way, you couldn't tell from the voice. Both had an intelligent quality to it that smacked of an affluent childhood where the best education was not only within reach but expected. Both had a slight treble to it that hinted at a southern accent but were free of the heavy twang. That's where the similarities ended.

Lillian's voice was warm and husky; the voice of a socialite who was schooled to fit in anywhere. Hayley's voice was crisp and direct; the voice of a woman used to being in the center of business.

Allison listened to the message one final time before saving it and moving on to the next. Three more from her mother were quickly deleted and two were from Ira, warning her about her mother before the answering machine filled with a silence that was thick and heavy.

It stretched along the seconds, her nerves stretching with it before a gravelly, male voice said, "I know what you are working on, you need to stop before someone gets hurt."

The steady drum of her heart stopped for a split second before it began racing. The anger in the voice was clear and it was directed at her. Allison shakily reached for the phone and flicked through the call display but without any luck. An unknown number flashed on the screen at the time the call had come through. She flicked through the rest and found the same unknown number another four times.

An angry click resonated on the answering machine, making Allison jump. She scanned the room, suddenly feeling exposed and vulnerable. She had dealt with angry calls in the past, but they always unnerved her. She couldn't help but wonder if this caller would be a violent one.

"Get it together Allison," she said aloud, and the noise made her nerves relax slightly. She stared at the phone. There was no doubt the call was regarding Lillian, but she had no idea why someone would leave those threatening messages. As far as anyone knew, Lillian had been a prostitute. Nothing more, nothing less. There was nothing for people to be afraid of and all of the other books about Lillian did nothing to counter that.

But Kai had mentioned angry citizens and she had said herself that Lillian knew the secrets of a lot of people. The thought was thrilling, and the call only confirmed what Allison had suspected; this was going to be the story of her career.

Her heart leapt at the possibility and with a renewed determination, she punched the numbers into the phone. She waited, the phone ringing in her ear before a crisp voice answered, "Wilson, Lockheed and Sturn. How can I direct your call?"

"Ms. McKinnon for Ms. Forester please."

"Hold please."

Muzak filled the ear piece and Allison pulled out a legal pad of paper to take notes. "Hello?" the same crisp voice from the message system filled the earpiece.

"Ms. Forester?"

"Yes, this is she. I can't say that I am glad to hear from you Ms. McKinnon."

Allison grimaced, there was definitely hostility in the woman's voice. "Well, you did ask me to call and I thank you for affording me this opportunity," she said. She had to be careful with this.

"I haven't afforded you anything yet," she snapped, and Allison wondered what the woman looked like. Would she bear any resemblance to her sister? "I am just making sure that you are not trying to run my family through the mud."

Allison paused and took a deep breath. She was used to hostility but if there was no mud...she couldn't pull anyone through it. "I understand your concern," she said carefully, "I have no intention of pulling anyone through the mud. I am simply writing a book about the murders and would like to gain your...and your family's...perspective about it."

"In other words, you want to grill us about our childhood and why my sister ended up as such a cold-hearted bitch."

"I will be going over some of your childhood," she offered, "Lillian has agreed to tell her story for the book. I need to speak to everyone involved in the case to ensure that I am writing the truth."

The laugh was harsh and cruel, "Lillian is a liar, so you are going to be disappointed when we put the record straight. She was a spoiled brat that ran away and got in over her head."

"Are you sure?" Allison asked quietly.

Silence filled the phone and dragged out for several minutes. Allison wasn't sure if she'd hung up on her or not. "Ms. McKinnon," the voice sounded tired, "I will meet you, so you can do your little interviews, but you are not to bother my mother with this nonsense. Do I make myself clear?"

Allison closed her eyes. This could make her life hell for the next few months if she didn't agree but she couldn't sign away access to Irene Ross. "I can't make that promise Ms. Forester. There may be some facts that only your mother can confirm," *such as whether he used to hit your sister*, she added silently. "I can promise you that I would only contact her if it was absolutely necessary and I will let you know before I do."

"That is not good enough. If you speak to my mother, I will contact our attorneys and have your book shut down."

"If you do, I will just write the book I can, and your family will have to live with what I put in. We have the permissions for the book. Your own mother signed off on the permissions for the book and for interviews. Did she not tell you this? I am allowed to move forward on this book."

"What?" the question was shrill, and Allison knew she had gotten under Hayley's skin. "When?"

"Several months back when I first started my research. As I said, this book will be moving forward with or without permissions. It was simply a courtesy that I asked your mother to sign off. The same courtesy I am offering to your family to know what is being said and to share the truth."

Allison held her breath. It was the truth, she didn't need their permissions but if the family decided to sue, it could lead to a lot of headaches for everyone; including her publisher.

The silence stretched out again, but Allison could hear Hayley breathing on the other end this time. Finally, she said, "Very well Ms. McKinnon. While I have my doubts about your book...or about how truthful my sister will be...I will meet with you to answer your questions. I will have my assistant arrange a time."

"Thank..."

Her words were cut off as Hayley said, "Don't thank me. I am simply doing this to minimize the damage your little book may cause for my family. As I said, my assistant will be in touch."

After a loud click, the phone went silent and Allison knew she'd hung up. She didn't care though; she had the interview...all she wanted. She needed to get inside that house and the only way in was through interviewing the family.

Dropping the pad and pencil, she picked up her coffee and headed back to her office to get started on her workday.

CHAPTER EIGHT

Corner's Scene Report:

Coroner Inspector(C/I) arrived at the scene at 10:27 PM on January 12, 2010. Environmental conditions at the scene: Ambient exterior temperature was approximately 32°F, Relative exterior humidity approximately 52%; Ambient interior temperature approximately 74°F, Relative humidity approximately 71%

C/I was directed into the apartment on the third floor of a four-story apartment dwelling. He was directed through the front hallway and to the right, which opened into a large, open concept kitchen and dining room. Victim One, a Mr. William Conrad Ross, was found in the center of the kitchen close to the refrigerator. The body was positioned with his feet pointing toward the door and his head pressed against the refrigerator. The body was on its side in a large pool of blood. His throat was slashed and there was evidence of multiple lacerations across the chest, arms and head. Victim was 6'1" tall. C/I verified the victim had no signs of life including respiration and heartbeat and pronounced the victim deceased at 10:34 PM.

C/I noted the upward-angled blood spatters on the walls, cabinets and ceilings of the kitchen that was consistent with violent slashes from an individual who was shorter than the victim. It was noted that slashes on the hands were consistent with defensive wounds and there was no weapon found near the body. Rigor mortis was established in the face and neck but had not spread throughout the rest of the body.

Body temperature of the victim was 91.4°F. Skin was waxy and cool to the touch. Eyes are open and corneas are cloudy. Preliminary estimate of time of death was within two to four hours before examination by C/I, subject to revision pending formal autopsy. Apparent cause of death is loss of blood due to large slash on neck.

C/I was directed down the hall and into bedroom. Victim Two, Ms. Lillian Ross was found on the floor of the master bedroom. Her feet were pointed toward the door and her head was near the bed. A cordless phone was beside her left hand. Blood was found on her hand and on the phone.

C/I noted bruising on the victim's face and exposed flesh. Her arm was at an odd angle, indicating a break and there were contusions on her body, neck and head. Victim was unconscious but there were vital signs. The victim was dressed in a white teddy and panties. Her feet were bare. Her clothes and skin were covered with blood, several were splatter drops. Ambulance was on route for victim during the examination of the scene...

~ Excerpt from Coroner's Scene Report, Dr. Amelio Rodriquez

Allison walked up to the bar and glanced at the fit man sitting on a stool in jeans and a t-shirt. He looked relaxed and the five o'clock shadow on his face made him look like all the other men in the bar. But she knew who he was, and it was time to get the work done, "Detective Modeure?" she asked as she sidled up to him.

He didn't turn to look at her and, instead, took another swallow of his drink...whiskey from the smell of it, "Ms. McKinnon."

She slipped onto the bar stool beside him as she shuffled her briefcase to her other hand. The bartender walked up, and she ordered the same as the detective. He raised an eyebrow at her and finally looked over. "I'm glad that you could meet me, Detective," she said when he did.

He shrugged his shoulders. "You said it was about the Ross murder. I was interested to find out what you wanted."

He was quite an attractive man, in his late thirties, maybe early forties. He had warm brown eyes, and a muscular jaw. She could tell he wasn't pleased. "As you know, I am an author writing a book on the Ross-Laurent murders. I have obtained the public police records on the attack, but I really wanted to speak to those involved in the investigation."

"Yeah, I know what you want. You aren't the first to come sniffing around this case," he said quietly before he drained his glass. He motioned to the bartender for a refill before he turned back to her. "So, what makes you different? Why should I discuss anything besides what's in that report?"

She narrowed her eyes at the challenge in his voice. He was definitely hedging, and she'd run into this before. They hated having a journalist sniffing around their files. Hated having someone else see something they had missed. If you asked her, the police were harder to work with than the criminals. "Really," she said between sips of her whiskey. "There isn't anything I can say to make you think I'm different. I can be honest...I want to make this book the best one on the market."

His eyes shimmered with laughter and Allison couldn't help but notice how nice they were. Honestly, if she'd met him at a different time, she might have tried her hand at flirting. *Yeah, right,* she silently scoffed. "Again, Detective..."

"Roger," he interrupted her. "Look, I have heard all of this before. We want to write the best accounting of the crime...we want to find the truth behind the story...we want to shine new light on it. The files have been poked to death. They've been ripped apart and that poor family is pulled through the mud over and over again. I haven't been part of that for any of the books so I'm not sure what I can do to help you with this one. I thought I'd meet you to be clear that I won't offer much insight into this case."

She gave him a weak smile...it was clear she'd lost him before they'd even met. She could see the interest fading from his eyes. He'd been humoring her. "Roger, I understand what journalists have done in the past but, this time, it's different. Really, I'm just here to clarify some points that Lillian Ross may give to me. I also have questions about the reports and what you saw personally."

His eyes cleared and the small, self-assured grin that had begun to form on his lips slipped, he asked, "Lillian is talking?"

Allison nodded. "I am pursuing this book because she has agreed to talk. Without her, I would never have started it. She came to me to write the book, not the other way around."

He leaned back and scratched the stubble on his chin. He stared at Allison as though he was weighing not only her words but her very soul. She shifted uncomfortably under his perusal. "Why don't we go and sit over at that table?" he asked as he pointed to the corner booth.

Standing up, Allison grabbed her drink and headed over to the private booth. The bar was done in tasteful dark woods and burgundy fabric and while there was a slight air of desperation, it was a pretty common neighborhood bar. When she slid into the bench, she began pulling her pencil and notebook out of her bag until strong fingers touched her hand. She stared at the fingers for a moment before she glanced up at the detective, "Let's just chat for now...there is plenty of time for us to go over the case."

Allison shoved her notepad back into her bag and relaxed against the back of the booth. Roger slid into the bench opposite her and nursed his whiskey as he stared at her again. She fought the urge to shift under his gaze, but she didn't. She'd played this game before and she always won it. He wasn't going to intimidate her.

"How long have you been a writer?" he asked suddenly, and Allison smiled in triumph. He'd been the first to break the silence.

"Since I was a kid," she offered, "Professionally, about ten years now."

He nodded, "Has it always been true crime that you wrote?"

Allison shook her head, "No, not at first. I tried different genres...just writing articles...that sort of thing. I fell into true crime by accident when there was a series of murders in my home town. A number of women were raped and murdered. They caught the murderer, but the focus was only on the killer. They didn't focus on the women at all and they became nameless victims. I decided to write their story in my first true crime novel, Forgotten, and it took off from there. I have never looked back."

He nodded and took a draw of his whiskey as he sat back. The silence returned between them and Allison stared out at the other patrons of the bar. Several were off duty cops as this was a popular place for them to drink but it was obviously a mixed crowd. The bar didn't draw the young crowd, it was just a quiet place to drink and maybe watch a game. It was a place that her dad loved to come to after he'd spent all day in the courtroom.

She rubbed away the pain in her head at the memories. She missed her dad completely. He'd been there when she'd needed him the most, despite the divorce, and he'd been there for her mother. When cancer had taken him four years before, she'd been devastated.

"So, have you always worked homicide?" she asked to break the silence between them and to tamp down the direction of her thoughts.

He shook his head, "No."

"How long did you work homicide before you worked Lillian's case?" Allison asked. She wanted to grind her teeth because she'd need a crowbar to pry the answers from him.

His jaw tightened, and he took another swallow. Allison raised an eyebrow and he relented. "About a year. Before that I had worked Vice."

Allison's eyes widened in surprise. "For how long? Why'd you transfer?"

Roger scowled as he stared into his glass. "I worked Vice for five years and I was tired of it. Tired of seeing the girls busted up by their damn pimp; tired of the johns and the dumb girls who kept going back to it. Tired of going to girls that got off the street only to tell them that we couldn't charge their pimps." He paused and ran his hands through his hair— his eyes haunted. "Hell, we were picking up girls as young as eleven. Fucking eleven years old and these assholes are convincing them to run away from home...telling them shit like they are the only ones who ever loved them."

Allison nodded. She wasn't naive about the world and she'd interviewed a number of prostitutes for several books. She could imagine the frustration of pulling the women off of the streets only to have them go back. She couldn't imagine the heartbreak of watching little girls be victimized over and over again.

"After we pulled the body of a sixteen-year-old prostitute out of a ditch, I realized that I needed to go into a different department. Since I was seeing the bodies anyway, I figured it would be easier to go into homicide. Then maybe I could finally make a difference when I saw one of the girls I knew in a ditch." He spread his hands out on the table and stared at them.

Allison stared at them as well and wondered if he felt the women's blood was on his hands because he couldn't save them. "Did you know Lillian Ross before the murders? I know she was an escort in the past, did you ever bring her in or her johns?"

He shook his head. "No, before that night, I didn't even know the apartment was being used for escorts. We had some idea of who Adam Laurent was. Back before I was working Vice, he was just a small-time pimp. He had a couple girls that he ran but he wasn't worth our time. By the time I was in Vice, he was running an escort service. His clientele were rich men and politicians...he kept a few girls working a few corners, but I think it was just because he needed a girl to punch around. His escorts needed to be in top shape to maintain the clients they did."

Allison nodded and took out her notepad. She gave Roger a questioning glance and he said, "Go ahead, take your notes. Obviously, our interview has started."

She jotted down a few notes about Adam Laurent. "So, you didn't pick up Lillian, even as Lily Laurent?"

He shook his head. "I know she took his last name, but they weren't married. She may have been picked up under an alias, but I never saw her before the first day when we found the bodies. Of course, I wouldn't have been able to identify her when I first walked into that apartment...she was a mess."

Pulling the photos from the crime scene out of its file, Allison flipped it open, but Roger's hand fell on the top photo of William Ross lying on the kitchen floor, his throat slit as he stared unseeing at the ceiling. "I've seen all the photos, I don't need to see them again. The scene still haunts me when I close my eyes. There was blood everywhere and when I arrived on scene, she was still laying on the floor in the bedroom. Paramedics were on route and I was ready to call them to tell them not to bother...she looked dead. She was so busted up and there was just so much blood on her, we couldn't figure out what was hers and what were the two victims."

Allison picked up the photos and sorted through them as Roger spoke until her eyes fell on the photos of Lillian. She did look dead. Her eyes were closed, already swollen from the beating she'd taken. Her lips were split, and she had angry red marks on her cheeks and around her neck. Allison could clearly see the shape of a thumb in one of the bruises on her neck. She was wearing a scrap of bloodied lace panties and teddy. Her long, blood-soaked hair stuck to her skin.

"I had an idea of what had happened the minute I had walked in the door. A trick gone wrong and a pimp that got involved. I wasn't sure who had beat her up, but my money was on the pimp. It wasn't until later that we found out who Lily Laurent was related to. At first, we just thought William Ross had hired an escort but when we found out he'd been there to see his daughter, it created more problems. Plus, it was a PR nightmare for the family, and we had to field a lot of calls concerning the murders."

Allison could imagine. The media had eaten up the story when it was leaked that Lillian Ross, the victim's own daughter had been arrested and charged with first degree murder. "Did you talk to her that first day?"

He shook his head and motioned towards the waitress for another drink. "No. Like I said, she looked dead and really, she wasn't that far from the grave. The doctors didn't think she would recover with the extent of internal injuries she'd suffered."

The waitress put down fresh whiskies and Allison thanked her before slipping her a twenty. She turned back to Roger and asked, "How long was it before you spoke to her?"

"About three or four days. She didn't regain consciousness for several days and then the doctors were not letting anyone speak to her until she'd recovered more."

"And what was your reaction to her?"

He scowled again and watched the game playing on the television over the bar. "Who do you think will win the World Series this year?"

Allison glanced up at the television and shook her head, "I have no idea who's playing...I stopped watching years ago when my dad passed away."

"Sorry to hear that," he said apologetically as his brown eyes searched her face. Allison felt like it was the first time he'd really looked at her since their interview had started.

"Don't be. It was four years ago." Allison tapped her notebook with her pencil and said, "So you didn't answer the question, what was your reaction to her?"

He rubbed his chin and laughed, his eyes twinkling, "Saw that did you?"

"What?"

"That I was avoiding the question."

She laughed. Surprisingly, she liked the detective. "You still are."

He held up his hands, "You're right." His smile slipped as he continued, "Look, it doesn't really matter what I thought of her. It was a case and we were looking at the facts. From what we saw, Lillian Ross...aka Lily Laurent...lured her father to the apartment and then killed him. For some reason, a fight broke out between her and Adam and she killed him as well."

"And the 911 call?"

"It was traced to that apartment and it was a woman who called. It is clear that it was Lillian Ross who had called." He spoke in an almost distracted manner as though he had said the same thing over and over again to countless reporters.

Allison nodded and flipped through the papers until she came to the 911 transcript. After reading it, she asked, "What do you think she meant by 'They killed me...'?"

Roger shrugged his shoulders, "Maybe she thought they had, I mean, she was half dead when we got to her. Christ, I'm surprised she didn't suffer permanent damage from her injuries."

"You don't think she meant anything else?"

"No." The answer was final, and Allison shifted the questioning.

"So, who do you think will win?" she asked, nodding towards the television.

"I don't know. I don't watch baseball," he smiled when Allison gasped in indignation, "Why are you writing this book? I mean, there have been a lot of different books about it."

It was Allison's turn to avoid the question as she pondered it. "Because she asked me to write it. She wants to tell her story for a change."

He nodded and sat back with a triumphant smile on his face, "And because it's too juicy of a story not to pursue."

Allison laughed, "That too." The laughter faded, and she asked, "While you were investigating the case, were there any signs of abuse in the Ross family?"

"No," he said but his voice was strained. "I suspected something, but the family always denied it. I was assured life was perfect in the Ross house. Even Lillian refused to speak about her family and, when she was forced, it was like she was reading from a script...life had been perfect...she hadn't been."

"And do you think that's true?"

"I'm a cop," he laughed wryly, "I see the worst in people before I see anything else. I think the Ross family hid a lot of skeletons, but they kept them safely locked away from the public...even through the trial."

He fell silent and they both watched the game...neither one interested in what was happening on the screen. Finally, Roger sighed, "Look, I felt sorry for Lillian. When she woke up, she was a mess. I went to that hospital every single day and she didn't talk about what happened. By the time her body healed, I knew her spirit was broken...she'd given up and she wasn't going to fight anything that was done to her."

"Look, I didn't know her before the murders, but I don't think she had so little hope before she was pulled out of that apartment. There was no light in her eyes, no hope that anything would ever be okay again. I don't think she deserved the death penalty. I don't think she committed first degree murder but I'm just a cop, I don't have a say in how the jury decides."

"Do you think she murdered those men?" Allison asked. Part of her knew what he was going to say, after all, it had been in the reports, but she needed to hear the words from him.

Roger leaned forward, his eyes shining with anger. "Yes, I think she killed the men, but I don't think it was the way the prosecution constructed the crime. I think Lillian is a survivor and when those men walked into that apartment, she was left with only two options...survive or die."

CHAPTER NINE

Adam Laurent was a minor player in the grand scheme of things. He had a few girls that he was pimping out, but he was a small-time pimp. No big aspirations, just enough bank roll to live the easy life. I ran into him a few times, usually picked him up when one of his girls got scared enough, or beat up enough, to lodge a complaint.

But I never got a charge to stick. This one girl, damn, he'd taken a bat to her and messed her up pretty bad. Then he'd left her for dead. I mean, everything was broken on her...ribs, cheeks, arm and she looked like a corpse. Actually, when we got the call for her, we thought she was a corpse, then she woke up a little and started moaning in pain...scared the shit out of the uniform waiting for forensics. He ended up fucking up the scene so bad getting to her that we couldn't collect a viable piece of evidence.

And the girl, Teresa, wouldn't talk when she finally woke up. Said some john jumped her, but she didn't have a good look at him. What could we do? We'd picked up Adam, he'd had some bruising on his knuckles, but we never found the bat he used and when she woke up and said it wasn't Adam, we had to let the bastard go.

Then Teresa killed herself, jumped off a goddamn parking garage, and nothing else could be done against Adam. If you ask me, I think he pushed her. Several of his girls went missing or killed themselves and I think he was just disposing of the human garbage...the girls that were more hassle than a benefit to the game.

About ten years ago, Adam went a lot bigger than I expected him to. He opened up an escort service that skirted the laws. Everything looked legit, but he still kept a few girls on the streets, seemed to love beating them up. But his real money was in the escort service.

We watched him but, over the years, he seemed to learn from his mistakes, and it was harder to catch him running prostitutes or beating them up. And while I wanted to investigate him for the disappearance of some of his girls, we didn't have funding. As my chief would say, "Who cares about a few missing hookers? They probably just went home."

~ Written Testimony of Detective Owen Burnham: People vs. Lillian Ross

Lillian leaned back in her chair and blew out a ring of smoke before she sucked in another from her cigarette. She seemed more at ease today...as though the process of telling her story was relaxing. Allison knew that, in some way, it was...she'd seen this process before.

Every time a person was able to share a part of their story, they were able to free up their conscience. She wasn't sure why it happened like that but as the story unwound, it was easier for the storyteller. They could relax and just allow their memories to flow.

"Adam was amazing when I first met him. He was everything I thought I wanted in a man," Lillian said. "He was handsome, charming and he smiled so much. I didn't meet a lot of men who smiled as a child. They were all austere like my father...they smiled when they were tucked in my father's study with their whiskey and cigars but nowhere else."

Allison nodded but didn't reply. Today there had been no dance, and Lillian had just launched into her story without even taking a breath. "But Adam...Adam loved life and he loved all the fine things his career afforded him."

"How long were you with him before you realized he was a pimp?" Allison asked.

"A few months...maybe even half a year," Lillian replied on a breath heavy with smoke. She watched it float up to the ceiling; Allison watched it as well as though she could see the memory that was clouding Lillian's eyes with emotion.

"He was so patient," she continued, "After that first meeting at the bus stop, he started coming by on a regular basis. He would always bring hot chocolate and then he would take me to the restaurant. I would eat alone at first but, after a while, I asked him to join me. I figured that was the only thing I could offer him, and he would chat about his life."

A dry laugh interrupted her words but there was no mirth in Lillian's eyes, "At least, I thought he was talking about his life. I was such a naive little bitch at the time. I thought I was providing him with a sounding board. I thought he needed me as much as I needed his generosity but all he was telling me was a rehearsed script he had created. He knew it so well...knew exactly what to say that made a girl think he was harmless. He was the good guy...the rest of the world was out to get us, and he was the shore where we could weather the storm. He'd used it many times and I was as easy a victim as every other girl."

Leaning back, Lillian ran her nervous fingers through her hair. She caught Allison's gaze and for a brief second, Allison could see the young girl in her eyes. Tired, hungry, scared...she'd needed her knight and the only one the world produced was a predator.

"I moved in with him after about three months. He'd been so careful about how it was offered to me that I actually thought I was the one who'd asked. And that first night when I'd slept in clean sheets, I was so grateful to him and believed that he could do nothing wrong. I was already in love with him when I moved in."

"So, you admit that you loved him?"

"Sure, I loved him. And Jessica loved him...and Tracy...and Brie...and every other girl that used that guest room before and after me. We loved him because it was easy to. No matter where we came from, Adam was offering us so much. He gave us gifts, gave us a beautiful condo to live in, he gave us security after living without it. He had enough style and wealth to pass as the dream guy we all wanted to save us."

Lillian shook her head and stood up. She moved towards the window, one of her favorite perches in the room. She stared outside but Allison knew she wasn't seeing anything but a world from long ago. "Did you sleep with him?"

"No...not at first."

"When did you sleep with him for the first time?"

"About two months after I moved in with him. I thought I was in love. I thought he was in love." She glanced over her shoulder, "I had nothing to give him in exchange for everything he did for me. What else could I give him except myself?"

"Did he force you?"

Lillian turned back to the window, "No. But he didn't give me much of a choice. When I first moved in with him, he didn't touch me...didn't even notice I was a woman. At first, I was grateful. After everything I had gone through..." her voice trailed away before she shook her head...and the new memory that had surfaced in it. "It was wonderful to not be looked at simply as a woman. Then I started getting frustrated. Why wasn't he looking at me like a woman? What was wrong with me?"

She leaned against the cool glass and Allison could tell Lillian was staring at her faint reflection, "Then it changed slowly. First, it was the compliments about how beautiful I was. Then it would be the way he watched me...as though he really saw me. Like he understood who I was inside my body."

She sighed, "Then he would caress me. So light, sometimes I thought I was imagining it, but I knew he was sexually attracted to me. I just needed to feel loved by someone. When he finally kissed me, it was easy to allow him to do more. I cried when he made love to me; it had been so tender."

"Was it your first time?"

Her body shifted, and Allison realized she'd asked the wrong question. Lillian glared over her shoulder, "I was nearly sixteen so what do you think?"

Allison shook her head, "I don't know." Her hazel eyes met Lillian's green ones and she sat still, waiting for the anger to drain from Lillian.

As though she saw something in Allison's eyes, Lillian nodded and then turned back to the window. "No, he wasn't my first...my first was long before I'd ever met Adam."

She leaned against the window again and was lost in her thoughts as Allison sat at the table and focused on the familiar black smudge.

Finally, Lillian took a deep breath and turned away from the window. She crossed the room and slid into the chair before she palmed the beat-up package of cigarettes.

Allison watched Lillian's hands shake as she pulled one out and lit it. Finally, after she had drawn a breath of smoke, Lillian said, "But we were talking about my first time with Adam, weren't we? Not my first time being fucked."

Lillian's eyes narrowed, and she snapped, "So, do you want to know what we did the first time we fucked? Do you need all those little details of how he touched my tits and how I sucked on his cock?"

Allison shook her head; it was like a sudden tornado of emotion. One moment Lillian had been still...the calm before the storm and the next, she'd been filled with rage. Swallowing, Allison tried again, "If you want to. This is your story Lillian, think of me as a tape player...I am simply here to record everything."

Lillian grinned but there was no warmth in it; it was a cold grin when matched with the anger in her eyes. "Yeah, I highly doubt that is all you do. After all, my story is just one facet of this piece of shit we call a diamond. You have to polish it all to make it sparkle for your publisher...and that means you are doing a lot more than recording."

Nodding, Allison didn't see the point to argue. Really, in a way, Lillian was right. If she just wrote what Lillian said, verbatim, the story wouldn't sell. But Allison could sense Lillian swimming around her...waiting for the first sign of blood to finish her...her book and everything that was riding on this. Instead, Allison treaded the water, watching as the anger began to drain from Lillian as smoke swirled around their heads from the ignored cigarette.

Lillian's hand reached out, "I'm sorry," she muttered, "Why don't we just talk about what happened after I slept with Adam?"

And like that, the storm was gone. "Okay," Allison said, "What happened after you slept with Adam?"

"We just went on. It was like we started dating but we weren't dating. At first, I always went back to my bedroom to sleep after sex but, eventually, it was just easier to sleep with him."

"Why?"

"Because, sometimes, he would wake me up in the middle of the night to fuck me." The words were edged in that barely contained rage. "I mean, what we did at the beginning of the night was different...tender... but when he woke me up, it wasn't Adam who did it. It was some monster that shared Adam's body."

Lillian raised her head and stared at Allison, the anger gone completely and all that was left was a sad and broken girl...a girl who didn't understand anything that had happened to her. "He would grab my foot from under the blanket and drag me onto the floor. I would always fight, I don't understand why; maybe because of how jarring it was to be woken like that. He always seemed happy when I did. Then his hands would be on me; punching, scratching, slapping."

Her voice rose with panic as she continued, and her eyes flashed white as terror seemed to grip her. "He seemed to enjoy hurting me and he would tell me how I was his and no one else's. He would tell me that he could fuck me if he wanted to and how he could kill me—snuff out my life—and no one would care that a dumb whore was dead. Then his hands would rip away my clothes before he wrapped them around my throat. I always lost consciousness before he was finished but I knew he was raping me." She wrapped her arms around her waist, "I knew that he was right, that no one cared what happened to me, that I was his to fuck and to kill. His to punch and slap. I was his dumb little whore and he'd seen my color the moment he'd found me at that bus stop."

Allison blinked back the tears she felt brimming in her eyes. She wanted to stay detached but something about a fifteen-year-old girl being in that situation was playing havoc with her emotions. "So you moved into his bedroom and you didn't leave?"

Lillian shook her head, "How could I leave? Where could I go? Most of the time, Adam was gentle. He loved me and he treated me like I was everything good in his life. In the mornings, I would wake up sore, but he would be there with breakfast and an apology. Adam had his demons and they surfaced at night; or, at least, that was his excuse. And I bought that. I wanted to heal him and a part of me believed his words. I was just a whore, not worth anything, not like Adam."

"How long did this go on?"

"Before it escalated? Four months. He was amazing most of the time. He took me out shopping, colored my hair and created Lily Laurent. I started to feel alive again. My hair, which I'd chopped off before I ran away," her mouth soured as she spoke and a hidden memory flashed in her eyes, "was growing back and the scars from my months on the street were fading. I looked normal again and felt beautiful. I was used to the finer things in life and having them back was bitter sweet after all those months on the street."

"Did you know he was a pimp by this time?"

"Yeah, after I moved into his room, he moved a new girl into my vacant one. Her name was Tiffany and I think she was thirteen or fourteen. I didn't care about her though. Adam loved me and he made sure everyone knew that. And I knew that he would never make me sleep with another man...he needed me to heal his scars. Boy, was I such a stupid bitch."

Allison didn't reply but she wanted to. She'd seen this before in other inmates she'd interviewed—the man who only wanted what was best for his woman but was flawed and damaged. A man who they could save with their love. It was a common trap—the tragic part was that it was such an easy trap and even the most intelligent person could fall prey to it.

"When did you start prostituting for him?"

Lillian pulled out a cigarette and lit it, signaling to Allison that she was ready to move into her story. "It was on my sixteenth birthday," she said dryly, "But a part of me knew it was coming. I could see it in the way he was treating me. For weeks, something had seemed off. The nights were more frequent...more violent. And then I came home one night and found Adam sitting on the couch, his eyes filled with anger and hate."

●————————————————————————●

The groceries felt heavy in my arms as I stepped into the apartment, but I couldn't stop the smile spreading across my lips. It was my birthday and Adam had promised that we'd do something special tonight. When I'd woken up in the morning, he'd said he had a surprise he'd been waiting to give me for weeks. Glancing into the mirror in the hallway, I paused for a moment as I stared at the girl...no woman...looking back at me.

I didn't look sixteen with my dyed blonde hair and perfectly applied makeup. I could easily pass for someone over twenty-one and I could pretend that nothing bad had happened to me. I looked like someone who'd never seen the darker elements of life. Except my green eyes, which I detested, showed an edge of unhappiness that I couldn't force away, no matter how much I pretended to be someone else.

"Lillian, is that you?"

Dad? The world dropped from below my feet and with it, I felt my stomach turn over as a wave nausea swept over me. The room spun and the image in the mirror blurred as tears filled my eyes. How? Why?

Turning towards the living room, I clutched the paper grocery bag against my chest and, my feet dragging, stepped into the room. Adam was alone, sitting on the couch. His face was twisted in anger and a trill of fear ran down my spine before relief flooded through my body. He wasn't here...I was safe...he would never find me...never touch me again.

Then my mind wrapped around the one-word Adam had spoken, 'Lillian'. "Wha—" I swallowed in an effort to moisten my mouth, which had gone dry. Shaking my head, I continued, "What did you call me?"

His eyes narrowed and he leaned back in his seat, his hand crumpling a piece of paper that he held. "That's your name isn't it? Lillian Ross?"

Tears slipped down my face and I felt my chest grip tightly on my lungs. I couldn't breathe, couldn't draw the oxygen into my lungs as Adam glared at me. "I know that Lily can be short for Lillian, but I didn't expect you to lie to me Lillian." He emphasized my name, making me cringe. "You acted like this dumb kid that came from a bad situation, but you were lying."

He flung the paper onto the coffee table and I stared at it. I couldn't see much due to the creases, but I saw my last name—my missing person's flyer. I shook my head, "I did," I cried, "You don't understand what it was like living with my father. You don't understand what he did to me."

The groceries slid from my arms as I fell to the floor. My hands cupped my face to block out Adam's snarling lips and to cover my shame. I couldn't understand why this mattered, couldn't understand why he was being so cruel. I was still the girl he met...I was still his Lily. "You bitch, what most of us wouldn't give for the life you walked away from," he screamed. "The money, the luxury and you just gave it all up. Then you expected me to give it back to you."

He stood up and I fell backwards as I tried to stay out of his reach. Raising his hand, he paused as he stared down at me, judging me, weighing me against everything that I had told him. "Please," I cried, "Please Adam, I'm sorry I didn't tell you, but I was scared to."

Adam cocked his head to the side, "Scared of what? Of me?"

Terror lanced through me and for the first time, I realized just how deeply Adam's monsters ran. I should have been more afraid of him than I was, but the fear of my father still clutched my heart. Adam could be fixed, he could be made to understand but my father couldn't. What he would do to me would be worse than anything Adam would do. "My f-fa-father," I stammered as my mind whirled around how I could make Adam happy.

His arm dropped and I winced. When I felt no blow, I slowly opened my eyes and stared up at him. The anger was gone, and he stroked his jaw, deep in thought as he stared at my missing person's flyer. "You're worth a lot of money you know. The reward for your recovery is a hundred thousand dollars. I could bring you home...be a hero and you would be back where you belong."

I stared up at him in horror—a grin spread across his face as though he liked my fear. "Yeah," he smiled before he picked up the paper, "What I could do with the hundred thousand. And you wouldn't have to worry about your next meal. You wouldn't have to worry about anything and your parents...your poor, poor parents could finally rest easy. Even your little sister wouldn't have to worry about you. You never told me about your sister, Hayley. Is she as beautiful as you?"

I winced when he mentioned my sister, but I shook my head, "How do you know about her?" I asked, my voice gaining strength as my tears stopped.

Adam shook his head and gave me a reproachful glance, "Do you really think I just found out? I found the flyer weeks ago and I have been sitting on it while I researched who you were. I needed to be sure that my Lily was this Lillian Ross girl." He leaned down and rolled one of my blonde locks between his fingers. "You looked a bit different, but it was the eyes that were the proof. You have such beautiful eyes and I knew there couldn't be two girls with the same ones."

I shuddered as his fingers slid through my hair and then behind my neck. His forehead touched mine before his lips caressed the corner of my mouth. It was so gentle that I wasn't sure if I imagined it. "I just don't know what to do with you Lily," he murmured against me, "I love you and then you hurt me. You put me at risk of being arrested and now I'm stuck having to decide between my heart breaking or my life being destroyed. Why did you do that to me?"

As I tried to pull away so I could think clearly without him touching me, his fingers bit into the back of my neck, causing me to go still. "I didn't know," I whispered, "I thought it didn't matter to you."

Tsking, he kissed me again, "It shouldn't but it does. Your family has money; money that I need and money they can use to find you. What do you think will happen to me if they find you here? Do you think they will see me as just a guy who helped a homeless girl?"

"I don't know..."

"What if you decide to say I kidnapped you?" he cut off my words with a shake of his fist. "What defense would I have?"

Letting me go, he stared at the paper in his hand, "No, I think that I need to send Lillian home and lose my Lily."

I shook my head as the sobs racked my body again. I needed Adam, I needed him to save me from my father like he saved me from the street. "Please Adam," I groveled, "Don't send me back to him."

"Was he really that bad Lillian?" I winced every time he called me that; it was like his decision had been made and he was killing the woman he had created.

I wanted to tell him everything. About my childhood, the cruel father and the cold mother but I couldn't. "Yes," I hissed.

He paused and stared at me and I knew that he was planning something; knew that he was looking at all his possibilities. Despite only knowing him for less than a year, I knew that he would do whatever benefited him the most—I just had to prove that keeping me was the best option.

"Don't send me back," I begged.

"And why shouldn't I?" he asked, "Why shouldn't I get the money? I mean, all you do is waste mine. You are a drain on me Lillian and you give nothing back."

"All the other girls that I take in, they repay me in some way. They work for everything that I give them," he continued, "But I never asked that of you. You were my Lily...my beautiful, untouched Lily...and I was happy to provide everything that I could for you."

He squatted down in front of me and cupped my chin. Tears slid down my cheeks and he murmured, "How is it possible that you are even more beautiful when you're sad?"

His fingers pinched my skin when I didn't answer so I said, "I'm don't know."

"Such fragility, such beauty and you hold it up for the world to grovel at your feet...for the world to long to have just one taste of you and then you deny them. How everyone must hate you Lillian. Is that why you ran away, because they all wanted you."

The words, so close to the truth, burned my heart into ash. I could hear the want in his tone and knew that while he'd fucked Lily, I'd never given him Lillian. "Please," my mouth felt bruised around the word, "Don't send me back. I thought you loved me."

"But I don't love Lillian. I loved my Lily and I want my Lily to stay with me."

He dropped my chin, stood up and I instantly wrapped my arms around his legs, terrified that his next step would be dragging me out the door and to my parents' home. "I will do anything to stay," I wailed.

"Anything?" he grinned, and I regretted my words the moment I saw the look on his face. "You'll do anything for me?"

I screamed in my brain, *Stop...don't agree to this.* But I whispered, "Anything."

"Well, my dear Lily. There is something you can do or, rather, someone. I told him about you, and he has wanted to meet you for months, but I was greedy...I wanted you for myself."

Terror slid through me as I stared up at him. "So tonight, your special night is going to be a date with this someone. You are going to do everything that he tells you to do and you are going to pretend to enjoy it. Do you understand?" His tone was cold, and I realized that this was the real Adam; the one who I should have been afraid of from the start.

Despair washed over me, and I knew that this was my life. I was worth nothing, just a whore like he'd said all those times at night. I nodded as he continued, "If you don't do what I'm asking, I have no choice but to send you back to your parents."

The sob ripped through me and I felt my heart break even more. I felt my body shaking and I clenched my fists to try to stop it. He reached down and dragged me to my feet like a rag doll. Even at sixteen, I was as tall as him and I stared directly into his eyes. "You know, my plan was to eventually put you on the street, and have you work a corner, but I quickly discovered that you were like a fine wine. Refined, cultured, educated, articulate; you needed a better client base, needed to be shared for the most money and not just fifty bucks to whoever could pay. You are the best commodity and only the best clients are there for you."

Wiping the tears from my cheeks, he leaned forward and kissed me again. This time, there was no warmth, no spark of gratitude from me—all that was left was a cold revulsion towards him. As I stared at him, I knew that I would stay with Adam and do everything he asked...nothing he did to me could be worse than my father. "Now I left you a nice outfit on the bed. Go and have a shower, then put it on. Your appointment is at seven."

He turned away, and I threw one last glance towards the door...towards freedom, before I turned my back on all of that and walked into the bedroom to find a private school uniform waiting on the bed.

●————————————————————————————●

"Who was the client?" Allison asked when it was clear that Lillian was finished. She wasn't surprised by what Lillian had told her. Predators had their own way of getting their victims to do what they wanted, and Adam was definitely a manipulator. It must have been more terrifying for Lillian to go home than to stay with him and Adam had capitalized on it. But why? Surely going home was the safer option.

Outside of admitting to being hit by her father, Lillian had shared very little about her family life before she'd run away. To understand the why, Allison really needed to know about that part of her life—those fifteen years that filled a young girl with so much terror.

"Carl Huntington," Lillian said, "He was a small-time politician. Really didn't amount to anything but he had a lot of money and he liked dress up. Actually, he wasn't that bad when it comes to clients. Sometimes he couldn't even get an erection so I would just lay there with him until he was ready to leave."

Lillian shrugged her shoulders and Allison couldn't imagine how sleeping with a stranger like that could be viewed as not that bad. "He became a regular," Lillian answered before Allison could ask, "He was an easy job."

"Did you just have that one client?"

Her laugh filled the room. "God no. Adam wasn't wrong, I was a rare commodity and I was quickly put to good use. I had tons of clients before I even made it a month. By the time I was eighteen and legal, I was working steady and had dates almost every night. I was a girlfriend experience. Wealthy men who needed a date for a gala or needed a travel partner would book me and I would give them everything a girlfriend would without any of the hassles, combined with the depraved sex they wanted. By the time I was eighteen, Adam's escort agency was busy, and he didn't need to go and groom girls like he used to. There were plenty of women looking for high paying work."

"Did he stop pimping and just run the agency?" Allison asked.

"No, he cut down but there was a thrill there that he couldn't give up." Lillian's smile slipped, "Besides, he couldn't rough up the escorts like he could his girls and he loved to hit women. He also loved the thrill of grooming them."

Lillian shook her head sadly, "Of all the regrets I have in life, my biggest is that I didn't stop him from grooming more girls," then she stood up and walked to the door...their meeting obviously at an end for the day.

CHAPTER TEN

Prosecutor Deveins (PD): Ms. Forester, you said that your father was a good man, a great father...can you describe what type of father he was?

Hayley Forester (HF): Yes...silence...

PD: Ms. Forester?

HF: I'm sorry, I'm just trying to gather my thoughts. I'm not sure how to explain my dad.

PD: Don't worry, take your time. Would you say he was a caring father?

HF Nods

PD: I'm sorry but can you give a verbal answer.

HF: Yes, he was very caring. He only wanted the best for us, especially for Lillian. He put a lot of his attention into her.

Defendant snorts.

PD: What type of attention?

HF: He would have her come into his study for hours at a time to make sure that her assignments were caught up. She often lagged behind, especially during that last year before she ran away.

PD: Was she struggling at school?

HF: I'm not sure how much she was struggling...one thing my father believed in was not dragging me into the problems. Instead, I watched Lillian as she screamed and yelled, and I would hear her crying in his study. He was strict, he took things away from her, didn't allow her to hang out with friends but he was trying to get her turned around.

PD: He was strict? Did he physically hit you or your sister?

HF: N...No, he didn't.

Defendant: That is a lie Hayley, you know it is.

Judge Abrams: Control your client, counsel.

Defendant: You don't have to keep lying Hayley, he's dead and he can't hurt us anymore!

~ Official Court Transcripts: People vs. Lillian Ross

●━━━━━━━━━━━━━━━●

    The bustle of the office created a low hum around Allison, and she shifted in her seat as she stared at the abstract paintings decorating the office. The well-groomed, distinguished woman sitting across from her looked up briefly before she returned to typing. Allison watched her for a few minutes, but the woman continued to ignore her as she tucked an errant black hair behind her ear and smoothed the gray suit jacket she was wearing.

Glancing at the clock, Allison jumped when she heard a buzz from the desk. The woman cleared her throat and said, "Ms. Forester will see you now."

Allison nodded, "Thank you," and gathered up her bag.

Stepping through the door, she found herself in another large room. The fall skyline stretched out before her in the floor to ceiling windows across from the door and the three other walls were filled with bookshelves and a large inventory of law books. In the center of the room, sitting behind an oversized mahogany desk was a woman, her blonde hair piled on the top of her head in a messy bun, her blue eyes scanned a document in front of her and she didn't even spare Allison a glance.

Allison stood on the threshold of the room, waiting to be acknowledged, and studied the woman, Hayley Forester. Really, the woman could have passed for a relative of Allison rather than a sister of Lillian. In fact, Allison couldn't see much that would tie the two women together. Then Hayley looked up and Allison saw the same intelligence she'd seen in Lillian's. The same sadness was there as well.

Ms. Forester stood up and extended her hand. The woman was tall and thin—another resemblance that the sisters shared—and she was dressed in a black pantsuit with a light blue blouse. Everything about her spoke of efficiency and class. "Ms. McKinnon," she said, her voice firm.

"Ms. Forester. Thank you for taking the time to talk to me," Allison took Hayley's hand in hers and was greeted with a firm handshake. Definitely a woman who was used to running in a man's world.

"Let's cut out the pleasantries," Hayley said as she sat down again. She motioned toward the chairs opposite hers. "You know as well as I do that I don't want you here. The only reason why you're here is because I am trying to control the damage that you are going to do."

Allison raised an eyebrow and stiffened. Despite her topic, Allison tried to prevent the damage that publishing could cause. She worked with families, gave them every chance to read her manuscripts and listened to their concerns. *But that's when you're writing the books for the victim,* a voice chided her. "I am not sure if I understand," Allison said slowly, "You set this meeting."

"I know I did," Hayley snapped, her eyes flashing with anger, "And god, how I wish I hadn't. But this book is going to be a family curse and it will destroy my mother when it comes out."

"Why?"

Hayley's mouth snapped closed and her cheeks went red. Opening her mouth, Hayley closed it again and stared down at her hands, which were folded on the top of her desk. Her well-manicured fingers were free of any jewelry and Allison made note of that.

Looking up at her, the fight was gone from Hayley's eyes and her voice was tempered as she said, "It just will. My mother has never been strong and what happened to my father destroyed her. She is not the same woman that she used to be."

Allison nodded, "The last thing I want to do is hurt your family, but you have to realize that Lillian never shared what happened in that apartment. She's never really shared anything about her life. Everything that has been written before now has just been suppositions. Despite what your sister did, she deserves to share her story."

"Yes, I understand that," Hayley whispered, "But I'm afraid of what she will tell and how it will affect us."

Hayley leaned back and stared at her...it was clear that she was sizing Allison up and trying to figure out the best way to approach the problem. Finally, she laughed, a harsh sound that filled the uncomfortable silence. "I was going to threaten legal recourse when you walked in here. I was all set to bring down the wrath of hell on you but there is no point. Lillian's story will get out there eventually. It might be next month, next year or ten years from now. It's like a knife hanging over my head...over my family. We can bury our heads in the sand and pray that it won't fall, but that isn't how I am. So write your story, ask your questions...and I will try to help you as much as I can."

A comforting smile filled Hayley's face and Allison realized that Lillian was there in the room with them—Hayley looked exactly like her sister at the moment. Glancing at her hand again, Allison said, "Thank you. Could we begin then, I do have some questions that I would like to ask."

Hayley followed her gaze to her hand and answered the unasked question. "I divorced my husband five years ago."

"I'm sorry, I didn't realize as it wasn't in any of the files I have."

Waving her hand in dismissal, Hayley said, "Don't apologize. It was the last tie that my father had to my life and I finally severed it. Really, I should have done it years before I did but it took me a long time to not be terrified of what life without David would be like."

Allison raised an eyebrow in question and Hayley seemed almost relieved to be discussing her divorce...maybe it was easier to talk about her ex-husband than to talk about her deceased father and her sister. "David was handpicked as my husband."

"An arranged marriage?"

She laughed, "Oh, god no! But my father made it very clear that he approved of David over other men that I was dating at the time. He was grooming David to become a congressman eventually. He had a lot of hope for him and it didn't matter that David is ten years older than I am."

"How did you meet your husband?"

"Through my father; he was at some dinner or other that my father was hosting. I didn't like him. I was nineteen and pursing my degree in law. David was already a lawyer in a very prominent firm, and he was close to becoming a junior partner. He was controlling like my father, which is probably why my father liked him."

Allison nodded, "How was your father controlling?"

Hayley's smile soured before it slipped completely. Memories chased across her eyes and Allison could tell that most of them weren't happy memories. She sighed as her vision cleared. "Before you start heading in that direction, I know that my father wasn't an easy man. He had his own flaws, but I did love him."

She continued, "But I also hated him. God! How I hated that man at times, and I hated David in the exact same way." Tears filled her blue eyes and she glanced out at the peaceful skyline. "The first time I met David, he didn't seem interested in me, but my father saw what he wanted."

"And what was that?"

"That his daughter become the happy wife of a congressman...and maybe even the president eventually. I was a commodity and, although I was going to school for my law degree, it was clear that I would have to give it up the moment my father found a suitable husband for me."

She sighed again and swiped at the tears that still hadn't fallen, "I'd always known what my father was grooming me for, but I hadn't expected it to happen so quickly. I knew that he hated the fact I was pursuing law, but it was the only thing that he didn't control me on. Really, law was my way to rebel against him...against being the perfect doll he wanted me to be. But I never took my bar exam after I graduated. Instead, I married David."

"So your father pressured you into marrying David?"

"Pressured? Pressured means I had a choice. I didn't and David knew there was no love in our marriage. He was eager to have a connection to my father and I was the perfect one. The marriage was flawed from the beginning and David had a mistress before the ink had even dried on the marriage license."

She shook her head and grimaced, "I begged my mother to help me out of the marriage, but she said it was our lot in life. We had to stand by our husbands. My father was adamant that I did not leave David and it was clear that if I wasn't the perfect wife, he would cut me off completely. I was terrified of displeasing my father, so I didn't leave David."

"Was your father controlling your entire life?"

Shaking her head, Hayley said, "Honestly, I don't remember. I do remember some faded memories of what he was like with Lillian and my mother. I remember Lillian stepping between me and my father one time when I'd come home late from a friend's. He was so angry that I had disobeyed his rules and I do remember feeling terrified by his reaction and then Lillian was there, her eyes filled with terror as she stepped in front of me and said, 'Run Hayley, lock yourself in your bedroom.'"

Her words stopped abruptly. Hayley stood up and began pacing the room like she was a caged animal needing to flee. Allison watched the woman worry away a patch of her carpet before she asked, "Did he hit her instead of you?"

Hayley spun around and stared at Allison. "I don't know."

"You don't."

Shaking her head, Hayley whispered, "I've hated her for so long that I can't believe that she ever took one of my beatings."

"Why?"

"Because she left!" Hayley snapped, "She left, and I was alone with him. He wasn't an easy man and he demanded so much from me. She'd always promised me that she would protect me and then she wasn't there, and father focused on me solely."

Her mouth snapped shut and her eyes widened as though she was surprised by what she'd said. She returned to her seat and sat down stiffly. "Look, this book is about Lillian's demons, not mine. All you need to know is that my father was a hard man to live with. And in his own way, David was even harder. The only blessing from my marriage was that we never had any kids so I could finally leave him."

Seeing the way Hayley's demeanor had stiffened, Allison realized it was better to talk about the marriage than her childhood. It was clear there were a lot of problems in the Ross family and pressuring her to share would spell the end of the interview. "Were you already divorcing him when your father died?"

Hayley shook her head, "No, we were both miserable, but my father would never stand for a divorce marring the image of a perfect family. Lillian's disappearance was a big enough stain, his youngest daughter had to be spotless."

She laughed, a wry sound that had no mirth to it, "You could say that I can thank Lillian for that. When my father died, I tried to hold onto the image for him...for his memory. I was so confused, and I felt trapped, but then, after the hearing, I realized that I was finally free and all I had to do was grab it."

"The divorce was easier than I thought it would be. David didn't have the drive to fight it and without my father, all the things he'd gained from marrying me were gone. He was more than happy to sign the divorce papers, especially since the pre-nup kept him very comfortable after. And then I threw myself into my career and here I am."

Allison sensed that Hayley was finished her story, but she asked, "Is there anything that you want to share about your sister?"

Hayley grimaced, "I don't have a sister. The woman in that courtroom was not Lillian, she was a stranger. I was still really young when Lillian ran away so the memories I have of her are faded...and really, I don't know anything about what happened to her after she ran away."

"Weren't you ever curious?"

"No, I heard enough in the courtroom. I attended every single hearing..." She paused and chewed her lip as though she was unsure if she should say anything else. "If you want to know more about who Lillian was during that time, I would recommend speaking to Eric Landersten."

Allison started, "Who?"

Hayley smirked, "Oh, Lillian hasn't told you about Eric yet, has she?"

"No," Allison replied slowly as she tried to gather her thoughts, "And I don't remember his name in any of the files."

"Why would you?" she asked, "My father wasn't the only one adept at keeping secrets. Lillian has plenty and I would never have known who Eric was if he hadn't come and offered to represent her in court. He'd even attended the funeral of my father and introduced himself to us."

"But who was he?" Allison wasn't sure how she knew this, but she had a feeling that this was one of the missing pieces that had eluded so many other writers who'd gone after this story.

"That would be something Lillian will have to tell you." Hayley said firmly before she turned back to her computer, "Now, if you excuse me, I really have to get back to work."

"Yes, of course, thank you for your time." Allison stood up and made her way toward the door.

As she was closing it behind her, Hayley looked up and said, "And Ms. McKinnon, I expect to read this book before it's published." Her words were firm, and Allison knew Hayley could be the greatest resource she had or the person who shut the whole project down.

"I understand," she said quietly, and then closed the door with a loud click.

CHAPTER ELEVEN

Defense Council (DC): Ms. Jackson, you were the housekeeper and nanny for the Ross family for how long?

Margaret Jackson (MJ): For about twelve years. I started when Lillian was born and was dismissed when she was twelve.

DC: I see, and what was the reason for the dismissal?

MJ: I was dismissed for fighting with Mr. Ross. We'd had a disagreement and he was not happy with what I said.

DC: And what did you say to him?

MJ: That he needed to be gentler with the children. Lillian was such a spirited child and he was rather harsh with her when he punished her. The more he pushed, the more she fought back. By the time I left, it was like we were living in a war zone.

DC: Were they violent with each other?

MJ: Not that I know, but I didn't think there was any love lost between them. It was like Lillian was floating through life waiting to die and I think her father was the result of that. I think something that he was doing to her was killing the spirit in that girl.

DC: Do you think Mr. Ross abused Lillian or his other daughter Hayley?

MJ: I...

PD: Objection. The witness is not an expert and cannot give a personal opinion on the matter.

JA: Sustained.

DC: Did you ever see Mr. Ross hit Lillian or Hayley?

MJ: No...but that doesn't mean I didn't suspect it.

PD: Objection!

~ Official Court Transcripts: People vs. Lillian Ross

The name whirled around in Allison's head and she ached to ask Lillian about. But she didn't. Instead, she saved the name for later when she'd have a chance to go and speak to Eric Landersten. She'd already done some digging and found out that he was a partner in a prominent law firm that specialized in criminal defense. He was Caucasian, married for the last seven years and had two children, both girls.

But she wasn't sure how he was linked to Lillian or even why he'd offered his representation. Why be linked to a scandal if he was part of the scandal? Outside of him hiring her as an escort,

Allison couldn't see any other reason why he would know who Lillian was. They'd grown up in different towns, but they may have met through the agency.

And that didn't add up as well. From the reports and witness statements, Lillian's clientele were usually older gentlemen...Eric was only two years older than Lillian, hardly the average client for her.

Shaking free of her thoughts, Allison watched as Lillian rubbed the tattoo on her wrist and wondered what regrets she was thinking of as she did. Deciding it was more than time to break the silence between them, Allison said, "I spoke with your sister earlier this week."

It was as though a bomb dropped in the room as Lillian's green eyes swiveled to where she was sitting. A look of pure rage filled them, and Allison's breath caught in her throat as Lillian said, "Why?"

She stared at the word as though she could see it. So simple but it held so much wrath. She tried to speak and choked on the words slightly. Clearing her throat, she said, "I needed to make contact..."

"Why?"

"I needed to speak with her to find out more about what you are telling me. I can't write a book solely from your story. I have to fact check..."

"And what, you think I'm lying? Why would I lie about all of this shit? What could I possibly gain from this?"

Holding up her hands, Allison tried to control her own anger, "I'm sorry but I need to do my job. My publisher won't touch the story if I don't follow it up with other people's point of view. I thought you realized that."

Lillian went still, her eyes flashing anger, her mouth a thin slit as she pressed her lips together...and then she fell back to the seat behind her as sorrow filled her body. It was like she'd wilted into nothing and her long fingers covered her face as her shoulders shook. "I'm sorry, I should have realized. I should have known you'd have to speak to my family."

She bit her lip and Allison was again reminded how the sisters shared some traits, "Tell me, how is she doing? I haven't spoken to her since the trial and, at the time, we weren't exactly on good terms," the last sentence was finished with a wry smile and Allison breathed in relief.

"I am not sure. We didn't really spend a lot of time speaking about how she was doing. I know that she is a lawyer now." Lillian nodded. "And she's divorced from her husband. But that is about all I know."

She nodded and leaned back, her head pressed against the dingy walls, "Did she seem happy?"

Allison thought about it, but she wasn't sure how to answer. What was happy? After all, she spent a lot of her time pretending to be happy, pretending to be this complete person while she ignored the holes in her own soul. How could she judge if others were happy? "I don't know," she offered, "I think she is happier than she used to be, but I don't know her well enough."

Lillian nodded again, satisfied with Allison's answer, "What did you talk about?"

"Her divorce. Her husband and how your father picked him for her." Lillian's mouth twisted in disgust as Allison quickly added, "And she talked about how you would get in the way of your father's anger toward her..." *And about Eric Landersten,* she said silently.

Lillian closed her eyes and drew her knees up to her chest before she wrapped her arms around her legs. "I guess I did. At least until I left." The words were so sad that Allison wondered if she would start crying.

"How would you protect her?"

"My father would sometimes go after her...sometimes there was nothing she could do to make him happy and he would go to hit her. I always stepped in and took the blow if I could. Sometimes, if I couldn't make it in front of him in time, I would go up and cradle her in my arms as she cried. My father hated that and sometimes he would come in and hurt me even more for taking care of her, but I didn't care...Hayley deserved to be protected, she was perfect."

"Shhh, don't say anything," I whispered to her as I crawled into the closet with her. Hayley stared up at me, her eyes bright from her tears, her cheeks red from her sadness and her arm red from the welt he'd caused on it. Her sobs grew louder as I snuggled against the small five-year-old. She shuddered against me and I rubbed her long blonde hair. It was as soft as my own, but it was a completely different color.

"Hayley," I whispered, "You have to be quiet or Daddy will come and get us."

I felt an urge to place my fingers around her mouth to stop the sobbing; maybe even to stop her from breathing. I could do it, I could kill her and then myself and Daddy wouldn't ever touch us again. I could stop him from having an excuse for the way his hands would touch me...I wouldn't have to protect her anymore.

I shook her gently when her sobs grew stronger, "Hayley, you need to stop or I will have to leave you alone and then Daddy will come for you and not for me."

The sobs stopped instantly, and I regretted scaring her like that as her eyes widened with terror. "Don't let him Lillian! Don't leave me!"

Any anger I felt at her faded. It wasn't her fault...she was just a stupid kid...she didn't mean to start crying when her toy broke. She didn't know that Daddy had come home like a thundercloud threatening to break. She didn't know her cries would cause him to crash against her, his hand snaking out as he grabbed her arm and throttled her.

Staring down at the bruise of his fingers on Hayley's arm, I knew she wasn't the one I was angry with. I was angry with him. I hated him and felt that hate in the pain across my back. I closed my eyes as I pulled Hayley against me again. "I won't let him hurt you anymore, Hayley. I'll protect you from him."

The words poured from my lips and I knew they were lies, just like I was sure she knew they were. I wasn't big enough to stop him, but I could try to minimize the damage he did to Hayley. Today when I launched myself at him, I'd broken his grip from Hayley as I screamed at her, "Run Hayley, hide!"

Then the blows had rained down on my back and I had curled up into a ball on the ground as I felt his fingers threading through my hair. And then I was thrown through the air. As I crashed down on the ground, I had scanned the room and seen no trace of my sister...the smile on my lips was the last happy thing I felt as my father turned toward me, and his fists crashed down on me.

I could feel my tears soaking Hayley's hair and I swiped at him. She'd grown still in my arms, but I knew she was awake...listening for him in the hallway. We always listened for his footsteps—if he came for us in our rooms, it was bad.

"You're going to leave me," she whispered and my heart broke. I had thought about it. Thought about running away or killing myself, but she was the only reason why I didn't. Someone had to protect her from him.

I pushed her away slightly so she could see the truth in my eyes. "I would never do that to you."

"Yes, you would, to get away from him." I closed my eyes and grimaced. At only five, she was so much older than she should have been.

"Hayley, I won't leave you but if I do leave, I'll take you with me...even if I have to come back for you." The conviction in my voice made it clear I was telling her the truth, but I wasn't sure if she believed me yet.

"You promise," her voice was so weak but there was a hint of hope in it.

"I promise."

"Pinky swear?"

I nodded and held out my pinky. She hooked her small pinky around mind, her eyes filled with hope, "Pinky swear."

She gave me a watery smile and I pulled her back into my arms. "Everything will be okay. We'll be happy one day and Daddy won't be able to hurt us anymore. He'll just be a memory and we can go someplace beautiful and happy."

"Will Momma be able to come with us?"

I paused and stared at her hands playing with a strand of my long hair. I watched as she twisted it with a strand of hers— light and dark forever connected. I wanted to tell her no...wanted to tell her that she shouldn't care about Momma—that she would hurt her eventually. "Yes, Momma can come too." I didn't have the heart to tell her no; Hayley still went out to the garden and saw how beautiful Momma could be. I hadn't been in Momma's special place for years; I wasn't welcome there anymore.

"And we could live in a beautiful house."

"Yes, Hayley, more beautiful than this house and there wouldn't be any tears in that house. Only laughter."

"And we would have a beautiful garden for Momma?"

"Yes, we will have a garden and we'll have a pony just for you."

"A pony? Really?"

"Yes, and I will have a horse I can ride until I can't breathe from the happiness that I feel. And we'll all be happy." I could see the house we would have without Daddy...and I could believe we would have it...almost. I closed my eyes like I knew Hayley was doing. This always calmed her down and we had the dream perfected. I only had to say a few things and then Hayley could see all of it from the colorful garden to the way her room was safe for her.

As though he sensed our small piece of happiness, the bedroom door swung open and I peered out through the door of the closet. There was no way that he could see us, but I knew he knew where we were. Hayley must have known it as well because she stiffened in my arms, her fingers still in my hair.

"Girls."

The word caused a swooshing feeling in my brain, like a rug had been pulled out from under my feet and Hayley whimpered. "Shhh," I whispered before I answered, "Yes, Daddy?"

"Come out here."

I closed my eyes, unwrapped our hair, and gently placed Hayley down on the pile of blankets in the closet. She often slept in here because the monster in the house was much scarier than any we would find in the closet. I kissed her forehead as she stared at me in terror. She didn't want to go out and I wouldn't make her. I would lie to him.

Pulling her hands from where they gripped my arm painfully, I crawled out of the closet and slowly closed the door on her. I stared at the closed door as I stood and steeled myself to face my father.

Turning, I felt that sudden rush of air again and wanted to cry out in terror. My heart beat against my chest and I bit back the scream as he took a step towards me. His eyes were on the closet door and I knew he wasn't done with Hayley. He wanted her and my skin crawled at the need in his eyes. "Hayley, come out here now!" He didn't yell but that only made it scarier. If he yelled, it wouldn't seem like everything he did was planned.

"She's sleeping," I lied and stepped into his line of sight. I wished I hadn't done that. Wished that I was willing to let him take out everything on Hayley, but I couldn't do that. She deserved what little happiness she could have with Daddy being here. I didn't deserve that happiness. I was worthless...something that could be used whatever way he wanted to use me.

"Lillian, go to your room." He stared at my face and I knew he was ignoring the bruises on my arms and legs. My short nightgown didn't hide the damage—new and old—that he had done to me. The new bruises covered older ones and it seemed like his attacks were growing more frequent. Nothing I did was ever good enough, but I didn't seem to care.

I felt empty and I used that emptiness to not feel what he did with me. The only time I felt anything now was when I watched him hit Hayley. "She's sleeping, Daddy." I stared at him as I repeated my words.

"And I said to go to your room!"

I shook my head, "No, Daddy. You need to leave Hayley alone. She's sleeping." I could hear her whimper slightly at his rage and I was glad I closed the door so she couldn't see what would happen next.

He took a step toward me, his hand lifting in the air as he drew back to slap me. I stared into his eyes, no fear...no emotion...there was nothing. Lillian wasn't here. She was in that house, dancing in the garden as Hayley's blonde hair sparkled in the sunlight. She was riding her black horse, racing through the fields and laughing; a sound I didn't know any longer.

I closed my eyes as his hand descended and then jumped open as his blow didn't land. Instead, his hand caressed my cheek and I stared up into the eyes I hated most of all. I could become empty when he hit me, but I couldn't lose myself in the dream when he looked at me like that.

"Very well Lillian. I supposed she is sleeping," he made a point of looking at the closet door. He knew I was lying! "So you can come to my study."

Tears sprang to my eyes and it felt like he had just punched me in the gut, "No, Daddy!" I cried.

He raised an eyebrow at me, his smile wolfish as he said, "Well, then send your sister."

I gagged at the thought of what he was asking me. Never! I would never send her to his study. I shook my head, "No Daddy."

"No?" His eyes filled with rage again and all I could do was pray that he became so angry he would hit me. It would be so much better than what would happen behind the doors of his study. Then the anger left them again and I knew there was no way out of it. "You will come or you will send your sister. Do you understand me, Lillian?"

I nodded and tried not to choke on the ash in my mouth, "Yes Daddy. But..."

"But?"

I knew the word was dangerous, but I couldn't stop myself from saying it, "Promise me you'll leave Hayley alone."

He went still and watched me until I began to squirm under his perusal. "Such a good sister, Lillian," he murmured, "I'll leave Hayley be if you are a good girl and listen to me."

I nodded and didn't say anything. It was a stupid request and I knew that no matter whether he promised or not, he would not keep it. He was a liar...he was a monster. His hand slid through my hair and he kissed my forehead, the feel of it slimy against my skin, "That's my good girl. I expect you in my study in five minutes."

And then he let me go and left. I stared at the door he'd just exited and collapsed to my knees as fresh sobs wracked my body. I could hear Hayley sobbing in the closet behind me and I realized that no matter how much I wanted to protect her; how much I loved her, a small part of me hated her for making me the protector.

But none of that matter and for the next five minutes, I cried and prayed that I would be struck dead on my way to the study

●━━━━━━━━━━━━━━━━━━━━━●

"Are you saying what I think you are?" Allison blurted out the question when Lillian stopped speaking. She couldn't bring her mind around it. Despite everything she knew about the world, she hadn't expected William Ross to be this type of person. Part of her had suspected when Lillian had started her story, but another part of her didn't want to believe it. His public image was one of a caring father and philanthropist...to find out that he was the antithesis of everything that the public thought he was was quite jarring...although it shouldn't be.

Shaking her head to stop her mind from traveling down dark corridors, Allison focused on Lillian. Her eyes were narrowed, and she was assessing Allison, who squirmed under her perusal, like the little girl had. From the way Lillian was staring at her, it was like she saw some of the secrets Allison hid.

"What do you think I'm saying?" Lillian asked, her voice low with a deadly tinge to it.

Allison stopped and stared at the woman. She could sense the storm brewing between them, and she knew when it broke, things would be different. If everything lined up the way Lillian was positioning it, it changed the way the murder occurred. Could it even be murder or was it something that had taken decades to come to fruition?

There was no doubt from Lillian's story, and the anger in her voice as she described it, that she'd been ready to kill or be killed even at the age of nine. The only thing keeping her from ending things one way or another was the fear that her father ruled his home with. Even Hayley was terrified of the man and, obviously, their mother was or she would have intervened. Wouldn't she have?

Allison stared down at her notes and felt her eyes fill with tears. No matter how many times she wrote these words...no matter how many lives she saw ruined by this type of violence, it never prepared her. She wanted to believe in the goodness of humanity. She wanted the black and white. The good guys, her poor victims and the police that helped lay them to rest, and the bad guys; people like Lillian—cold, calculating and bloodthirsty. She didn't want to see the victim in the bad guys, but she knew Lillian was one of those shades of gray she detested so much.

"Ask it Allison," Lillian broke into her thoughts, "Ask me the question."

"Ask it," Lillian's tone was clipped, "Ask me—did your father rape you?"

Allison opened her mouth, but the question didn't come out. She knew the answer. She could see it in the turmoil raging in Lillian's eyes and she knew that same turmoil was in hers. She avoided these stories because she didn't want her own memories to come raging back to life. She'd fought so hard to forget; or at least, pretend to forget.

"Ask it," Lillian snapped angrily, her hand slamming down on the tabletop. "I need someone strong to write my story and if you aren't, you might as well leave right now and forget about ever coming back."

Grinding her teeth, Allison drew in a calming breath and forced all of the thoughts and emotions down deep inside her. She was a professional and she would handle Lillian like she did all of her other clients. She would remain detached, an onlooker regardless of how much Lillian drew her in.

"Did your father sexually abuse you?" she asked, biting each word as she did but changing the question. She hated the taste of the words in her mouth, but they were important.

Lillian sat back and smiled but there was no warmth or happiness in it. She took a deep breath.

"Yes."

CHAPTER TWELVE

Medical Summary Report

Personal History: Jane Doe, later identified as Lily Laurent, was admitted to the hospital at 1:36am by ambulance. She was unconscious at the time of admittance and had substantial wounds on her body.

No personal history was reported at the time of admittance. Upon examination in the emergency room, several injuries were identified including:

- *Contusion on the back of the head, measuring two inches long and one inch wide.*

- *Blood loss from the contusion.*

- *Multiple fractures of the ribs, bilateral*

- *Third and fourth finger broken at the knuckle on the right hand*

- *Thumb and index finger broken at the mid-joint on the left hand*

- *Bruising on the chest, stomach, arms and legs*

- *Crushed larynx*

- *Possible internal bleeding*

- *Lacerations on fingers and palms from blade like object*

Lily appeared to have suffered from a severe assault and extensive medical intervention was needed. Medically induced coma was administered as there was some concern, from the extent of head injuries, that there was a significant risk of a brain injury or brain bleed.

~ Excerpt from medical report of Lily Laurent

Allison stared at the windows of her house, but she couldn't draw the strength to pull herself from the car. She'd driven home completely numb and she wasn't sure how she'd even managed it. One minute she was there, in the prison with Lillian. The word, such a simple word...yes...echoing through the room as she felt each letter like a punch to her gut. She should have known. Should have seen it in the medical and coroner reports. The rage Lillian had attacked him with wasn't the rage you would expect from an errant daughter.

Maybe the physical and emotional abuse could have caused that rage, but that anger made sense now. After all, hadn't she felt that anger herself? Wanted to throw herself against him and beat him to death with her own hands.

She caught her reflection in the rear-view mirror and shuddered at the rage she saw there. And the sorrow. She could see Lillian and Hayley. The little girls who just needed someone to love them, needed someone to take care of them and all they'd had was each other. They weren't strong enough to fight against William, and they shouldn't have had to.

Screaming, Allison jumped at the sound of a knock on the window. She glanced up and noticed her mother. Her short hair was a stylish bob and the silver suited her so much better than blonde ever had. Her eyes were squinting, producing more lines that she'd have to hide with Botox. Allison knew she wasn't happy.

"Allison?" The question was filled with so much concern, Allison was reacting before she could even process what she was doing.

Without thought, she unlocked her car door and slid out of it. She wrapped her arms around her mother's waist and sobbed. She sobbed for Lillian sitting in her cell, sobbed for the little girls that William had hurt, and she sobbed for herself and all the secrets she carried. All the scars she felt needling along her soul.

Her mother didn't say anything. She simply rubbed Allison's hair as she navigated the crying woman toward the door. Allison felt, rather than heard, Frank as he took the key and unlocked the door. Then he went into the kitchen, leaving the two women to stand in the foyer as Allison continued to cry.

Mercutio wrapped himself around her ankles before he slunk off, following Frank in search of food. She could hear Frank as he filled the tea kettle with water and set it on the stove. Then she felt her mother move away slightly, opening the space between them. "Ali, what in the world?"

Allison shook her head and accepted the tissue her mother passed her. "It's nothing. Just work."

The twist of her mother's lips made it clear just what she thought of Allison's work, but she didn't say anything except, "Let's talk about it over a cup of tea."

Nodding, Allison followed her into the kitchen and noticed that Frank had made himself disappear, along with the cat. He was good at that. Always finding somewhere else to be when his wife, Ruth, was on the war path about something. Since Allison hadn't been expecting her, she knew her mom was here to rant about something.

Probably work, she thought to herself as she watched Ruth maneuver around the kitchen as she finished making the tea. Allison studied her and realized she was still as beautiful as she always was. Ruth was tall, distinguished and elegant. She'd demanded attention in her youth and her presence still filled a room. Sure, she'd had a little work done but she didn't look her age. In fact, she looked like she was barely fifty.

Allison felt frumpy beside her, like she often did. Turning around, Ruth's eyes narrowed as she gave her a cold perusal. "You look like crap Allison."

"Thanks Mom," Allison said and rolled her eyes, although she murmured another thanks as she took the hot mug between her hands. The warmth of the tea spread through her and she hadn't realized she was so cold. She shuddered again as Lillian's face swam into her memory; she'd looked so defeated and maybe even relieved that she'd finally said the words.

How many times had she said it to herself? How many times had Lillian wanted to say something and then not said it? She wanted to ask her, but Allison knew it was useless. Nothing was going to change the past or the outcome that abuse had led to.

"You really need to quit Allison," Ruth said, and Allison glanced up at her. She realized that her mom had been speaking for a few minutes and she'd completely ignored her.

"What did you say? I didn't hear you," she murmured before she took a sip of the tea.

"I said that you should quit. Carl was talking to Frank on the course that you shouldn't be getting involved in this case. Too many people are worried about the story and there is even talk about lawsuits against you and your publisher. Carl really didn't want to see you get hurt."

Carl? Allison wracked her brain as she tried to remember who Carl was and then it hit her, Senator Carl Evans. He was a close friend of Frank and had known him for years. It surprised Allison that he would talk to Frank about her book...and how did all these people know about the book anyway? It wasn't like she, or her publisher, were advertising the book as they really didn't know what they had.

She shook her head to clear it of all the webs. Too many people were interested in seeing the book buried. "What did Frank tell him?"

Ruth's cheeks reddened and she said, "Well, he told him that we had no say in what you do but that he would ask me to speak to you. So here I am, asking you to drop this manuscript."

And there it was. Ruth was often blunt, at least she could credit her mother with that, but it didn't change anything. She wasn't going to drop the book, but she didn't want to fight, not tonight, not after everything. Sighing, Allison asked, "Is that what you really want?"

Ruth fell silent. Allison could sense what she wanted to say, and she was hoping she would say it. She needed to focus on something other than the pain in her heart.

"I feel," Ruth said slowly, "like you are baiting me into a trap."

Allison shook her head and Ruth pursed her lips before she added, "If I tell you I don't want you to write this story, what will you do?"

Allison stared into her tea as. "This isn't my first book and you have never been this vocal about my work before."

Ruth walked into the kitchen and stared at the neglected back garden through the window as she sipped her tea, "I remember when William Ross was murdered. Frank didn't know him directly, but he had friends affected by the murder. It sent a shudder through various circles and when it came to light who the murderer was, it made an even bigger impact."

"But I didn't really think much of those murmurs or gossip. I mean, I'm not naive, I know that Lillian was a prostitute. There were rumors about some of her clients, influential men and there were rumors that some of the men in our circles had hired her. But, most men in our circles have mistresses so we shrugged it off."

She turned toward Allison and there was real worry in her eyes, "But the gossip is starting again, and I think that, if things go bad, they will go bad for you as well. I just don't want you to get hurt by this."

Allison nodded. It made sense and the messages on the answering machine had become an indicator of just how much people wanted this story buried. She wasn't naive either. She knew most of the men Lillian had as clients were influential men...paragons of their community...and she also knew they were worried about what Lillian would say.

"I don't think I will get hurt," she finally said but she knew it as a lie. Already, what Lillian had told her had cut deep. She'd felt the fist raining down on her. She'd remembered the guilt and anger that had consumed most of her teen years. All because of one horrible memory that would never go away.

"You know," Ruth said, "I was right there with you during that court case. I cheered when he was sentenced to eight years and

I cheered even louder when he died of a heart attack three years later."

"But you also cheered when you met him and married the bastard," Allison snapped.

"And that's it, isn't it?" Ruth said, "The reason why you allowed your dad to take care of you so completely. You blamed me for everything because I fell for his lies. And you still blame me, which is why you are so intent on writing the crap that you do."

Allison rubbed her palms against her eyes to stop the hot flood of tears from falling down her cheeks. She thought of all those years... of how much he'd destroyed. The only reason why she hadn't killed Brian was because her dad had helped her heal...he'd helped his ex-wife heal as well, even though he hadn't been obligated to do that.

"If Brian hadn't died in prison and he walked into the room right now, do you think I would be right if I killed him after all these years?"

"No," Ruth managed in a strangled voice and Allison dropped her hands to really look at her mother, "There is no reason big enough to take another person's life. No matter what he'd done, I couldn't validate you for killing him."

Allison felt her stomach roll at the words. Despite every scar they shared, her mother was nothing like her. She didn't live with a monster inside her. "Well, I think there are some things that would validate killing another person and I think Lillian may have a reason she never shared. So, for that reason, I am not going to worry about some old perverts who are worried their affairs are going to be made public. I'm just going to worry about writing the story that she needs to tell. Despite who she is, or who she was, she deserves to be heard."

Allison took a step back, "Now, if you don't mind. I have work to do. Please lock the door behind you when you leave."

And with that, she turned on her heel and fled into her office.

CHAPTER THIRTEEN

We didn't keep accurate files of clients using the services of an escort. Adam wanted it kept that way so his clients could enjoy discreet and completely confidential services. When I started working the administration, I was given a number of rules regarding the booking of appointments. Lily handled the majority of it, but she started to get really busy with clients. Actually, it was almost like she came out of retirement.

At the end of every week, we destroyed credit card information for the clients. So I can't really tell you who Lily's clients were. She had about twenty regulars, but she organized them according to Disney names. She had her seven dwarves and that sort of thing. Dopey was one of her favorites as he was an easy job. Grumpy called a lot but she didn't allow him to book a lot of time as he was pretty rough from what I understand.

My job in the office, outside of making a few appointments for the girls, was to dispose of the numbers so the men didn't risk it being made public. But if you ask me, Adam was photocopying the files, just in case he needed to pull a few favors from the clients. I just have no idea where he was keeping them...and I don't think Lily did either.

~ Statement by Anna Serenchik, Administrator of Discrete Escorts

●━━━━━━━━━━━━━━━━━━━━━━━━━━━━●

M

"He wasn't always a horrible father," Lillian said the minute she walked into the room for their scheduled meeting. Allison nodded and didn't say anything in reply. She knew about the good times and how it was easy to focus on those times when they were happening.

She also knew that it was harder to see those good times when bad things were happening, and she had a feeling that the bad often outweighed the good. She watched as Lillian's restraints were taken off and the guard left the room.

Allison waited as Lillian got comfortable. Her usual cigarette lit within seconds of sitting down. Letting out a long breath, Lillian said, "I left you with a lot last time, didn't I?"

"Yes, although I did suspect something when you were talking."

"Really?" Lillian raised a brow and her nostrils flared as she let out the smoke she'd inhaled. "I always thought I was good at hiding it, but we never talked about anything that happened at home." She leaned back and watched as the smoke drifted to the ceiling. "I guess I never really talked about anything before so it was easy to lie about my childhood. I mean, Adam had probably guessed since I had been so desperate about not being sent back but he never said anything. Every girl that went to him was damaged, why would I have been any different?"

"So you never disclosed, not even to your mother?"

"I never said that. I disclosed or tried to once. My mother slapped me across the face. Called me a dirty little whore and a liar; said that my father was a good man, a great man who provided us with an exceptional life. She said that my words were just there to hurt him for everything that I fucked up."

Her eyes were bright with unshed tears as she turned toward Allison, "Do you know how that felt? To have your own mother not believe you. I was devastated and it was probably one of the reasons why I ran away. All I needed was for her to listen to me but by the time I was fifteen, Daddy didn't focus on her anymore. She could go out and pretend to be this wonderful mother and a pillar of the community. She fundraised and threw these lavish parties where she could parade her daughters for all to see. Daddy would let her, always willing to lend a hand, or an ear, to the right politician or businessman. Since he had us to throw around and fuck, Momma was free to live without him. I think the last time I saw him hit her, I was about eleven. The next night, they ended up in separate bedrooms and I never heard him in her room from that day until the day I left."

She swiveled in her chair slightly and placed her feet up on the chair beside her as she leaned back. "I did hear her lock the door every night though. It was like she was terrified of him coming to her room and savaging her." Her lips twisted into a bitter sneer, "And I am positive she heard him open my door some nights but, who knows, she was often taking Valium to wind up dead to the world until morning."

Allison pressed the tip of her pencil into the paper so hard that she jumped when the lead snapped and tore the legal sheet.

She closed her eyes. No matter what her own mother had done, she would never have left Allison to fend for herself. She would protect her daughter with her life and she'd almost given it up for her once.

"Do you think she knew?"

Lillian stared at the ceiling and didn't answer. Finally, she said, "When I was a child, I wanted to believe that she didn't but now, after all these years of thinking about it, I think she did. I think that she traded my happiness for a little slice of her own. I think, if he'd allowed it, she would have given him full custody of us and left without a moment's hesitation."

The words were sad but free of bitterness. As though she was simply resigned to the truth about her mother. "Allison," Lillian whispered on a breath of smoke.

"Yes?"

"Do you think it is wrong that I hate my mother?"

"No."

"Would you hate your mother if she was like mine?"

Allison shook her head automatically. The truth was that Ruth could never be Irene Ross. She didn't have that type of ability for subterfuge and was often too honest. But, if she could lie and put her own needs before her daughter's, would Allison hate her for it. "No." She wouldn't hate her mother. Irene was a victim, just like Lillian had been. A shitty mother, yes, but a victim nonetheless and no one could know how they would react to the situation until they were in it.

"Then you're a better woman than I," Lillian said dryly before she turned back to stare at the ceiling. She drew another long drag from her cigarette and said, "I can imagine killing her like I killed my father. I often wish he'd brought her to the apartment that night with him, but Daddy always liked to be in control."

Allison didn't answer as Lillian was obviously fishing for a reaction. "I don't hate Hayley though. Not anymore."

"You did?"

She laughed, "God yes. I hated how she looked like Momma. Hated how Daddy didn't seem as interested in her as he was in me. Hated how I couldn't just leave because once I did, he would be after her."

Allison stared at Lillian's hand as she twirled the cigarette around between her fingers. "Then why did you leave her?"

"Because I knew that I was going to kill him if I'd stayed. I stood over him at night sometimes, a knife in my hand, and I was more scared of what I wanted to do than of what he would do to Hayley if I left." A tear slid down her cheek and, for one of the first times, Lillian didn't swat it away. "I began to believe that he would leave Hayley alone. It was me that he wanted. It was my fault that he was so sick. I made him that way; something in me caused him to react and Hayley didn't have that. I thought if I left, then things would change. They'd be a happy family and he wouldn't hurt Hayley. She'd get her big house and her beautiful garden. She would get a Momma who laughed in the sunshine and taught her all about the birds and the flowers we saw in the garden. I thought that once I was gone, the sickness in our house would leave with me."

She looked back at Allison, her eyes filled with turmoil. "I was wrong, wasn't I?"

Allison shook her head, "I don't know."

"Yes, you do. You saw Hayley. You saw the pain in her eyes, heard the secrets in the lies she told you. He hurt her, didn't he?"

Allison wanted to tell her no. Wanted to tell her that William Ross had become the father every little girl deserves, but it wasn't true. Hayley hadn't admitted to anything, but it was there in the way she spoke of her father and in the ways that she wouldn't. "She didn't say anything, but I think he did," she finally answered.

Lillian's eyes squeezed closed as fresh tears slipped down her cheeks. "Are you going to see her again?"

"Probably."

Her eyes opened again, "Tell her that I'm sorry. I thought about going back to get her so many times, but I had nothing to give her except Adam, and all the bullshit he brought with him. I thought she was better off where she was."

"You were probably right," Allison said quietly and winced at her opinion. It was the truth though. There had been nothing for Hayley in Lily's world except more hurt. Lily would have been just as helpless protecting her sister as she'd been against her father.

Lillian fell silent and stared back at the ceiling. Allison watched her for a few minutes but when it seemed like she wasn't going to say anything else, she stood up and crossed to the barred window. She stared outside at the fall sky, which was a soft blue with a brilliant sun. Outside, it was warmer than the cold that clung to her in this room. She wanted to be outside and she pressed her palms against the window, feeling the heat where the sun had warmed it.

Turning around, she noticed Lillian had shifted slightly so she could watch her. For the first time since she'd started this process, she wasn't scared of the woman across from her. She felt like they were two sides of the same coin. Both of them had been damaged to the point where they were drowning in memories as bitter as the storm swept ocean, but they had both held on to a small part of their humanity.

She should be terrified of this familiarity, but she wasn't. She was curious about it and wanted to explore this strange bond growing between them. Lillian seemed different today. As though a weight had been lifted off of her; Allison wasn't sure if Lillian was curious about this new relationship as much as she was.

"How long did the abuse last?" she asked in an effort to break the comforting silence between them. For some reason, that silence seemed more dangerous than any other silences they'd shared.

"I don't really remember. Maybe seven or eight years," her words faded away as she thought about it, "No, that's not right. It was probably about ten years."

"So it..."

"It stopped about three months before I ran away," Lillian interrupted her. "I was almost fifteen when I ran away."

"When did it start?"

"I don't remember the exact date when it started," Lillian said dryly, "But I think I was four years old...I might have been five," she laughed but there was no mirth in it, "Hell, I could have been three for all I know. Maybe it started from the moment I was born but I just remember the first time at four. I don't really know."

Allison sucked in a deep breath, the smoke from Lillian's last cigarette still clung to the air and she fought the urge to cough on it, "Did it start with a rape?"

Lillian shook her head. "No. Does it ever start with a rape?"

Allison had no answer to that question. The truth was, she had no idea if there was a way that sexual abuse started. She'd never really sat down and tried to figure out if there was a concrete pattern. Lillian frowned, "No, it didn't start with rape. It started with different things. The way he would get me to sit on his lap in his study and I would feel his erection. At the time, I had no idea what I was feeling. Then it grew from there. When he was hitting me, he would start touching me in places I knew were wrong, but I was so scared that I was making it up, I didn't say anything. Why would he touch me there when he was hitting me? Maybe I'd imagined it because he never said anything about it."

"Then he started giving me little gifts after he touched me in the wrong way. At first, I thought he was apologizing for hitting me. I'd seen him do it so many times to my mother but then I realized, he was giving me the gifts so I wouldn't tell anyone about the other things he did."

She stood up and walked to the window beside Allison. There was less than a foot between them and if Allison wanted to, she could reach across the gap and touch her. She didn't, although her fingers tingled with the need to do it.

Lillian shook her head and Allison knew she shouldn't touch her. She took a step to the side so Lillian could touch the warmth on the window. She didn't move to the other side of the room...she wanted Lillian to know that she believed her completely; something all survivors needed, especially when they were let down by the adults in their lives.

"The first time he actually raped me, we were alone in the house for the weekend. By that point, I already knew to stay away from him when we were alone. Momma had gone to the coast for the weekend with Hayley. She'd said she was feeling extremely stressed, but I knew that it was due to the fact that her face was beat up. Daddy had an important business meeting on Friday evening, and he didn't want Momma there with her beat up face. It would be clear that she hadn't just fallen. She was going to take both of us, but Daddy said no. I think he wanted to make sure she had a reason to come home."

●━━━━━━━━━━━━━━━━━━●

The picture book laid flat in my lap and I stared at it unseeing. Instead, my entire brain was listening to my daddy as he walked around the house. Everyone was gone for the night and I knew it was just daddy and me. It was terrifying but maybe he would just go to bed. He'd been drinking all afternoon with the men in his study. They'd all left smelling of whiskey and cigars and I had watched them from where I'd hid in the closet across from the study door.

I paused and listened to his feet on the stairs. He was stumbling a little bit and a tremor of terror filled my stomach with acid. It hurt to swallow, and I was scared he would hear me. Daddy was always angrier when he was drunk. I held my breath as I heard him pause outside of my door. I stared at the light beside me, hating the fact that I was scared of the dark. Maybe if the light was off, Daddy would leave me alone.

His hand fell on the doorknob and I closed my eyes, "Please God, please let Daddy go away," I whispered.

But he didn't listen, and I tried to look calm as the door started to swing open. Any sign of being scared sent Daddy into a rage. I glanced up at him and tried to smile but I knew it was a fake one. "Hi Daddy," I said as cheerfully as I could. I schooled my features into a pleasing mask the way I had seen Momma do so many times before.

"Lillian?" he asked, and I was so confused; I didn't know what Daddy was asking. "What are you still doing up?"

"Reading Daddy," I said quietly.

"That's a good girl," he said as he slumped onto my small bed. He patted the quilt beside him. "Come here girl."

I felt my body stiffen and I wanted to say no but I was so scared of his fists. I stood up slowly, the book hanging from my hand as I hesitated before I took the step. I crossed the room and sat down gingerly on the edge of the bed—as far from Daddy as I could get.

His hand reached out and his fingers caressed down my back as his other hand pulled the book from my limp fingers. "I used to read this book to you all the time."

"I know Daddy," I said, "It's my favorite." I wanted to add that it was because it was one of the few times when Daddy hadn't been cruel or scary.

He flipped the book closed before he opened the oversized cover to the first pages. His lips pursed as he looked at the whimsical images and the easy to read story. His hand on my back started to press harder, no longer a light caress and I knew he was going to hit me, but I didn't understand what I had done wrong. I had been quiet all night and I had been a good girl. He didn't have to think about me or even come to my room so why was he getting angry with me?

"Once upon a time, there was a little girl," he murmured, and I knew that he wasn't reading the book. Momma had read that story to me so much I had memorized it. There was no little girl in this story.

I glanced up into Daddy's face and realized he wasn't seeing the book in front of him and I knew that something bad was going to happen. There was no way to get away from it. I felt my body begin to shake and I knew that Daddy could feel it too, although he didn't say anything. "And that little girl became her daddy's special girl...they shared special things together and he brought her special presents."

I realized that I hadn't heard part of his story. "You'd like that, wouldn't you Lillian? To be Daddy's special girl?"

Nodding, I didn't know what to say. I wanted Daddy to love me and not hurt me anymore, but I felt so confused. Was he saying he wasn't going to hurt me anymore? "And you won't tell anybody about the special things that you and daddy do?"

"No, Daddy," I murmured and cried out slightly as I felt his fingers dig into my back. Terror clawed at my brain and I wanted to start screaming but I knew he was going to hurt me if I did. All I could do was make him happy and then, maybe, he would leave me alone.

"That's a good girl," he said, "And if you tell anyone, you will get taken away and you'll never see Momma again...you'll never see Hayley again. Do you want that to happen?"

For the first time since he'd come into my room, I knew the exact answer to that question and wasn't confused at all. "No Daddy, I don't want to lose Momma or Hayley."

He smiled and it was a scary smile that made me move away from him. His hand curled around my arm before he pulled me against his side. "Then you can never share with anyone what you and Daddy do together. You have to promise me Lillian, or they will take you away and Hayley will have to become my special girl."

Tears welled in my eyes as I thought of those men coming and taking me away. They all looked like the men from Daddy's study. Drunk men, fat men laughing as they sucked on the smelly cigars they all liked. "I promise Daddy. I want to be your special girl."

His smile deepened and I should have felt safe, but I didn't—I had never felt as scared as I did in that moment. Tears slipped down my cheeks and I hadn't realized that I'd been crying. He wiped one of the tears away and said, "That's exactly what I wanted to hear baby girl. Lillian, you are such a good girl."

He stood up and I watched as he started to loosen his cuffs and collar. I stared up at him in surprise. Daddy never loosened his collar around me. He was always perfectly dressed in a suit and tie. The fear dug harder into my stomach and I wanted to run but I felt paralyzed to the bed. "Now Lillian. Daddy is going to do something that might hurt at first, but you are not to cry or say anything."

And then he moved against me and I could remember nothing but that story, "Once upon a time, there was a girl..."

Her voice stopped abruptly, and Lillian slumped to the floor. She pulled her legs up to her chest and wrapped her arms around her knees. "I couldn't stop him," she said.

Allison slid down the wall so she was at the same level as Lillian, "I know you couldn't. You were just a child." She felt her own tears slipping down her cheeks and knew that she looked as shattered as Lillian did.

"He only did it that one time and then waited for a few more weeks before he did it again. I was so confused. I thought I was supposed to be his special girl, but he acted like he hated me half the time. The next morning, he took me to the zoo and then bought me a beautiful doll. I was so happy that he was being nice to me that a part of me forgot about how much he'd hurt me the night before."

She shuddered and closed the distance between them until her shoulder was touching Allison's. Allison started, tensing at the sudden contact they shouldn't have been having, but then she relaxed. If the broken woman needed that contact, then she would let her have it. "Do you remember what he did to you?"

"Some of it. I know he raped me but when he lay on me, I went to a magical place where he couldn't touch me. I would only remember the pain. When I got older, I couldn't escape to that place and, sometimes, my body reacted to what he did."

Allison nodded, "That wasn't your fault, you have no control over how your body reacts."

"I know, but it doesn't change anything or take away my guilt. I still feel it. Sometimes, I still feel echoes of his touch on my skin and I want to cut it off of me so I will never have to feel it again."

She didn't say anything in response. Really, there was nothing she could say. Lillian needed to seek help from a trained counselor to deal with the pain of her childhood. An author with her pencil wasn't going to help her in any way...except, maybe telling Allison her story was cathartic for her.

"Did it happen frequently?"

"Sometimes," Lillian murmured. "Sometimes we could go months without him touching me. Sometimes we couldn't go days. But however our life was, our special time was like an axe hanging over me, ready to drop at any second."

Lillian's hand reached across the small space between them and she captured Allison's hand in hers. She twined her fingers between Allison's and they both stared at the fingers. Allison closed her eyes as Lillian's warmth flowed through her and burned away the horrible words...the horrible secrets...she had shared today. She felt Lillian's head rest against her shoulder and they both fell silent.

The sat like that for a long time, the silence keeping them safe from the horrors of the world...both outside and inside of them. For a few moments, Allison thought Lillian had fallen asleep on her but then Lillian whispered, "Thank you."

"For what?" she asked.

"For letting me tell you this story. I have never told anyone about what Daddy did to me. Not really, I never talked about it, just made reference to it. I needed to tell someone."

She scrambled to her feet and walked toward the door where she paused. "Will you come next week?" She sounded so vulnerable, as though she was expecting revulsion after telling her secret.

Allison nodded and said, "Yes, I'm here for you to share your story."

"Good," Lillian said and then she banged on the door.

The guard opened it and glanced toward Allison, raising an eyebrow when she saw her sitting on the floor, before she led Lillian from the room and closed the door on Allison and her thoughts.

CHAPTER FOURTEEN

External Examination:

The autopsy began at 13:05pm on January 14, 2010. The body is presented in a black body bag and when first viewed, he is wearing a pair of beige cargo pants, a blue polo sweater and white undershirt. The hands have been bagged to preserve any possible evidence and he is wearing a Timex digital watch on his left wrist. No other jewelry appears to be present and none were included with the body.

The body is of a white male, measuring 70.8 inches, weighing approximately 154 pounds and the male is stated to be 45 years of age.

The eyes are open, and the irises are dark brown, almost black, with cloudy corneas. The sclerae is clear. The hair is approximately 5 inches in length and is dark brown. The hair and clothes are encrusted with what appears to be blood. Both the upper and lower teeth are intact with no injury to gums, cheeks or lips, however, the top right incisor, bottom front teeth and the third molar on the left are artificial caps. He still has his wisdom teeth, and none are impacted.

There are two tattoos on the body. One is on the rib cage and is of a snake that starts under his left nipple and ends just above his navel in a winding pattern. The second tattoo is on his arm and is a Celtic knot. There are several scars on the body, including a small surgical scar over the appendix, a scar that looks like a knife wound under his right nipple and a straight scar on his lip.

The head, nose and mouth are not remarkable. The left eye has been punctured by some type of sharp object. It is a new wound. There is a knife protruding from his chest and appears to be the fatal injury. There is bruising on the back of his knuckles. The genitalia are that of a circumcised adult male and show no evidence of injury.

Evidence of Injury:

1.   Stab Wound 1 of 2 located on the midline of the chest.

The stab wound is located 19 inches from the top of the head and 6 inches from the side of the body. It has a long, 10-inch butcher knife protruding from it. From the vertical angle, along with the depth of the wound, it appears that the wound was caused by the force of a body falling, either the assailant falling on the victim or the victim falling on the assailant. It is vertically oriented, and the wound is tapered. It measures 3 inches in length and shows a pathway through the skin, subcutaneous tissue, through the right rib and into the heart. The direction of the cut is from bottom to top.

Opinion: This is a fatal wound that is associated with the perforation of the heart. The trauma around the wound site indicates excessive force was used to create the wound...

~Excerpt from Adam Joseph Laurent's Coroner's Report, Dr. Amelio Rodriquez

Allison stared at the heritage home and admired the white exterior and the perfectly manicured lawns. Eric Landersten had definitely done well for himself and it seemed strange that he had a connection with Lillian when she'd been an escort. Allison would have expected the connection when they were teens, although it was clear that they hadn't gone to the same school.

It had taken her a few days to find him. It wasn't like he was trying to hide, but his private address was not public knowledge. Allison had tried calling him at his law firm, but he'd been away on vacation with his family. She'd left a message with his service and had thrown herself back into the research.

Lillian's confession had been hard for her and she'd ignored the work for two days before she'd gone back to it. Instead, she'd spent a lot of time sleeping and cleaning. And she'd spent a lot of time nursing a drink at the bar with Detective Roger Modeure. He hadn't spoken about the case again and, really, Allison hadn't wanted him to. Instead, they'd been silent companions, both lost in their own thoughts as they drank. A few times they talked about the small things...where they went to school, how they grew up, where they lived but the moment it started to grow too personal, or they started talking about Lillian, they would finish their drink and then leave.

Allison wasn't sure what the attraction was between them, but she was enjoying sitting with someone who saw just how shitty life was. Misery loved company, didn't it? She shook the thought away and straightened her skirt and jacket. She looked like she was perfectly together and not a shell like she felt. And she did feel like a shell...or rather, like an empty vessel that Lillian was slowly filling with her memories. It scared her but, at the same time; it was exciting to know she'd broken through the woman's barriers.

She walked up to the gate and pressed the button. "Yes," the voice of an older woman echoed out of the intercom.

"I have an appointment with Mr. Landersten. This is Allison McKinnon," she replied. It had surprised her when Eric had called her back. It was clear he was still off with family, but he'd been adamant about setting aside a little time for her to talk.

"One moment please," the woman said before the intercom went silent. Allison waited and stared around at the neighborhood. Mansions spread out on either side of the road, each one with its own gated garden and driveway. She heard the door to the house open behind her and she turned to see a tall man walking out the door.

He was stunning! His blonde hair was slightly long and styled so it swept across his forehead while a light dusting of five o'clock shadow covered his square jaw. He glanced up at her and smiled, his dimples hollowing his cheeks as his blue eyes sparkled.

The dress shirt and khakis clung to his body, and she could see that he was in excellent shape. As she stared at him, she knew, without a doubt, that he had never been a client of Lillian's. So why had he offered so much to help her win her court case?

"Ms. McKinnon?" he asked as he drew closer to the gate. "If you don't mind, I thought we would talk out here. I know it is a little cool, but it should be warm enough."

Allison nodded and held out her hand when he opened the gate. "Yes, of course."

He led her through the garden and around the side of the house where she found a lovely deck with a small patio table and chairs. It looked out at the side garden and she could see a pool and other furniture toward the back of the house. "You have a beautiful home," she said as she looked around.

"Thank you," he said quietly, "I did a lot of work to it when I bought it about twelve years ago. I'm still working on it if truth be told but it looks nice on the outside."

"Well, you've done an amazing job," Allison said as she took the chair Eric had motioned to. "You bought this twelve years ago. Was it before you met your wife?"

Eric's smile slipped slightly. "Yeah." His eyes grew hard as though the question brought back some memory for him, so Allison decided to stay quiet and look around the space. Late-blooming fall flowers brought some color but, mostly, there were evergreens surrounding the space and some large oak and willow trees losing their fall foliage. It was a peaceful space and she wondered if he came out here to think. "I inherited a large sum of money when my dad died, and I invested it in this house. I had planned to start a family here with another woman, but that relationship failed. And then I couldn't give up the house after that. I met my wife about three years later."

He looked sad; heartbroken actually. Allison wanted to ask about the woman, but she'd have to pry enough without bringing up his lost lover. Maybe he'd lost her because of Lillian. Clearing her throat, she said, "I don't want to take up too much of your time. I know you are on vacation with your family."

He nodded and leaned back. "Thanks. What did you want to know?"

"I am writing a book on Lillian Ross and the crimes she committed." Allison ignored the way Eric's jaw tightened at the mention of her name, "During some of the interviews, your name came up and I was wondering if you could share how you knew Lillian."

"Did Lillian ask about me? Did she talk about me?" Hope filled his voice and it suddenly all clicked into place. Eric had offered his help because he was in love with Lillian.

"I'm sorry, but no," Allison felt instant guilt at the look of devastation that flashed across his face. He stared down at his hands and the plain, gold wedding ring on his left one. "Her sister, Hayley Forester, mentioned that you had offered your counsel to Lillian."

Eric nodded "Hayley is a damn good lawyer. I've worked with her on a few cases but when I first met her, it was at her father's funeral. I couldn't believe how different she was from Lillian. She was like a little mouse where Lillian was a falcon. Wild, beautiful and so out of reach for anyone to love."

He turned back to Allison, "I loved her, you know? But I guess you wouldn't. Lillian didn't tell you about me and Hayley didn't know the extent of my relationship with her sister. I thought we were in love."

"Did you date her or did you use her..." Allison's voice trailed off and she felt the blush on her cheeks. She didn't know how to word the question.

"Was I a client?" Eric asked for her. "No, I didn't even realize that she was an escort until we'd been dating for about a year. She had a completely different persona for me. I like to believe that she was the real person when she was with me, but I don't know."

"You dated for over a year? Why did it end?"

"I found out she was an escort," Eric said bluntly, "And, to be honest, my ego couldn't handle it. I broke things off with her and it was the hardest thing I have ever done. I'd been ready to ask her to marry me. I'd wanted to bring her to this house and start a family together but after learning what she did for a living, I couldn't stomach even looking at her."

"Then why did you offer to represent her after she was arrested?"

He sighed, "Because I still loved her and couldn't imagine the Lillian I knew to be capable of killing two men. I thought that I could save her and, maybe, we could find each other again. It was stupid, really. I was about to get married, but I would have left Diane the very second Lillian said she'd take me back."

"It's something that I have felt guilt over for years, although my wife and I went to counseling for it—even before we got married. She knows how I felt about Lillian and she accepted it." He ran his hand through his hair and stared toward the house, probably looking for his wife. "Don't get me wrong, I love my wife with everything in me and I am grateful to have her but there will always be a small part of me that belongs to Lillian."

Allison nodded. She thought of Lillian's fingers entwined with hers and how she'd felt that bond. Maybe Lillian had that power over people...the power to haunt the dreams of everyone she showed a piece of her soul to. "Did you know her as Lily Laurent?"

He shook his head, "No, she told me her name was Lillian Smith. I should have known that it was a fake name because I couldn't find anything out about her. It was like she'd just plucked a name out of the air when she met me."

"Where did you meet?"

"At a bookstore," he laughed, "I was there looking for a book for my niece's birthday and she was looking through the horror fiction. She had a Stephen King book in her hand, and I noticed her from across the store. She was beautiful with her long blonde hair and she was dressed in a stylish smock dress. I made a fool of myself trying to introduce myself to her. Said something corny about the book she had, and she'd laughed. The first sound of it and I knew that I was lost. I never believed in love at first sight until I met her, but I was in love."

Allison could picture the two of them together. They were both beautiful people and they must have made a stunning couple. "I asked her out right there and took her to dinner from the bookstore. I wasn't letting her get away with leaving before I could charm her number out of her. She'd hesitated a bit but I, eventually, won her over."

He smiled at the memory. "Then I got her number and called her the next day. Before she could even catch her breath, we were dating. She was reserved at first, but then we were together as much as possible. I was pretty busy and very career driven. She didn't seem to mind and was often leaving for trips as a consultant." He laughed and the bitterness was clear. "I thought she was a business consultant that helped businesses grow and expand...I guess she did get things growing."

Allison winced at the same time Eric did. It was clear that his ego was still slightly damaged from his relationship with her. "Did you suspect anything?"

He shook his head, "No, nothing. We didn't sleep together until we'd been dating for three months. I always thought she wanted to sleep with me, but something was holding her back. When we finally made love, she cried and curled against me. She said it was the first time she'd ever made love...that all the other men she'd been with had only ever fucked her. Maybe that should have been a clue, but I didn't want to see it."

"After that, we were together as much as possible. She would often sleep at my house and six months into our relationship, her business trips started to slow down. Then they just stopped, and she didn't go on them anymore. I thought she'd lost her job, but she assured me she was just promoted to a different department that meant more office work and less travel."

"Did you ever go to her office?" Allison asked. It was surprising that Lillian had been able to keep so many lives from colliding.

"No, but she never came to mine either. We kept our relationship away from our work. I was selfish and wanted her to myself." He glanced back to the house, "I never met her family either. I'd asked but she said they were dead."

He sighed, "Actually, I'd met her family without realizing it. Several partners were friends with William Ross, and I was invited to a few of their fundraisers. I had to attend for the firm."

"How did you find out?"

"Lillian started pulling away. She avoided our dates, didn't come over to my place. I thought she was just nervous because it was clear where I wanted the relationship to head. I even showed her the house and we made love in the kitchen. But then she didn't call me for days. I thought she was dead. I don't know what was happening until I received photos in the mail of Lillian with a client. I ended the relationship the same night...didn't even wait for her explanation."

His eyes were bright from unshed tears and Allison could see the turmoil on his face. It was clear that he was haunted by his decisions. "Did you see her after that?"

"Not directly. I would park in front of her condo from time to time. I would sit there, aching to go in and talk to her; needing to tell her I loved her and would forgive her for anything. I dreamt of her. Stared at the counter where we'd made love until I couldn't stand it and tore the entire kitchen out to rid myself of her. I got rid of everything she'd touched, everything she'd left at my apartment. I threw myself into work, but it didn't stop me from driving by her house at night."

He clenched his fists and his mouth became a hard line. "Then I met Diane at an event put on by the firm. She made it easy for me to forget Lillian and leave her behind. I stopped going and checking on her and, eventually, I stopped even thinking about her. Diane healed all the hurt Lillian had caused."

"I'm glad that you found someone," Allison said, and she was, but she couldn't help wondering what would have happened if his relationship with Lillian had ended up with marriage. Would she have still ended up killing?

"So am I." Eric murmured, "But all the hurt came rushing back when I saw her photo in the paper and learned who she really was. I was angry at first, but it made sense why she lied. She was trying to protect the one good thing in her life from all the shit in the rest of it. I felt so guilty that I went to her and offered to represent her."

"You talked to her directly?" Allison was surprised by that. She figured he had just her council or the family.

"Yes, when she was arrested and before bail was set. She was cold. I'd never seen her so cold and she told me to go back to Diane and to get married. I guess she'd been keeping tabs on me as much as I had been on her." He looked down at his hand and twisted the ring on his finger. "She told me she never wanted to see me again and, if I ever loved her, I would do what she asked. I would go away and get married. I would fall in love with my wife over and over again and I would have a family. That if I ever loved her, I would walk out of that prison and never look back."

"And I did. I didn't look back, but I wish I had. I wish I had told her that I would always love her, but I didn't. Instead, I was angry she'd rejected me as bitterly as I'd rejected her. Then I did everything she'd asked me to do."

The sliding door slid open. Allison watched as a tall brunette walked outside holding the hand of a pretty, little, blonde girl and held an infant in her other arm. The pain and heartbreak in his eyes vanished and Allison could see nothing but love in them. Despite a part of his heart still belonging to Lillian, it was clear that Eric loved his wife and family. "I'm glad I did," he murmured, "In a way, Lillian gave me the family that I needed."

The little girl cried out and Allison watched her race toward her father before she jumped into his outstretched arms. "Are you ready to go Daddy?" she asked as she hugged her father.

"In a moment, Lily; I just have to walk this nice lady to the gate. You go and get in the car with your mom and I'll meet you there." He handed the girl to her mother, who was staring at Allison, a frown on her lips.

Allison gathered up her bag and walked with Eric to the gate after she gave Diane a polite nod. "You named your daughter after her?"

"Yes. It was a hard sell to my wife, but I needed it to finally say goodbye to Lillian. I wanted a piece of her to survive all the nightmares she'd endured, and I wanted to remember that happiness I'd felt with her."

Allison fell silent and they continued walking. It seemed strange, but maybe it had been something he'd needed to do. When they reached the gate, Eric held it open for her, but he caught her arm before she could slip through. "If you need anything else, please contact me."

"I will," Allison said as she stared down at his hand.

He didn't let go and when her eyes met his in question, he said, "Please tell Lillian that I will always love her, but that I am happy."

"I will," she said but she knew she wouldn't. She had no doubt that Lillian had been destroyed the moment Eric had ended their relationship and she didn't want to bring that heartbreak back to her.

CHAPTER FIFTEEN

The day my husband died, eighteen months ago, my world ended. William was my world, he'd become the rock I leaned against after Lillian disappeared. When she ran away, I thought that nothing could be as devastating as the loss of a child...I was wrong.

I remember the police coming to the house and telling me. I remember collapsing on the floor and crying for hours. No one could console me, and it took me days to pull myself out of bed. Hayley, my youngest daughter, tried to help, but even she couldn't reach me.

To learn that my husband was dead shattered my heart, knowing that it was my own daughter who had killed him will forever prevent me from picking up those pieces. The last thought I have before going to sleep is to question what I did as a mother to create such a horrible child. The first thing I think about when I wake up is how empty my bed feels and how alone I am.

I suffer from severe anxiety attacks now and I find myself worrying about the safety of my remaining daughter. I have lost so much because of Lillian and I am terrified that I will lose even more. I attend counseling to try to overcome the terror I feel on a daily basis and sitting in this courtroom, hearing about the horrific manner that my husband was murdered, has only intensified that feeling.

Writing this victim impact letter was so difficult. As a mother, I want to ask for lenience for my daughter—the little girl that used to garden with me. The little girl who used to cuddle against me when she woke up from a bad dream—I still can't believe that little girl killed her father.

But I have to be realistic. That little girl is gone. Lillian has taken everything from our family. She has destroyed the happiness that we filled our house with and there is no way for us to ever get that happiness back.

I have blamed myself for what she did, but as I watched her through this trial, I have realized she doesn't regret anything. She seems to feel no remorse for the murder and that is why I had to stop being her mother and admit to how much of a victim I have become because of her.

I believe that, if Lillian is given a light sentence, she will destroy the rest of her family. So, considering the violent nature of the crime, I ask for the maximum sentence allowed by law. I understand that you, your honor, have the final say, but I ask that you consider the death penalty when you sentence Lillian Ross.

~ Victim Impact Statement of Irene Ross: People vs. Lillian Ross

The room felt awkward today. As though the bond, that had formed between them the last time, had created a barrier they couldn't get past. Allison wanted to launch right back into that quiet space where Lillian seemed real...seemed human...but Lillian pulled back from it.

Maybe it wasn't Lillian. Maybe it was the fact that Kai had been at the gate for her this morning. She'd been upset and had threatened Allison with locking her out again. "I'm not happy with how upset Lillian has been coming out of the room after the visits," she'd said, the Southern drawl completely missing.

"I also have it under authority that you were sitting on the floor of the interview beside Lillian," Kai's eyes flashed with anger. "Need I remind you, Ms. McKinnon, that you are to remain on your side of the table. You are being given a luxury and I can revoke it whenever I choose to."

Allison hadn't argued. Instead, she'd apologized until Kai had seemed mollified and she'd been admitted to the meeting room. Maybe it was Allison who had pulled back to ensure she could keep coming to see her and Lillian had reacted in response?

And to make matters worse, they were being interrupted every ten minutes as the guard checked in on them. It didn't make the environment conducive to getting Lillian to talk. For her part, Lillian didn't seem to be in the mood to talk. She sat on her side of the table drawing in her smoke before she filled the room with the bitter smell. The only acknowledgement she gave to Allison was the occasional glance when she thought Allison wasn't looking.

The door swung open and Allison glared at the door as Officer Cronin looked in. It wasn't the usual guard today and that might be the reason for the interruptions. "We are okay for the next half hour," she snapped, and the woman's smile dropped in surprise. "I think Lillian needs a little uninterrupted time to talk." She tried to smile to soften her tone, but she didn't think it worked.

The guard nodded and said, "I guess a half hour between checks is okay."

Thank you god! Allison said silently before she added, "Thank you, I appreciate it."

The door closed shut and they went back to sitting in a silent room. Allison was tired of having to rebuild a relationship with Lillian every time something happened between them. Every time they took a step forward, Lillian panicked and ran ten steps back.

"Do you want me to come back another day?"

Lillian raised an eyebrow at her. "No, why would you think that?"

"You aren't talking. I have been here for forty minutes and the only conversation I've had is with the warden and Officer Cronin. You've been silent."

A red blush covered Lillian's cheeks. Finally, she said, "I don't know what to say now. I think I just needed to say what my dad did to me out loud. I needed someone to hear it and believe me."

She paused and searched Allison's face, "You believe me, don't you?"

Without hesitation, Allison said, "Yes, I believe you."

Lillian smiled and Allison realized that it was the first time she'd seen the real smile. It was filled with a melancholy that made her heart ache. She wanted to reach out and reassure Lillian, but she knew they were being watched by the camera. She had to be on her best behavior so Kai would have no reason to close up her prison to Allison.

"Did you want to talk more about what he did to you?" Allison asked.

Shaking her head, Lillian said, "There's no point. It is more of the same. He would hit me, berate me, put me up on this pedestal where I knew that, at any moment, I would tumble off. I couldn't be perfect like he wanted me to, and he knew it. I was flawed and he delighted in setting me up to fail so he would have an excuse."

Allison couldn't imagine how difficult that would be to grow up with...even without the added stresses of abuse. "Was he like that with Hayley?"

"Yes, to a lesser extent. But I was his special girl and he promised me that he would only do those things with me if I didn't tell anyone. At first, it was because I wanted Daddy to love me differently than he loved Hayley but then it became about me needing to protect Hayley. I didn't want him to touch her and destroy something so beautiful."

"Do you think he kept his promise?" Allison knew the answer, but she still needed to ask it. Grooming was almost textbook, and she often wondered if they handed out how to guides.

"No. I knew he didn't. That's why I started fighting back I guess. The times when he wouldn't touch me, it was like he knew I was ready to break and tell the world. He would give me that time and use fear to control me instead of the little gifts and the promises. And it worked; I was always terrified of him."

"What drove you to leave?" Allison asked and Lillian stiffened.

"I don't want to talk about that right now. Let's change the subject or we are done here today."

"Why?"

~ 169 ~

Tears filled her eyes, "Because I don't want to. William Ross is dead, and it is exhausting talking about him. Let's talk about something else."

Allison fought the need to push deeper on this matter. It was clear Lillian was getting ready to close herself up and Allison didn't want that to happen. "Okay, what do you want to talk about?"

Lillian fell silent and she stared at the clock on the wall. Maybe she was willing time to speed up so the meeting would come to an end. "I don't know. Maybe we could talk about my life with Adam."

"If you would like," Allison said, careful to keep emotion out of her voice and off her face.

"I lived with Adam for about two years as he tried to set up his escort business. The girls on the street weren't making enough bank for him. I mean, twenty-five for a fuck, ten for a blow, didn't leave much money for him in the end. The girls had to work twice as hard to even get a fraction of what he earned off of me."

"And how much was that?"

Lillian seemed proud when she said, "When I first started, it was about two hundred and fifty for an hour. When I was at the peak of my career, I charged a thousand for an hour."

Allison's mouth dropped. She would never had thought that a woman could make that much as an escort. She shook her head and jotted the number down.

"Surprising, isn't it. But I was refined, which was a rare commodity. I knew how to act at influential social engagements and men wanted that. I was usually hired on as a girlfriend, which included me going to expensive places. I had to represent class and sophistication."

"So what was the girlfriend experience?" Allison asked.

Lillian smiled, "It was easy." Then she laughed, "Really, most of my clients just wanted a beautiful face to show off. They would book me for a weekend, or a week, when they attended business trips. I would tag along and spend my day exploring whatever city we were in. Then I would make sure I was there for after the business meeting. They would take me to events, dinners, galas and I would act like they were the only man who could please me. Then we would go back to the hotel and fuck. Sometimes not even that. Some of them couldn't get hard without help so I would rub their feet or give them a back massage. Most of them spent a lot of time talking. It was actually quite easy."

"And you charged a thousand an hour?"

She shook her head, "No, I would charge a flat rate for a weekend. Usually about five thousand, sometimes as high as ten thousand depending on how many appearances I needed to give."

Allison was floored; she couldn't imagine anyone spending that type of money for sex. But maybe it wasn't about the sex. Maybe it was about having a companion who didn't judge them. They could let down that facade of the moral senator or husband and just be themselves. She could see plenty of people paying top dollar for even five minutes to drop those masks with someone.

"Didn't it bother you, sleeping with all those men?"

"No. When I started, it did. I didn't have a choice but give in to Adam. He always kept that axe over my head. That one phone call to my father to send me back to the worst thing I could imagine. For some reason, sleeping with those men felt like it was my decision."

Lillian smiled wistfully, "And I felt sorry for a lot of them. They just wanted some type of companionship that they didn't get elsewhere. Sure, there were a lot of sick fucks out there, but once Adam started to understand the high-quality escort service, he got better at selecting the best clientele for us."

"How many escorts did he have?"

"Escorts or whores?" Lillian asked, a tremor of humor edging her words, "Escorts, he had twelve regular girls. Whores, I think he had about twenty, maybe twenty-five. It was hard to keep track of the prostitutes because he went through them so quickly. I tried to step in when I realized that my position with him was different than other girls but then he just hid what he was doing to the girls from me. I never saw another bruise, but I did see some of the girls just disappear. And there were a few who killed themselves. Part of me thought he'd killed them, but I didn't want to believe that. I was safe. I was an escort living a life apart from Adam."

"Why didn't you take your suspicion to the police?"

"Because I knew that police placed very little value in us. I tried to get help in the early years but then I just stopped. We all have our demons to fight and we need to learn to fight them by ourselves or we'll be consumed by them."

It was a bleak outlook on life but maybe Lillian was right. Maybe the only way to survive was to learn how to fight on our own. No one was going to save us. No, that's not right, Allison said to herself. She refused to believe that life was as grim as that. There were still good people in the world and Lillian had met her share of them...she was sure of it.

"Adam started selling some of the girls...I mean, not as prostitutes," Lillian said, breaking into Allison's thoughts.

"What? How?"

Lillian laughed, "I thought that would get your attention." Then she went serious, "But I shouldn't laugh about it. Those girls went through so much, but I am almost happy he sold them when he did because most of them ended up having a good life. I even pushed for him to sell the girls."

Allison was confused. How could being sold really save the girls? Why was she happy about her part in it?

As if reading her mind, Lillian said, "After he met me, he realized that some of the girls were worth more money with their family than they were on the street. He would often find the girls with the biggest reward for any information resulting in their return and would wait until it grew a little. Then he would contact the family and sell their daughter back to them."

She smiled as she remembered, "I used to talk to the girls and then try to get him to send as many as possible home." Wiping her face, she sighed, "I guess that it was my way to make a difference. Adam didn't care about the girls, he just wanted the most money and some of the girls he used to put on the street before he took them home. I hated that, but I thought it was a small price to pay for getting them out of Adam's clutches."

Allison jotted down some of the details before she said, "How many did you send home?"

"I can't remember. Not as many as I would have liked, maybe twenty or thirty over a ten-year period. The first few years, I didn't really notice the girls. I thought they were all dumb for getting involved, but when I shifted to escorting, I saw that Adam was getting more violent with the girls he groomed. I started stepping in and would actively look at the missing persons reports. When I matched a girl to a missing family, I would bring it to Adam. Some of the girls would fight going back...just like I did, but I would talk to them about the alternative. He could make upwards of a hundred thousand in 'finder's fees' when he sent a girl home."

"Did you keep tabs on any of the girls that you sent home?"

She shook her head, "Not all of them. A few of the girls ran away again from what I understand but they never came back to Adam or I...can't blame them I guess. Some ended up finishing school and living a much better life than they could have with Adam...if they'd have survived Adam."

"Survive?"

A strange mixture of anger and sorrow flashed across Lillian's face, "Adam was made from the same fabric as my father. He would hit us when he felt like it and that was a lot. When he realized that the high paying clients didn't want bruised escorts, he had to rein in how he treated us. I think that is why he kept a few girls working the streets. People didn't care if their prostitute was beat up."

"Did you witness a lot of beatings?"

She grimaced and fumbled with the cigarette package, her fingers shaking as she lit a new smoke. "I witnessed my fair share. Actually, that is why I ended up getting my own apartment. By the time I was pulling in a thousand an hour, Adam and I were more like business partners. He was making a large amount of money at the escort agency and was as legit as he was willing to go...at least in that line of business. I was doing my own thing and we had an understanding that I wouldn't leave but he couldn't touch me. We'd stopped sleeping with each other and I was sleeping in a spare bedroom of his new condo."

"I was about twenty-two when he brought in Kaitlyn. She was fourteen and she looked so much like my sister that I instantly became protective of her. I stepped in between her and Adam whenever he was ready to hit her, but nothing I did to get her to go home would work. Her family wasn't rich enough to pay a reward so there was no leverage for Adam."

"But she wasn't capable of being a prostitute for him and she suffered for it. She wasn't the first girl that had suffered like that. Over the years, a number of girls disappeared or killed themselves. I used to think it was just the way life was. The weak were swallowed up and it really wasn't Adam's fault that so many of the girls killed themselves. I figured that it was the nature of the beast."

"Then there was Kaitlyn. She was with Adam for about a year before she killed herself and I don't believe she did it. I saw her; I knew that no matter how hard her life was, she wouldn't do that. It went against everything that she was."

"Are you saying you think Adam killed her?"

Shaking her head, Lillian wiped away the tears from her eyes and said, "Yes...No...I don't know. I suspect that he did, but even if he didn't slit her throat, I am positive he drove her to it. He gave her no other choice."

⬤———————————————⬤

"Lily," her voice was frail, and my heart broke at the sound of it. I checked the number on the phone again and realized that it was from Adam's apartment. What was she doing there? She was supposed to be staying with me so we could find somewhere safe for her to go. Adam wasn't happy with Kaitlyn and I didn't think she was safe with him.

"Why are you at Adam's?" I asked, taking a deep breath to remove the fear that was smothering me. "I told you I'd be home after I was finished with my client and to wait for me."

"I know," she said, and I could hear the tears in her voice. "But Adam said he wanted my stuff out now or he would be calling my mom. I can't go home," she finished with a sob.

"Where are you now?" I asked but I knew the answer. I stared at the hotel bed and cursed myself for taking the date tonight. I could hear my client cleaning up in the bathroom behind me. Jason was a regular and he was an easy hour—most of it spent with me spooning around him.

"Adam's bathroom. I took the cordless in here with me..." She stopped talking abruptly and I could hear banging on the door. I closed my eyes and could picture the scene in my head. Her cowering in the bathroom as Adam swore and beat at the door.

"Tell Adam you are on the phone with me and that I am on my way there," I said as I started picking up my clothes from the floor and sliding into them. I still had a half hour with Jason, but I was going to cut it short. The last thing Kaitlyn needed was to be alone with Adam for any longer than she had been.

I could hear her tell Adam that through the door and I heard Adam swear, "Fuck, why did you call that bitch?"

Wincing, I ignored the venom in his voice. I knew that Adam loved the money I brought in, but I was positive that he hated me now...maybe he always had. "Kaitlyn," I said before I repeated it again when she didn't answer. "Listen to me. Stay in the bathroom and do not go out. Do you understand me?"

I could hear my voice growing in pitch as I spoke, and a hard lump filled my stomach—something felt so wrong and I had no idea how to fix it. "He hurt me Lily," she said quietly. "He hit me when I came in and I ran for the bathroom. I think he broke something in me."

Tears stung my eyes. She was such a sweet kid, she didn't deserve to experience the shit that Adam brought with him. "I'm sorry, honey," I soothed, my fingers aching as I wished I could be there holding her and comforting her. "But I will be there in less than twenty minutes. I am leaving now. You just need to hold on until I get there."

"I'll try," she said, and she sounded completely lost, "I'm just done with all this, Lily."

"I know, honey, and that is why I'm going to get you out of this. You can go home, or we will find somewhere safe for you to go to school and graduate." A part of me wanted to keep her at my house. I could get her the fake ID like Adam had done for me. Then she could be my daughter and grow up in a safe place. *But she isn't safe if she's with you,* I silently chided. Adam was still in my life and he would have access to her...just like today.

"Don't do anything, just stay in the bathroom and I will get Adam to leave you alone." I said.

"Okay," she said silently and then I heard a click as she hung up. Closing my eyes, I tried to fight the nausea washing over me. She was alone and it would take me twenty minutes to get to her. Writing a short note for Jason to find, I left the hotel room, closing the door behind me. The race to the parking lot was blinded by me constantly redialing Adam's cell number...only to get no answer.

I sped through every red light I could until I found myself outside of Adam's building. It was the same building he took all of his girls when he first groomed them since it afforded him more privacy than his actual condo. I rode the elevator up to his floor and even more dread filled me as I walked up to the door. The apartment was too silent.

Pushing the door open slowly, I paused on the threshold and listened, but I could hear nothing. From the silence, I would say no one was home but I knew there was. I could sense Adam in the living room. I closed the door and dragged my feet down the hallway. I found Adam sitting on the sofa, his hands covering his face—he looked destroyed and my heart plummeted.

"What happened?" I asked hoarsely.

He jumped at the sound of my voice and I wasn't sure if it was an act or he really hadn't known I was there. Tears glittered in his eyes and I shook my head as I realized why he was upset. "No," I said quietly.

"Lily," he started as he stood up and crossed the room. He captured my arms in his and I broke free. I slapped his face...once...twice...his lips curled into a snarl and I knew he was going to hit me. I pushed him away, his hands biting into my arms before I broke free and raced down the hallway to the bathroom.

The door was ajar, and I could see blood on the floor. I gagged as I pushed into the bathroom, my eyes searching the blank face of the dead girl on the floor. "Kaitlyn!" I cried and fell to my knees. I went to touch her blonde hair, my hand hovering above her...unable to make contact. Her blue eyes staring up at the ceiling. A straight razor in her hand, her wrists and throat slashed.

The sob that ripped through me ripped my heart apart. I felt my sanity rushing away as I tried to take in the damage on her small frame. I felt Adam in the doorway and heard his voice, "Lily, I tried to get in, but I was too late. She came over ranting about how she was going to end it. She had the razor with her and flashed it at me...then she raced into the bathroom."

I turned around and glared at him through tears. He sounded like he was telling the truth, but I didn't think he was. I knew Kaitlyn wouldn't do this. The shriek that came out of me surprised me before I launched myself at him. I felt my fingers raking at his face and then I was flying through the air into the hallway.

"You stupid bitch!" he growled, "Look at what you did to my face."

He crossed the distance between us before I could stand up and swung his leg. The air exploded out of my lungs as his foot connected with my stomach. I couldn't scream, couldn't think, couldn't react. Instead, I could only collapse on the floor as he kicked me a second, and then a third, time. I could hear him ranting, "The dumb bitch killed herself. I had nothing to do with it and you are just as stupid if you think I did."

"She called me," I said when I finally managed to catch my breath. My throat was sore, my words weak. I was positive that he had broken a rib. "I heard you trying to get in. She wouldn't have killed herself."

He stopped and stared down at me, worry mixing with the anger in his eyes. "Yeah, you heard me trying to get in to stop her," he replied. "The damn bitch was suicidal. Didn't you see that when you were taking care of her?"

I shook my head as I curled up on the floor. I couldn't cry despite the pain in my body and heart. I thought about Kaitlyn and how I'd known she wouldn't survive this world. Maybe she had killed herself. She'd seemed so lost when she called me but that didn't explain it all. I wanted to believe Adam...it would be the easier choice. If I believed that he'd killed her or driven her to kill herself, I wasn't sure he would let me survive.

Adam squatted down beside me and touched my side. Fresh pain blossomed where he'd kicked me. It had been a while since he'd hit me, and I knew that he'd done enough damage to put me out of commission for a few days...maybe even weeks. "Now, you need to get control of yourself Lily or I will have to make you. That girl in there killed herself and you will need to accept that. You aren't this great savior Lily. You're shit, just like that girl, a fucking whore. You were made for men to fuck...you weren't made to think or to help the other girls who were made for fucking just like you."

I stared at him in disbelief. He usually used different tactics than this. I don't ever remember him saying something like this to me. Fresh tears filled my eyes and I began to sob. "Shhh," he cooed, "She couldn't be helped, and you need to accept that. Lily, you need to get yourself together, go home and I will deal with Kaitlyn."

My body began to shake as I thought about what he would do. He couldn't call the police, or he would be busted...I had no idea what he would do with her. I shook my head to argue with him but before I could say anything, he shook his head and I felt his fist against the side of my face. I groaned as he hit me again and then the world went black.

"The next day, there was a report of a girl's body being found in one of the drug dens in the city. Cause of death was determined to be suicide, but again, who really looks into those things. Adam moved me into his apartment for the next few months so he could watch me. I think it was so I wouldn't call the police. By the time I was able to go home, I believed that she'd killed herself. I blamed myself for her doing it. I should have gotten her out of there sooner."

Lillian's voice faded away and Allison watched the war of emotions on her face for several minutes. "You don't believe that she killed herself, do you?"

Shaking her head, Lillian said, "Not now, not after what Adam did to me. I know that he pushed the knife into her hand...even if he didn't make the cut himself."

CHAPTER SIXTEEN

Mildred Schuntz (MS): I saw Lillian arrive at about seven-thirty. I know it was that time because I was just taking my nightly meds and I always take them at that time. I heard the steps in the hallway, so I glanced into my peephole and saw her.

Officer Timmons (OT): Did you make contact with her?

MS: Yes, I opened my door and she smiled at me. She said I looked radiant and she gave me a bouquet of daisies from her shopping bag. She always brought me daisies because she knew they were my favorite.

OT: Is that all you spoke about? Did she seem agitated in any way?

MS: Oh, no. She was happy and smiling. Her usual self, but she said that she was late for an appointment and a client was coming over. I didn't pry, but I think her clients were men she slept with. But I'm a modern woman, you know, and I didn't think that anything was wrong with what she was doing.

OT: Have you seen a lot of her clients?

MS: Through my peephole, but I've never talked to them, unless they were passing when I was coming home.

OT: Did you see anyone else coming to the apartment?

MS: Oh yes, two people. There was a man at about eight-thirty. He was very tall and distinguished looking, but I didn't really pay any attention to him as all of Lily's clients are distinguished looking...although some aren't so tall, and a lot are fat.

OT: Did you speak with him or hear anything?

MS: No, he didn't knock, just went into the apartment. I didn't worry about it though, I saw a lot of men who just slipped into the apartment without knocking.

OT: And did you hear anything?

MS: After a little while, I heard screams, but I didn't think anything of it. It wasn't the first time I have heard screams and I figured they were just having sex. You know, some play acting.

OT: At what time did you hear screams?

MS: I'm not sure, probably around a half hour later. It might have only been ten minutes though, but it got quiet about five or ten minutes after that. Then at about ten, I saw that other man, the shorter one, head into the apartment. That was when I heard a lot of yelling.

OT: Did you see anyone leave the apartment?

MS: No, I decided to go to bed shortly after that and didn't know anything had happened in there until you knocked on my door.

Allison slid into the seat at the bar and ignored Roger, who was already on the stool beside her as she ordered a whiskey on the rocks. She swallowed it in one gulp before she ordered a second from the bartender. Without even glancing over, she said, "Do you ever think someone is justified in killing another person when it isn't self-defense?"

Roger didn't say anything at first and continued to stare at her in the mirror above the bar before he replied, "I thought we weren't going to talk about cases anymore...that we were just friends."

The blush that filled Allison's cheeks made her curse silently. The heat wasn't because of the whiskey, although that had helped. The quiet nights she'd spent in this bar, chatting with Roger, had been a break away from this case. It made it easier that he understood what she was going through, since he'd lived it himself. It made it even easier that a huge part of her found him attractive and she wanted to be around him.

But tonight, they weren't friends. Tonight, she was an author who detested her job. Not because of the writing, or even the interviews and the research, but because she hated how bad people could destroy so much around them. Lillian hadn't stood a chance to be anyone other than what her father and Adam had made her. If she believed in fate and destiny, Allison was positive that Lillian had been destined to that one, final, bloody scene where two men ended up dead and she was clinging to her life.

"You didn't answer me. Do you ever think it's justified?"

"I should tell you no," he said slowly, "But I won't. We have self-defense laws for a reason, and I think there are times when a person is justified. Is it right to take a life?" He paused and then sighed, "I don't think so. I think if we start saying this was justified or that was justified, we start skating over a very important line that defines us as people. Unless it is between you or the other person dying, then all attempts to not take a life should be made."

"But what about in cases of abuse? What if you lived through so much abuse that you finally break and kill the abuser?" Allison pressed.

"I would still say no. Unless the person was trying to kill you, then no matter what was done, you have to make the decision to leave or to get help. Killing that person won't take away the pain you've lived through."

He turned slightly and searched Allison's face, but she stared into the mirror and ignored him. "I don't know if I agree with you on that. I think a history of violence could be justification, especially if you knew that person was a horrible individual."

"And who are you to judge?" he asked and there was a sharpness to the question. Allison cast a glance over at him and saw a storm in his eyes that she wouldn't have expected from him. He didn't seem to have that edge to him but maybe that was why he was a cop. "I have to make judgments every day at work but in the end, the only people who can judge someone is the jury. I see the horrible people, the bad guys for want of a better word. I see the abusive husbands, the neglectful mothers. I see the shit that everyone avoids looking at and I have to make a choice on how I am going to handle it."

He shook his head and motioned to the bartender. His jaw twitched as he remained silent while his fresh drink was poured, but Allison could sense that he wanted to say something. When the bartender walked away from them, Roger turned on his stool and pulled her to face him. "I have been there, Allison. I saw some pretty awful shit, including an infant dead in a crib because her parents were too busy playing a fucking game online. They let her starve to death and as I looked down at that innocent soul, I cracked. I was so angry I wanted to pull my service pistol, walk into the living room where the pieces of shit were sitting, and fire two bullets into them. I didn't think they were worth the skin they were sitting in and I felt justified in my opinion."

Allison's eyes widened even more. She thought she'd seen some horrible things in all of her research, but she'd never imagined anything like that. From what she knew of Roger, he'd been a homicide detective for about seven or eight years now. Before that, he'd worked Vice. "Maybe you were," she said quietly.

His eyes hardened and his jaw seemed even tighter, "Maybe but what life would I have ruined by my choice. Instead of destroying more, I made the choice to do my fucking job and put those pieces of shit in jail. And that is what life is about...choices. We could all say that the choice was taken from us because of circumstance, but it isn't really. What we do is make the choice to close our eyes and allow life to happen to us—good, bad, or just ordinary; we make that choice to let things go out of our hands."

Allison turned back to the bar and her drink as his words sunk in. She nursed her whiskey and thought about Lillian. Had she closed her eyes and let go, or was the circumstance out of her hands? No matter how she looked at it, Lillian never had a choice with her father...and really, she'd never had a choice with Adam. All the choices she made were tempered by her past and what she believed of herself. "Maybe you are right," she said bitterly as the words bit into her heart, causing it to ache, "But sometimes you have no choice about what happens to you. No matter what you choose to do, the outcome is still going to be bad."

His eyes softened with concern and he placed his hand over hers. She glanced down at his long fingers and how his hand engulfed hers. The heat of his skin played over hers and she felt the goose bumps rise on her body. She definitely reacted to him and, if he wasn't involved in this case, she might have thought about going on a date with him...at least if he had been interested.

"Are you thinking about Lillian or about yourself?" And just like that, a bucket of ice water was thrown on her.

"W-what?" she stammered.

"I know about your past, Allison. You aren't the only one who does research, and I decided to do some digging on you. Oh, your name was kept hidden to protect a minor, as was your parents, but if you know the right questions to ask, you can find out about anything."

Allison shook her head, "I-I don't know what you are talking about." Even to her own ears the words lacked any strength or conviction.

He cocked an eyebrow towards her, and she realized that he looked as tired as she felt. "Come on, Allison. We've become friends over the last few weeks since you started coming in here. At least be honest about this. I know what happened to you and your mother. The rape, the attempted murder...he was a sick fuck and I'm glad that you survived what he did to your family. He made choices to be who he was, just like you made the choice to survive and write what you do."

Every word felt like a slap and Allison couldn't do anything but stare at him. Was it really so easy to find out these things about her? But what did he gain from this? "I think I need to go," she said as she moved to stand up. She made it only a few feet when she felt his hand on her arm.

"Don't, let's talk about this," he said as he pulled her onto a bench. She tumbled into the seat rather than sat and she stared at his hand that still trapped her arm. All she wanted was to escape and she felt the tears on her lashes. "I assume that Lillian's story is similar to yours and that's why you are asking about justification."

Allison nodded, not really processing his words.

"I suspected abuse when I first took statements, but Lillian would never open up to me. Her sister, her mother, hell...even the housekeeper kept singing the same song. William Ross was a saint, an amazing father, just pure goodness through and through, but the key was off, and I thought if I pushed hard enough, I could find the proof as to why Lillian reacted the way that she had."

He shook his head and Allison blinked back her tears, "And I thought she was justified. Adam was a bastard. I knew him from my days in Vice. I didn't shed a single tear about that bastard dying, but I needed to have more of a reason to stand with Lillian on the murder of her father. For all we knew, they hadn't seen each other in almost two decades. What drove her to kill him? Were the injuries on her body from her father or from Adam?"

"Why are you telling me this?" Allison asked.

Roger looked over at the bar, "Because you are asking about justification and I know you are thinking about Lillian. I know that you are comparing yourself to her and it is so easy to do that. I wanted to help her when I met her. I thought she was an innocent, but Lillian Ross is anything but innocent. She's seen a lot of life and she made choices to be who she was. After all, she could have run from Adam as easily as she ran from her parents and she had a lot more money to do it."

He grew quiet and turned Allison toward him. He grabbed her upper arms and stared into her eyes, his brown ones searched hers as he said, "You should never think that you are like her because you share a similar story from your childhood. You each made choices, you just made different ones. Be justified in that...don't look for justification on what she did because there is none. Lillian made the decision and she kept making that same one when she turned down my help and didn't fight the charges."

Allison stared at him. She didn't fight when he pulled her against his chest and held her. She knew tears were falling but she didn't feel them or hear her sobs. Instead, she thought about the choices everyone made. She thought about her own, which had led her to Lillian, and she knew from the files that Lillian hadn't fought any of the charges of first-degree murder. She'd just gone through the motions.

"Why did you set the charges to first degree murder?" Allison asked as she pulled away slightly.

He stiffened and seemed reluctant to let her go. "The DA set the charge, we just finalized it," he said carefully.

"But why two counts of first-degree murder? Even the DA said that Lillian Ross and Adam Laurent acted together in the murder of William Ross and then they got into a fight and it resulted in the injuries to Lillian and to Adam's death. Why not one manslaughter and one first degree murder count? It just doesn't add up."

"Because the DA wanted first degree murder. He also hid the fact that Adam came after William Ross did. We had first hand testimony from the neighbor that Lillian arrived first, then William Ross, then over an hour later, Adam Laurent. The focus of the trial was never really Adam, it was William that was important. I recommended a charge of second degree in the murder of William Ross and manslaughter for Adam Laurent." He sighed, "Look, I shouldn't be telling you this, but the DA had a lot of people demanding that Lillian be sentenced to the maximum. He never said who, but he was firm on the first-degree murder charges, and I made the choice to support him in my testimony."

Allison gasped in shock, "You chose to testify against her? Why?"

"Because life is all about choices. I was tired of Vice and I was new to homicide. I wanted to stay in my career, and I wasn't secure enough in my department to butt heads with the DA. I tried my best to help her, but she didn't want my help—her very words—so I began to believe that she was guilty. It was a decision I made, and I have had to live with it since I made it."

He sounded so tired that Allison realized it was a choice he regretted. "Do you think she killed them?" she echoed the question that she'd asked the first time they'd met.

"Yes, I think she killed them," he answered firmly.

Shaking her head, "Do you think she was justified in killing them?" she worded the question in a different way.

He shook his head. "I don't know, Allison." He stood up and opened his wallet where he counted out a few bills. He motioned to the bartender and, as he dropped the money on the table, he added, "What I do know is that she didn't deserve the death penalty like she got. Now, if you'll excuse me, I want to go home...I'm feeling tired."

He took a step away and Allison cried out, "Wait, would you help Lillian if I tried for an appeal for her?" Roger stopped and drew in a steadying breath before he turned around.

His eyes were filled with so much sorrow that her heart ached for him. "I would help you, Allison, with anything that you asked, but before you go charging in on your white horse, ask yourself one question," he said quietly, "does Lillian want you to help her or does she just want you to hear her story?"

"I don't know."

"Then you better find out before you make another decision that Lillian doesn't want because, as far as I could see, Lillian's choice to not fight and be convicted of first-degree murder had been the very first time she'd made a choice of her own free will."

CHAPTER SEVENTEEN

(Jury not present; time noted: 11:56am)

The Court: I have a note from the jurors, which is marked Court Exhibit 112. It reads as follows:

'I, Robert Jamenson, foreman in the case of People vs. Lillian Ross, notify the court that the jury has reached a unanimous decision.'

We will now call the jurors in to receive the verdict.

(Jury present; time noted: 12:01pm)

The Court: Mr. Jamenson, has the jury reached a verdict?

RJ: Yes, your Honor, we have reached a verdict.

The Court: Mrs. Weber, could you please read the verdict for the record.

Deputy Clerk Laura Weber: Yes, your Honor. Ladies and gentlemen of the jury and distinguished members of the court, listen to the verdict of the jury as it stands on record.

09 CR 2282 People vs. Lillian Ross

As to Count One: Murder in the First Degree, Guilty.

As to Count Two: Murder in the First Degree, Guilty.

~ Transcripts of Verdict Reading, People vs. Lillian Ross

"Mr. Deveins?" Allison's voice rang out and echoed around the foyer of the old courthouse. She noticed the tall gentleman, his hair receding and his gray eyes scanning the crowd with a nervous interest. Here was the man she wanted to speak to, the same one that had been avoiding her calls for the last few weeks, ever since she started questioning some of his ethics.

She raised her hand in the air and felt a chill race down her spine when she noticed that there was no warmth in his glare. "Mr. Deveins, I'm Allison..."she started when she got closer and held out her hand to him.

"I know who you are," he snapped and looked at her hand with disdain. His hawk like features were even more pronounced when she was close to him. "I thought you would take the hint and know that I have nothing to say to you about the Lillian Ross case or any case. I do not discuss my cases with the media."

Allison bristled at the contempt in his voice but plastered a fake smile on her face. "I understand and while I do have questions about the case, there were a few other matters that I wanted to discuss with you."

He shook his head and started walking, his long legs forcing Allison to jog slightly in an effort to keep up. "Mr. Deveins, I really need to speak with you."

"And I, Ms. McKinnon, really need to get back to my office and work so just spit out what you want to know, and I will decide if I want to answer."

Grinding her teeth, she chased him down a flight of stairs. At the bottom, she asked bluntly, "Have you ever suppressed evidence to secure a guilty verdict either for yourself or for an interested third party?"

Harold Deveins stopped abruptly, his spine stiffening as he turned his wrath filled gaze on Allison. She didn't move, didn't fidget but instead, stared at him with equal ire. "Exactly what are you implying, Ms. McKinnon?" his voice was cold and void of any emotion other than pure rage.

"I'm not implying anything. I have a witness who will testify that you suppressed some evidence in order to charge and convict Lillian Ross of two counts of first-degree murder." She knew she was lying—Roger hadn't agreed to help Lillian or testify on her behalf—but she was furious with how this man was treating her. "I also understand that the original charges were second degree murder and manslaughter. Had she been convicted of those charges, she wouldn't have faced the death penalty."

His mouth puckered up like he was tasting her words before he moved back toward her, "Lillian Ross got the sentence she deserved. She was a cold murderer and she didn't feel any remorse for her crimes. If it was manslaughter, she would have shown some emotion, but she sat there, day in and day out, without emotion."

Allison shook her head, "You know that isn't completely true. There were times in the hearing when she spoke out, but you all ignored it. Tell me, did you get paid off for the murder conviction? Earn some favors to further your career?"

Her eyes flashed with anger and she knew they matched Harold's. She'd never detested a man so quickly, but she couldn't see anything worth liking in this man. His very presence made her skin crawl. "Watch yourself little girl," he hissed, "I have never taken a bribe. I did my job when Lillian Ross was on trial. I proved that she cared little for those men that she killed. She killed her own father! Do you not get that?"

"But did you look at what her father did to her to make her react like that?"

And she watched in amazement as the fight drained from Harold's face along with his color. He took on a pasty white hue and, for a second, Allison felt awful for starting this fight. It wasn't like her to be so forward and she wasn't even sure if Lillian wanted her to start pushing for an appeal. But did that matter? Why wouldn't she want that appeal? Why would she prefer to sit in jail for the rest of her life? Because she didn't fight for her freedom in the first place?

Shaking the doubts from her mind, she waited as Harold stared at her. She couldn't be sure, but it seemed like he was debating on how much he should say and how much he should keep to himself. Finally, he said, "We did. But there really wasn't much to look at. He was a private man, despite having a lot of contacts in Congress and having a lot of money. He could get things done, that was certain, and he had a lot of powerful friends."

"I know that," she said quietly, "Everyone knows that side of him, but did you delve into his family life?"

He smirked and then began walking again, although this time, he walked slow enough for Allison to keep up. "Yes, I delved. And the defense delved even deeper. There was nothing to find. The only controversy was when his eldest daughter went missing."

"No one wondered why she ran away?"

"No one thought she'd run away," he said as he cocked his eyebrow at her. "Everyone was positive that she'd been abducted. There were no signs that she ran. She just left her house one morning and didn't return. She took nothing with her, and she left a half-made breakfast in the kitchen. The police searched for leads but there had been nothing to go on."

He stopped and turned back to her, "Lillian wasn't talking, but from what we could see, Lillian was happy where she'd been. We weren't sure if she'd gone into it willingly, I mean, that Adam Laurent was a real piece of shit. Pardon my candidness." He grimaced and shook his head. "The guy was a pimp and there was some belief that he'd killed a few of the girls he controlled. No proof, mind you. Honestly, if Lillian had only murdered Adam, I would have offered her a plea deal, so she'd never see the inside of a prison. It was a happy day when Adam wasn't on the earth anymore."

"But William Ross was an upstanding citizen and that was the focus of my case. That wasn't a little struggle and an accident. Lillian went at him with such rage that it was terrifying. Did we really need that type of person on the streets, especially with her mother still alive?"

Allison shook her head, "But she isn't that person. She had reasons for what she did. Her father abused her, her sister and her mother."

"And where is the proof," he said smugly, "Her sister and mother said that nothing had happened in their family. Friends, family, business associates—all people who knew Lillian as a child and were often in the home—all said they were a happy family...as happy as the next person."

"But..."

"But what?" He gave her a pitying look, "Did Lillian tell you that she was abused for your little book?"

"She is telling me her story, yes, and I believe what she is saying." Allison glared at the man. She could see the direction he was heading, and she felt like screaming at him. He was being obstinate on purpose.

Harold shook his head, "I'm not going to say whether she is telling the truth or not, but I will tell you that Lillian Ross is a manipulative person. She has some gain in this. Maybe it is just an easy way to finally destroy her family before her execution or maybe she actually believes her lies now. What I saw throughout the trial was a cold woman and a family devastated by the loss of a father. I didn't see a victim who was struggling to survive."

"But that is your own perception of the case," she argued, "You could have read her wrong or you could have missed something. I think there is enough to support an appeal on the case. Maybe she should be in prison, but she didn't deserve the death penalty."

He stiffened again, his eyes flashing, "And what would be the new facts that would mean an appeal?"

She raised her chin in defiance as she said, "The fact that you buried evidence. The fact that you allowed public opinion to sway how you handled the case. The fact that you allowed the pressure of 'concerned citizens,' men who had hired Lillian as an escort, to suppress testimonies and evidence. There is a long list of reasons why we could get an appeal and win it. But the main reason is that I believe Lillian was acting in self-defense."

He scoffed, "Self-defense?" Shaking his head, Harold laughed, "Maybe with Adam but not with her father. What could have possibly triggered that rage? What could her father have done for a self-defense plea?"

"I don't know," she said slowly.

"And that is exactly the problem. Only three people know what happened that night. Two of them can't talk, one didn't and even if she is now, we have no way to prove if she is telling the truth."

He was right. As much as she hated to admit it, he was speaking the truth. But she couldn't let it go. She knew that Lillian had a chance for a lighter sentence at the least. Grasping at the last straw, she said, "But we do have proof that you suppressed evidence."

His eyes went cold, and his mouth twisted harshly, the smug smile erased completely. "You're playing with fire if you plan on going that way. I don't know who you think you are, but I won't let anyone drag my reputation through the mud. Sure, I received phone calls from a few concerned citizens and even from a few men who used Lillian's services, but I did my job, little girl. I didn't suppress any evidence that was relevant, and I don't regret how I handled the case."

Turning on his heel, he took a few steps before he stopped again, "Before you are so quick to judge, you should ask some of the people you know who used Lillian's services. You would be quite surprised how close to home she was and how many people you knew were the concerned citizens."

Allison's mouth dropped and she felt the world spin around her as he stalked off. What could he possibly mean by that? She turned away from the direction he went and headed back the way she'd come.

When she reached the foyer, she stared at the large staircases leading up to the second floor. The wide, marble floors were a favorite place for her to perch when she'd waited for her dad to be finished in a courtroom. She'd loved the building as a child and then hated it as a teen when she'd been here for the trials. Glancing around, she spotted a familiar face and called, "Ira!"

He turned and his eyes filled with warmth as a smile crossed his lips. It was the complete contrast to the hostility that had been in Harold's eyes before he'd stormed off and it was a welcomed look. "Allison? What brings you here today?" Ira said as he crossed the space between them. He gave her a quick hug when he reached her and then beckoned for her to follow him outside.

"I was going to ask you the same thing," she said.

Ira smiled, "I was just walking a friend to court after lunch together. I rarely see the inside of a courtroom these days."

She nodded and walked in silence with him. Harold's words still bothered her. She glanced sidelong at Ira, but the question wouldn't form on her lips. Finally, she said, "I was here to see Harold Deveins."

Ira glanced at her before he looked in the direction they were walking. They were passing through the large park opposite the courthouse and one of the familiar spots where Allison would sit with her dad. Her heart ached with the bittersweet memories the area brought to her. "Why did you need to see him?" Ira asked quietly.

Allison breathed in the fresh air, already nipped with a touch of winter. It wouldn't be long before the snow arrived. Her goal had been to be finished with the interviews before winter but from everything she was learning, she wasn't sure if that would happen. "About the Ross case," she answered as she turned to study his reaction.

A pink blush filled his cheeks and Allison couldn't help the warmth flow through her. She really did love Ira. He was a shrewd contract lawyer, but he always seemed flustered about women. She figured he was blushing because of the meeting at the prison. "What did you need to know that wasn't in the documents you have?"

She chewed her lip and wondered what she should say. She'd spent so much of her career talking to Ira about a case and he'd always offered her a lot of helpful advice. Sighing, she said, "I have it from a witness that he suppressed evidence, which could have led to a lesser charge against Lillian, maybe even a not guilty verdict."

Ira stiffened and he stopped walking toward the park bench where they'd been heading. "What?" he coughed and then started again, "What evidence?"

Allison motioned to the bench and they sat down on it.

"He didn't enter in some statements and he was also surprised at how a detective was going to testify. Finally, he listened to what the 'concerned citizens' wanted instead of adhering to the law."

"Are you sure about this?" Ira asked.

"Am I sure? Well, before I went to speak to him, I wasn't a hundred percent sure but after, I all but got a confession from him."

"I see," Ira took out his handkerchief and mopped his brow. Allison's eyes narrowed as she watched him. It wasn't hot outside and the sweat was only caused by his nerves. "Did he say who the concerned citizens were?"

And then it hit her like a fist to her stomach. She closed her eyes as the thoughts whooshed in her brain and she slowly shook her head, "Oh Ira, please tell me that you or my father weren't involved in this."

She opened her eyes and stared at him. He was looking out at the park and his gaze seemed like it was looking years into the past. "Not your father," he said quietly.

Allison couldn't help the flood of relief flow through her. She didn't want to know that her father was flawed in any way. He had been there for her, for her mother. He was the white knight and a part of her still needed to believe in that. She didn't ask if it was him. It all made sense to her now. Why he'd been so against this book? Why he'd broken confidentiality and spoken with her mother about it? He had something to hide and he didn't want her getting to the bottom of it.

"I'm surprised," she said numbly, "I wouldn't have even guessed that you and Lillian had met from your reactions to each other. There was no look of recognition on either of your faces."

His face had grown redder and he dropped his hands to his lap as he pulled at the edges of his handkerchief. Finally, he said, "I didn't know her."

Allison glanced at him in surprise and he continued, "I knew of Lily Laurent and later that she was Lillian Ross. I knew her father actually and helped him with a few contracts that he had. Never liked the man personally, but professionally, he was a shrewd ally. But Adam Laurent, I knew him only through his escort business."

She wasn't surprised now. She'd figured that was the reason why he'd called. He'd been one of those credit card numbers the police had been so interested in. "About ten years ago, I started seeing a few of his girls. I would take them on business trips, and they would fill the hours when I was away from home."

Tears stung her eyes, but she wasn't sure if it was anger or sadness that caused them. Ten years ago, he would have still been with Rebecca. They got divorced eight or nine years ago. "How could you do that to Rebecca?"

"I didn't do anything to Rebecca. We were married in name only. By the time I called the escort service the first time, Rebecca and I had been sleeping in separate rooms for five years. We hadn't signed the papers, but the marriage was as good as dead. I clung to the hope that maybe we would reconnect but then I realized it was no good."

He sighed, "I decided to use an escort service because I didn't have the energy to start dating and, until the divorce was final and made public, I didn't want to hurt Rebecca. Adam Laurent ran a very discreet business."

"And you never hired Lillian?"

"No, not once. I think I tried to hire Lily, but she wasn't taking new clients at the time or something."

"Did my father know?" It hurt her heart to ask but Ira and her dad had been friends and partners for years. How could he not know what Ira was doing and how did that look for the law firm?

"Not when I was doing it," Ira offered as he shook his head, "Afterwards, when Lillian was arrested, I panicked. I had hired a girl, one of the ones that I saw regularly, only two weeks before the murder. I didn't know that he destroyed credit card numbers to protect his clients and I freaked out. Being linked to the escort agency could have ruined me...could have ruined your father. So I admitted to what I had done."

His eyes were filled with sorrow as he turned to her, "Your father made a few calls, turned in a few favors but ultimately, I am the one who called Harold and asked him to squash the evidence on the johns. It wasn't just me, several of our biggest clients were also clients of Adam Laurent...some were even regular clients of Lily. If that list had been made public, the devastation it would have brought to families would have been catastrophic."

"For who," she snapped, the anger inside of her was starting to heat up. Knowing that her dad had called in favors was almost the worst part of all this. "For the families or for the assholes who cheated on their wives and didn't want to get caught?"

Ira winced with each word as though she'd struck him. And maybe she had. Maybe she wanted to do more than strike him. "Do you even know what those girls were living through? Adam was not a nice man. He used those girls for his own gain. He abused them physically, mentally and emotionally. Sure, they made money, but they never made enough to break free of him."

She speared him with her glare. "I don't know why this hurts so much but it does. Maybe it's because you weren't honest with me. Instead, you tried to do what everyone else is doing...burying Lillian before she can affect your precious little life."

Allison stood up and Ira grabbed her arm, "Allison," he pleaded, "I didn't know who Adam was as a person. I thought the girls were there because they chose to do it. I was lonely and I saw what I wanted to see. I'm sorry but I can't change the past."

Grinding her teeth together, Allison stared down at his hand. It was old and covered in liver spots. It was the same hand that had tossed her up in the air as a child. The same hand that had held hers when her father had died. She wanted to hold it again and tell him that it was all right, but it wasn't. She felt betrayed that he hadn't told her about this when she'd first talked to him about the book. She was angry that she'd found out this way and that, in the very same instance, found out that her dad wasn't as perfect as she thought he was.

"No," she whispered, "You can't change the past, but you can make the effort to right the wrongs you've done. You should never have asked my dad to help you and you should never have silenced the evidence."

She sighed and blinked back the tears, "You should have told me."

Taking a step away from him, Ira pleaded, "Allison, what can I do to make things right between us?"

Allison paused, her back to Ira as she thought about it. Finally, she said, "You can pull some favors so that Lillian can have an appeal."

With that said, she walked away and didn't even look back at the sad, old man sitting on the bench.

CHAPTER EIGHTEEN

Opening argument from Defense Counsel Noah Mann

Good people of the jury. I would love to tell you that life was easy. That everything is found in shades of black and white, but life isn't like that. There is no black and white and life is a myriad of colors. Some colors are beautiful, and life can be easy when you enjoy them, but a lot are dark and violent and people who find themselves lost in those colors are lost forever.

People like Lillian Ross. She started life in those beautiful colors but there were problems in her life as a teenager that drove her into a darker, violent path. One where it was survive or be consumed. The prosecution will tell you that Lillian had a choice in her life. She had a path to take that would see her safely back in her home with her parents and her family, but she didn't.

Adam Laurent, the very man that she is accused of murdering, was a violent and dangerous man. He preyed on the weak, the young girls who thought life was so unbearable at home...for whatever reason...that they had no choice to run away. He would find them: tired, scared and beaten down by the cruel world that they were facing alone, and he would offer them safety.

Lillian was one such girl. An innocent who, due to mental health issues, had tried to kill herself in the only way she knew how. She ran away. There, on the streets, scared, alone and terrified by imagined demons, Adam preyed on her.

But he didn't remain nice for long and he shattered that little girl's innocence by forcing her into prostitution. By the time she realized what was happening to her, she was destroyed and more afraid of leaving than she was of staying.

And that is how we found Lillian; broken, scared and when her father came to that apartment, she was too scared to fight, too tired to run as Adam picked up the knife and plunged it into William Ross's body.

Yes, members of the jury, remember that. There were three people in that apartment and Lillian was the weakest after years of abuse from Adam Laurent. She nearly died in an effort to save her father from that man and in the ensuing scuffle, she killed Adam Laurent...but it was too late for her father.

The prosecution is going to tell you a lot of half-truths. They are going to say that it is black and white. That Lillian was the murderer, but I am going to prove to you, without any doubt, that life is not about black and white. I am going to prove to you that Lillian Ross was a victim as much as her father had been and Adam Laurent was the monster that destroyed her family.

After all, in transcripts you will hear during this trial, Lillian Ross, herself, called 911. She was the one who asked for help and she was the one who said, "They killed me."

If she was a cold murderer...tell me...why would she have said those three powerful words.

~ Official Court Transcript: People vs. Lillian Ross

"How dare you!" the voice screamed out within moments of Lillian being left in the room by Officer Taylor. Allison started and almost leapt from her chair as the woman glared at her. The plump lips were a hard line on her face and an intense anger shone in her eyes. "He was mine...not yours," she yelled as Allison tried to figure out why Lillian was so angry.

"Who?" she asked as she stared at the room across the table from her. She was ready to jump out of the way if Lillian lunged at her.

"You damn well know who," she snarled, "Eric. You were never supposed to go and see Eric. Who told you about him?"

Allison blinked in surprise. She wasn't sure how Lillian had found out, but she realized she had to tread carefully or she would set her off more. "Your sister mentioned him when I was interviewing her."

Lillian stopped and it was like a switch had been flicked off. Her eyes filled with unshed tears and pure sorrow filled her face. Allison fought the urge to run over and hug her. "Hayley?" Lillian murmured as she sank into her chair again, "How did she know about Eric?"

"He contacted your family when he realized who you were," Allison said quietly. "He'd wanted to represent your case to save you."

The tears slid from Lillian's eyes, but she ignored them. Instead, she stared down at the table and Allison watched as each tear splashed on hard surface, creating a larger puddle as she continued to quietly sob. "I didn't know," she whispered, and it was as nerve wracking as the scream, "I thought he only came to me."

"No. He said he contacted your family too."

She watched Lillian, who was gently rubbing the tattoo on her wrist and all her suspicions were confirmed, he was her regret. "How did you know that I went to see him?" Allison asked after Lillian's tears had slowed.

Lillian stared down at her tattoo and didn't answer. She seemed like she was a million miles away and maybe she was. Maybe where she was surpassed time and space and she was living her life with Eric. Maybe it was the life she'd lived or maybe it was a different life...a dream that she'd tried to experience.

"Lillian?"

Her eyes flicked to Allison and she looked shattered...like nothing was worth living. "Do you want me to come another day?" Allison asked—maybe Lillian wasn't up to this today and she couldn't afford to have her shut down now. She didn't know why she thought it, but she felt like Lillian was almost finished with her story.

"He came here." The words were so quiet that Allison thought she'd imagined them.

"What?"

"He came here," she repeated louder, ignoring the other questions Allison had asked.

She raised her head again and this time, that anger boiled just under the surface again. "I didn't know why I was getting a visitor, but I went anyway. I don't know why I did, I usually just say no but I didn't last Monday."

Tears burned in her eyes and her mouth twisted wryly. "And then I sat down, looked up and he was there. He was so..." She swiped at the tears and buried her face in her hands as a sob shook her shoulders, "He was so beautiful and I felt it all again, the betrayal, the way he had destroyed my heart and left me in a million pieces and I couldn't talk to him but I needed to hear his voice."

She shook her head and Allison watched in horror as Lillian sank her nails into her face. Small, red crescents bloomed on her skin, but she didn't press hard enough to break the skin. Glancing toward the door, she opened her mouth to scream for the guard, when Lillian said, "He told me he still loved me."

Her voice cracked and she stared up at Allison...she looked like a little girl who had no hope ahead of her. "What am I do with that?" she sobbed, and Allison wasn't sure if she should answer her, "What can I say? Wait for me...maybe when I'm done my sentence, we could start a family together," her laugh was broken and coarse. "I have nothing ahead of me but death. I was given the death sentence. He couldn't wait for me even if he wanted to."

"What did you do?" Allison asked as her heart broke for Lillian. She could not imagine the despair she'd felt at seeing Eric. She wasn't sure, but she would guess that Eric had been the only man Lillian loved.

"I told him to love someone else. I told him that there was nothing for him here," she sobbed, and it was a strange mixture of heartbreak and anger. "What else could I say to him?" she snapped.

Allison nodded. There really wasn't anything that she could offer. The future for Lillian was as dark as her past but, if they could arrange an appeal, it didn't have to be. There was still hope for her, although there was no future with Eric. "Did he tell you he was married?"

She nodded, "Yes, and that he has two daughters. He showed me pictures as I sat there staring at him. I had nothing to say and all I could think about was that he was here, and I couldn't touch him."

"Then he told me that he'd talked to you and that is why he wanted to see me. He needed to say the words he hadn't said all those years ago. That he forgave me." She started laughing and it had a hysteric edge to it, "He...forgave...me!"

Lillian stood up and Allison moved with her, keeping space between them. She wasn't sure what was happening, but her moods were shifting as quickly as the sea. Lillian narrowed her eyes and it was clear she'd caught the motion and seen the nervousness in Allison. "I laughed when he said it and told him to go home to his little wife and his perfect family," she spat into the air, "I told him that I heard what he said and that if he truly loved me, he would never come back."

She turned towards Allison again and glared at her. Her body was filled with energy and she swayed in her spot as though she was ready to launch herself through the air. "He was mine Allison," she sneered, "My memory that this..." she waved her hands in the air, "shit...didn't touch. The one thing that I could remember without thinking about my dad or Adam."

"I'm sorry. I didn't know who he was to you until I went and met him. I thought he was a..."

"A john?" Lillian laughed, "You dumb bitch. Did you think my life was just about fucking some old pervert? I had a life outside of the escort agency and I had someone that I was able to go home to."

Allison winced at her harsh words, but she took the anger. She didn't blame Lillian, but she wouldn't apologize again. "Yes, I thought he might be a john, but he talked about your relationship and what happened at the end."

Lillian's shoulders slumped and Allison watched as the anger drained out of her again. She leaned against the wall and pressed against the tattoo on her wrist, almost like she was trying to make it disappear. "And how did he say it ended?"

"That he was sent photos of you with a client and he broke it off." It sounded cold but it was the truth.

Her laugh was devoid of happiness. "Yeah, I guess you could say that. The photos were courtesy of Adam. I had been a stupid bitch when I asked to buy myself from him."

Allison felt it in the air...the fight was done, and Lillian was ready to talk. The air didn't crackle anymore and the energy that had had her dancing in her spot was gone. She was calm—or at least, as calm as she could be considering everything. Allison took her seat, despite the fact that she closed the distance between them. From where Lillian was leaning against the wall, there was less than ten feet between them, and it would be easy for her to attack Allison if she chose to.

"You tried to get out?" She wasn't sure why she was so surprised. Maybe because she, like everyone else, expected the worst from the woman in the room.

Lillian laughed, "Don't look so surprised. It wasn't like I really enjoyed what I was doing. By the time I met Eric, I had five regular customers and I wasn't taking any additional ones. Most of the time, I worked in the office for Adam, setting up dates and so on. Two of my clients saw me once a week, the other three were once or twice a month. All of them were easy jobs and were, mostly, just about spending time together."

She smiled and it was brilliant and filled with a touch of happiness. "They were nice men and I enjoyed their company. Most of the time, we didn't have sex unless they decided to pop a Viagra. But even then, it was over so quickly that it didn't bother me. And I made a lot of money from just the five of them...even with what Adam was taking off the top."

"Did you stop escorting when you connected with Eric?"

Shaking her head, Lillian's smile slipped into a sadder version of itself, "No, Adam would never have allowed that, and I wasn't sure what was happening with Eric. I didn't want to believe in our relationship because I didn't want to be hurt, but he was so persistent. No matter how many times I pushed him away, he was there pushing right back until it became easier to let him be a part of my life than to drive him out of it."

She straightened and walked toward the table where her cigarette package had been tossed when she'd walked into the room. She lifted it up and took one out of the package, but she didn't light it. Instead, she just cradled it in her hand as she sat on the edge of the table.

"We dated for fourteen months and I was so nervous about everything. What I wore, the people that we met. I spent the first three months expecting an old client to run into us, but I kept away from his work and avoided talking about mine. When I finally felt safe with him, we made love."

Lillian sighed and a single tear slid down her cheek, "I had never made love before. I felt like I was a million pieces...shards, but he, he managed to put all of me back together. I finally felt like who I was supposed to be from the moment I'd been born. After that, I started scaling back my clients and what we did."

"And Adam allowed that?"

Shaking her head, she said, "No, Adam didn't allow that, but I worked things out with my clients. I explained about falling in love and I set up another girl to go in my place. She lied to Adam for me and never admitted to him that I wasn't seeing clients. Since the money was going into his pocket, Adam never even realized what I was doing. I had enough in savings to survive and I took a small portion from the girl helping me."

Allison thought about it all and realized that a lot of the information was correlating with what Eric had told her. "The girl didn't threaten you for the rest of the money."

Lillian slid her feet into her chair and wrapped her arms around her legs. Her back was to Allison and her hair fell forward, hiding her face. "No, she wouldn't. I kept Adam off of her for the most part...there were a few times I couldn't stop him, but I protected her. I protected a lot of the girls from him...obviously not enough. Candi, as she liked to be called, was a low range escort. Maybe two hundred an hour. When she worked for me, she pulled in about a thousand an hour, so she made a lot more. She didn't want to risk that, or risk losing my protection."

Lillian shrugged her shoulders. "Once I stopped escorting, I threw myself into the relationship. I was happy for the first time in my life and I didn't think anything could change that...but I'd been so wrong. I made a mistake and asked Adam to let me go. I offered him everything that I had saved, but he laughed and said he wouldn't give up his best pussy for any amount. He would make triple keeping me around than what I had set aside in my savings. He was angry that I even had savings, but he wouldn't hit me...he had other ways to destroy me."

Her voice cracked as she said, "I knew that I couldn't be with Eric any longer. That he would be targeted by Adam and I wouldn't put it past Adam to kill him. There'd been enough rumors, enough speculation, around Adam killing people who got in his way. So I pulled away and Eric kept pushing and trying to find out what was wrong with me. But I couldn't tell him, so I avoided him."

"Then what happened?" Allison asked. Her fingers burned with the need to touch Lillian's back and give her some comfort, but she remembered Kai's warning. If she touched her again, she'd be out of the prison for good. No more interviews.

"Then Adam happened, and he destroyed everything."

Opening the door, I stepped into the dark apartment and sighed. Home. I needed to be home and away from the office and Adam. He'd been watching me even more than he did in the beginning and our relationship was on a razor's edge. I wasn't sure what he would do to me, but I knew I couldn't say anything to set him off.

Pulling off my heels, I tossed them towards the closet and walked through the dark condo. The lights of the city spread out below me and I watched the headlights as people made their way. Probably going home...to a family. My hands slid to my stomach at the thought and I felt the empty seed inside me like I always did. There would be no family for me; no happiness, no husband, no children. There would only be Adam until I breathed my last breath...and that might not be too far away.

Stepping into the kitchen, I screamed as the light flicked on and I found Eric sitting at the small, kitchen table. "Eric?" I gasped as my heart beat in my throat. "What are you doing here?"

His eyes were red rimmed, and he looked awful. I wanted to run to him, but I couldn't, Adam would know, I was sure that he was having someone follow me, and I couldn't risk what he would do to Eric. "Waiting for you," he croaked.

"In the dark?"

"I figured that was the only way I'd get to see you. If you saw a light on, you'd run like the coward that you are."

I jerked at the words and felt like he'd hit me right in the stomach. I stared at him in disbelief; this wasn't my Eric. "I don't understand why you are acting this way. I haven't been running, I've been really worried about work."

He sneered and the cruelty in his eyes was worse than anything Adam had ever done to me. Worse than anything any client had said or done. I felt a shiver run up my spine and I knew I should run. I should cover my ears and run as quickly as I could and for as far as I could before he said anything more, but I didn't. Instead, I stood there, knowing this was the moment when he would break me like all the others had. "Work? Is that what you fucking whores call it?" he snarled.

He picked up a stack of papers and a large manila envelope. Throwing the stack at me, he screamed, "I know all about your work Lillian! I know all about how you earn money as a fucking whore!"

The papers flew around me and I caught images of me with various clients. I knew what they were...Adam's collateral; images he'd taken over the years to keep control of me. I stared down at a large, eight by ten photograph, my arms were bound in rope and a masked client was fucking me from behind as he pulled my head back by my hair. I remembered that client, the abuse he would get off on. He'd treated me like the garbage I was, and I let him. I did more than that, I would pretend to love it as he beat me...and a part of me had. I had deserved it all. I had loved it because I was worth nothing. The photograph was over three years old, well before I'd even met Eric.

Tears slid down my cheeks and my throat closed around my words. I wasn't going to plead...*Oh god, please don't let me plead.* "I won't defend myself against this," I said flatly.

He stared at me in confusion as I moved back to the counter, careful to not step on any of the photographs. I poured a glass of wine, the red liquid splashing over the rim and onto the counter from the shake of my hands. I picked up the wine glass. I took a long swallow as he said, "You won't or you can't. Tell me those photos aren't real. That they are just doctored photos to fuck with me."

I shook my head and closed my eyes. This was it, the moment I needed to save him. The moment I needed to let him go so that Adam would never bother him again... "I can't do that. It is me in those photos and that is my job," I was surprised by how calm my voice was. "If it is any consolation, I haven't been fucking anyone else but you since we started fucking."

He stood up and then sat down as he clenched his fists. I didn't look at him, didn't give any acknowledgement that I saw his anger. It would hurt my heart a lot more than my body when he finally did hit me. I took a long swallow of my wine as I stared out at the sparkling lights. They blurred with my tears but I blinked them back so he wouldn't see them. This would be easier on him if he didn't see me cry. "It can't be true," he hissed, and I could tell he was losing his anger.

"It is. I'm a fucking whore and I have been for a very long time...since I was sixteen actually. Maybe even before that if I stop to think about it."

He stood up again and began to pace the small space, "How can you be such a cold bitch about this?"

"Because I am a cold bitch, Eric. I fuck men for money and I'm good at it. I make more on my back for an hour than you do in twenty hours of work." My words were tinged with emotion and I swallowed another sip of my wine in an effort to push aside what I was feeling. I needed to be numb for this, but I could feel my heart breaking. I could feel the breath catching in my throat and the tears stinging my eyes.

He shook his head, "What the fuck was our year together? What the fuck was I to you?"

I swallowed the lump in my throat filled with all my emotions. I wanted to tell him how he was my world...my soul mate. How I didn't think I could live without him. I wanted to tell him I loved him with everything in me and that was why we couldn't be together.

But I didn't say any of those things. Instead, I stared at those sparkling lights outside and I said what would hurt him the most, "You were a...distraction."

I felt, rather than saw him deflate and I was sure it was my tone more than anything. "A challenge to see how far I could drive you and make you want me. You were a plaything for me when I was bored with my *work*." I emphasized the last word.

"I don't believe you," he murmured, "There was something more between us than just fucking."

I turned toward him and forced my eyes to be dead. "If you really believed that, you wouldn't have come here with those photos. You would have thrown the envelope away and you would have believed me when I said there was no one else while I was with you."

He winced but I continued on, taking a step toward him as my rage finally snapped and I couldn't fight it any longer. I speared my finger at him. "You know the truth and that's why you are so hurt. The big man couldn't take it that I'd been fucked better than he'd ever been able to do. You walked up to me remember. You didn't ask about who I was, and you were always willing to look past the missing information I gave you."

I laughed, "I mean, you didn't even ask me what consulting firm I worked for. You were perfectly happy to ignore the truths poking out from our life together because...why?" The part of me that was Lily wanted to hit him and she was taking the reign tonight. She would break this thing between us. The part of me that was Lillian wanted to cheer her on, but I could feel her heart breaking and almost hear her cries in my head.

I shook my head to clear it of this child's fancy as I said, "Because I fit the perfect little checklist you had. The right looks, the right colored hair, and the perfect speech that made you think I was refined. You fell in love with me through your cock and you didn't want to know anything about who I really was."

Finished, I felt the fight drain from me. All I wanted to do was curl up in my bed and sleep for the rest of my life. Perhaps I wouldn't wake up and this travesty named Lillian would be no more.

Eric stared at me, his mouth opened in surprise and the anger flashed in his eyes. He looked down at the floor in shame and then his jaw tightened as he stared at the photograph of me being fucked from behind. The anger spread through him like a wildfire and he swore, "Cunt!"

I reeled backward, the insult stinging my skin with an angry flush as he took a step toward me. "You don't get to act all high and mighty. You are nothing but a fucking whore and I hate you for everything you did. You are a disgusting bitch and I regret the day I saw you in that bookstore. I should have just kept walking."

Each word took him closer and, before I could process it, he grabbed hold of my upper arms. His fingers pinched my skin and I cried out in pain, but I didn't tell him to stop. I deserved this, deserved everything he did to me. I laughed, "You don't have the fucking balls to do what you're thinking."

He snarled as he whipped me around and threw me against the wall. My teeth snapped together as my back hit the hard surface, but I didn't scream. I'd been hit worse than this...this wasn't even a spanking. "Fuck you, Eric," I spat at him and then he was there, his hands gripping my shoulders as he shook me.

Each shake thumped me into the wall and fear started to claw through me. Maybe he was going to kill me! I didn't care. Instead, I snarled, "Do it, show me that you're a piece of shit like all the rest of them. Prove me right Eric."

And like that, the world grew still around us as Eric stopped shaking me. He pressed me against the wall, the heat from his body overwhelmed me and I reacted. As fucked up as this all was, I wanted him to make love to me...right there against the wall...amidst the photos of me being a whore.

His eyes filled my vision and I knew what I saw in them...heartbreak and a loss of innocence I hadn't realized he'd had before that moment. His hands slid up to my neck and I felt his fingers press into the sensitive flesh of my jaw. He leaned in; his breath on my lips a second before his mouth closed over mine.

The kiss was tender and sweet. It tasted of everything that was between us and everything that was behind us. It lasted for agonizing minutes as I tasted the love I had for him and the future we would have together. Then he broke away, placed his forehead against mine and the future turned to ashes in my mouth. "I could have loved you forever," he whispered as his eyes burned with unshed tears.

"I know," I whispered as the tears slipped down my cheeks, "I know."

He dropped his hands from my arms, walked over to the counter and dropped the key...my house key...onto it before he left. He didn't turn back, didn't say anything else and I stood there, tears streaming down my face until I heard the click of the door behind him.

—————●———————————————————————————●—————

Lillian buried her face into her knees and Allison was grateful she didn't look at her as the tears flowed freely down her face. The only man who'd shown her love had destroyed her thanks to Adam. He'd played into Adam's plans so easily.

Finally, after she was able to get her emotions together, Allison asked, "Are you sure it was Adam?"

Lillian raised her head from her knees and glanced over her shoulder at Allison, her eyes were red, and her face was puffy from her tears. "Yes. He admitted to it, but he didn't have to. I saw his handwriting on the envelope."

"What did you do?"

Lillian stood up and turned to sit in the chair so she could face Allison. She threw the broken cigarette onto the table and fished out a fresh one. Lighting it, she said, "I spent the night on the floor, crying until I fell asleep. When I woke up in the morning, I saw all the pictures and I felt that rage again. I picked them up and ripped them apart before I shoved them into the garbage. Then I grabbed my keys and drove to Adam's house."

Her voice was filled with anger and her eyes flashed like they did earlier in the day, "I stormed into his house, pulled the bitch he was sleeping with out of bed and launched myself at him. I got in a few good punches before he threw me off. Then he was calling me a dumb bitch and asked me what I had expected him to do when he was about to lose me."

She drew in a long pull from her smoke and it seemed to calm her a bit. "I lost it when he said that and called him every foul name I could think of. And then he was hitting me, but I fought back that time; one of the few times I actually fought back, and he was surprised by it. When he drew back, I told him if he ever hit me again, I'd kill him."

Allison shivered at the premonition in her words...she'd killed him, and it had been clear that him or William...or maybe both, had hit her. "What happened after that?"

Lillian shrugged her shoulders. "I went back to my clients. They were happy to have me back and I began taking on new ones. There was nothing left for me. Eric wouldn't take me back, even if I had gathered up the courage to beg him for forgiveness. Adam wouldn't let me go if I tried so I did what I was good at, I fucked the clients that Adam brought in and I accepted the more violent johns. The ones with rape play and hitting...the real sick fucks that none of the other girls wanted to deal with."

Allison's heart ached for her. "What happened between you and Adam?"

Lillian stopped and cocked her head to the side as if she was thinking about it, "I continued my job, he continued his, but we never really talked again after that. I hated him more than I ever thought I could, and he knew that if he pressed any harder, the life he was building for himself would be threatened. I knew, one day, we would kill each other."

The room echoed with her final words and Allison shuddered from the chill of her tone. If Lillian had ever loved Adam, the feeling had died when he destroyed her relationship with Eric. As she opened her mouth to ask another question, Officer Taylor slid the door open and said, "It is getting late and the Warden feels it's time for you to head out tonight."

Allison nodded and started packing up her things as Lillian watched her. Glancing up, she thought Lillian looked lighter than she had before. Lillian smiled at her, "You know, I think I needed to tell you this, although I was so angry with you for talking to Eric, I really do feel better now."

CHAPTER NINETEEN

Defense Council Noah Mann (DC): Mrs. Ross, what would you say your relationship with Mr. William Ross was like?

Irene Ross (IR): He was my husband for thirty-one years...almost thirty-two and it was a good marriage. Sure, we had our lows, but every marriage does. He was the love of my life.

DC: I see, and how would you say his relationship with your daughters were?

IR: They were close with their father. Sometimes I thought that they were closer to him than they were to me.

DC: Were they always close throughout their childhood? Or more specifically, was Lillian close to her father?

IR: Yes.

DC: Yes? They both were or Lillian was?

IR: They both were. Lillian thought the world of her father.

DC: Hmm, seems strange for a woman who thought the world of her father to run away, doesn't it?

IR: I...

DC: Did you and your husband have a volatile relationship? Did you fight often?

IR: No, William was a gentle person. He wouldn't hurt anyone.

DC: Did he ever strike you?

IR: I...

PD: Objection...Mr. Ross's relationship with Irene Ross is not on trial here.

Judge: Sustained.

DC: Did William Ross ever strike Lillian?

PD: Objection...Mr. Ross is not on trial here.

DC: Your Honor, I am simply trying to establish why a fifteen-year-old girl would run away from a seemingly happy family and choose to live with a known pimp.

Judge: I will allow the question, please answer it Mrs. Ross.

IR: No! He would never hit her; she was his princess.

DC: And what was she to you Mrs. Ross?

IR: I...We...she was my daughter.

DC: Yes, we know that. How was your relationship?

IR: Like every other mother and daughter relationship.

~ Official Court Transcripts: People vs. Lillian Ross

She stared at the large house before she glanced back to the clock on the dashboard. Ten in the morning, she was definitely awake, but should she go through with it? Allison sighed as she gripped her steering wheel. She'd been sitting outside Irene Ross's house for the last hour, debating on whether she should take this step.

She knew that it went against everything she'd promised Hayley, but she needed to meet the woman herself. She needed to see if Irene was as cold and distant as Lillian had said she was...No, that was wrong...not cold, just calloused in the way that she sold her daughters for her own safety. She ground her teeth as she thought of the repercussions for interviewing Irene Ross.

If Hayley was as adamant as she'd seemed, she would sue Allison the second she found out about the visit. But what if she didn't find out? Maybe Irene would just answer the questions and she could be on her way.

As she chewed on the decision, Allison stared at the notepad sitting beside on her the passenger seat. There were so many questions written on it and none of them could be answered by anyone other than Irene Ross. Taking a deep breath, she reached for the pad when a loud knock on her window caused her to startle.

She turned and stared into the blue eyes of Hayley Forester. A rosy blush heated Allison's cheeks and she hung her head in shame, like a child caught doing something wrong, as she hit the button for the window.

Hayley waited until the window was rolled down fully, "Ms. McKinnon. Fancy meeting you here," she said on a breath of cold air.

"Same, Ms. Forester," Allison said weakly. She looked Hayley over and noticed that she was wearing sports pants, a sweater and her long hair was tied back into a ponytail. Despite the crisp air, loose strands of Hayley's hair clung to her sweaty forehead.

"I was just finishing my run for the morning. I spent the night at my mother's house. She occasionally has night terrors and when she does, I spend it here," Hayley offered, although Allison had already figured out most of it. "But that doesn't explain why you are here."

Deciding honesty was the best course of action, Allison said, "I was here to speak to your mother." Hayley's eyes narrowed in anger but before she could say anything, Allison continued, "I don't plan on upsetting your mother but there are some questions that have been raised since I started working on this book. Only your mother can answer them."

Hayley held out her hand and snapped her fingers, "Let's see the questions."

Reaching over to the pad, Allison placed it into Hayley's hand and waited patiently as Hayley scanned the questions. She motioned for the pen and scribbled some notes on the pad before she passed it back to Allison.

Allison stared at the answers Hayley had given for some of the questions and wanted to scream. These were the same answers that had become almost routine during the trial. Everything had been Camelot in the Ross family and home, but Allison knew that wasn't the case. She took a deep breath and said, carefully, "I know these answers, Hayley, because they are the carefully groomed answers every lawyer trains his clients to say. What I don't know is the truth behind them. I have heard a lot of different things—from you and from Lillian, but I need to hear from your mother."

Hayley crossed her arms over her chest, and it was clear she was not convinced by Allison's words. She looked toward the house and Allison followed her gaze, but she couldn't see anything or anyone looking back. "Do you agree to leave if she gets upset?"

"Yes, but there are things being said that I really feel Irene needs to defend herself from. If I write this story from just one side, people may be misrepresented...for the worst."

Chewing her lip, Hayley stared at her silently for a few minutes and Allison knew she was contemplating it. Pushing for the win, Allison said, "Doesn't she want to tell her story?"

Hayley glanced toward the house again as though she could see the woman waiting for her inside. She nodded slowly and Allison felt a moment of triumph. She would get her interview without having to worry about Hayley and a lawsuit...or the latter at least. "You can come in to speak to her," she said slowly, "but I'm not sure how open she will be to you, especially since you are representing Lillian."

Allison nodded. She rolled up her window before she grabbed her bag, slipped the notepad into it and stepped out of the car. Shutting the door, Allison paused when Hayley said, "I need to say one thing..." Her eyes hardened and it was clear she wouldn't accept any argument. "If you hurt her or make her upset, you will be out of that house and you will never have access to another Ross, do you understand me?"

Allison nodded, although she wasn't sure how she would accomplish not upsetting her—she was positive Mrs. Ross would be very upset about the topic of her wayward daughter. Instead of arguing, Allison fell into step beside Hayley as they walked in silence up to the front door. Hayley fished out a key and opened the door before she gestured for Allison to enter.

The foyer of the house was beautiful with hardwood floors and a winding staircase that wrapped around the large space. Off to the side was a heavy oak door that must lead to a study...William's study...and a long hallway led to the rest of the house. Allison hovered in the room, feeling a whirlwind of emotions as she realized that the house was so familiar to her from Lillian's stories. She could almost hear the tears of a little girl echoing from the doorway.

"My father's study," Hayley said, quietly, "Would you like to go and see it? I'm sure you heard enough about it." Her voice was haunted, and Allison turned to study her. Stress lines were furrowed on her brow and small lines around her eyes hinted at a sadness that was hidden from most.

Without waiting for an answer, Hayley crossed the room and placed her hand on the doorknob. She took a deep breath and seemed to hesitate before she turned the knob and swung the heavy door open. Allison walked up beside her and through the door to find herself in a large, masculine room. A huge desk sat in the center of the room and was surrounded by bookshelves filled with heavy, leather-bound tomes. She'd read a few of the books in the room, such as the Shakespeare collections, but the majority leant to law topics and were probably there more for show than actual reading.

The air in the room was heavy and pulled down on her. She could picture Lillian in this room. Could see her flying through the air seconds before her father was punching and kicking her. She could imagine Lillian's mother standing outside, waiting for her husband to call her. It was a dark room, and not just because of the heavy wood paneling and shelves.

As if reading her mood, Hayley said, "This is Dad's room. We never went into it unless Daddy asked us to come into it. Even with him gone, it's still his room and only the cleaner comes in here."

Allison realized that Hayley was still standing on the threshold...glued to it almost. "You left it the same? Nothing has changed?"

Hayley shrugged, "A few things were removed by the police and my mother threw them out when she finally recovered them. A few other things were removed by business partners since the items were part of their business. Everything else has been left the same. Momma insisted on it." She smiled weakly, "She said, if she touched his study, the man would probably come back to haunt her."

"Is it just her in this house?" Allison had been surprised to learn that Irene Ross still lived at the same address as she had before her husband had been murdered.

Nodding, Hayley took a step back into the foyer, forcing Allison to follow. She looked nervous, as though she was afraid of being caught out in the study, "No. She does have a live-in care worker and a few of the help live in guest houses on the property. She isn't as young as she once was, and the murder aged her. She is only sixty-two but, some days, it's like she's ninety."

"Why didn't she sell it?" Allison asked. She didn't understand. With all the memories, the anger that had been contained under this roof, why wouldn't she just let it all go? Besides, the house was too big for a large family, let alone a widow.

"She loves this house," Hayley said simply as she motioned for her to follow her. "It was exactly what she wanted in a house and she spent thirty plus years getting the gardens just the way she wants them. You can't see very much right now, but, in the spring and summer, the gardens are spectacular. She didn't want to leave that, she didn't want another part of her life to be destroyed."

As they walked into a large kitchen, Hayley pointed to a breakfast nook looking out over a large, indoor pool. "If you want to have a seat there, I will make some coffee and then find my mother. She is probably in her room."

Allison nodded and she watched Hayley as she brewed fresh coffee for them and brought the carafe, along with several mugs, cream and sugar to the table. She set them down and said,

"Feel free to have a coffee as it may take me a little while to convince Momma to speak with you."

"Thank you, "Allison said, and she reached for her hand. When she caught it, she gave a gentle squeeze. Hayley's eyes widened in surprise and she looked from Allison's hand to her face. "Thank you for the coffee and for sharing your story with me."

She shrugged and the anger was there again in her eyes before it was replaced with nothing but grief. "What choice did I have? Either I share or you print Lillian's lies."

Turning, she left Allison alone with only the coffee and her thoughts.

●━━━━━━━━━━━●

"I really do appreciate you taking the time to see me," Allison said, "I know you are a very busy woman."

Irene Ross's mouth puckered into a tight, coral pink, smile as she stirred the sugar into her coffee. After nearly a half hour, Irene had appeared in the kitchen. Despite being sixty-two, and what Hayley had said, Irene looked no older than her mid-fifties. She was slightly taller than average height, around five foot eight or nine, and her dyed hair was curled and cut into a stylish blonde bob. It was clear that she had a natural beauty, although the smoothness of her skin definitely hinted at a few Botox treatments.

When Irene had walked into the room, a chill had followed her. It was clear from the scowl on her face that she didn't want to speak and the nervous way that Hayley was shifting in her seat spoke volumes about the tension in the room. The first ten minutes had felt like she'd been in contract negotiations...without her lawyer. The thought had made her think of Ira and she'd felt that anger surface along with her guilt—who was she to judge him?

Irene's nostrils flared in frustration, "What choice do I have Ms. McKinnon?"

"Please, call me Allison," she interjected.

She gave her a cold smile and continued, "As I was saying," the reprimand for Allison's poor manners was clear in her tone, "I didn't have much of a choice. I assume that Lillian was telling lies, she often told lies about her childhood. She liked to make up stories...but I am sure you know all about making up stories."

Allison ignored the barb and said, "I'm not in a position to really say what Lillian has told me, but that is why I am here, to get all of the points before I move forward toward publication. If anything she has said is untrue, it is better to identify it now so it won't make it into the final book."

"So you are still going to publish the book?" Hayley asked.

Allison nodded, "I am contractually bound to finish the book for my publisher. I never even started it, outside of the initial research into the case, before they were on board. At this point, I have to produce a book about the case. I am trying to make it the most truthful representation out there."

Irene winced and her lips puckered like she'd just tasted something bitter. "How can you have no guilt over destroying what is left of my family? My husband is dead, my eldest daughter is in prison and awaiting execution...I live with constant grief and my youngest," she looked at Hayley, "has no happiness in her life. The whole affair resulted in a divorce from her husband. Lillian is bent on destroying this family and she has found a new way to reach us from her prison cell."

As she spoke, a tightness around Hayley's eyes increased and she looked extremely uncomfortable...and even angry...when her mother mentioned the divorce. "Momma," she said slowly, "Lillian wants to tell her side, Allison is simply doing her job so you can't blame her for it."

Irene's mouth snapped closed and she gave her daughter such a withering glare that Allison watched as Hayley shrank into her seat...literally. It was clear nothing had changed in how the Ross family dealt with their children. "I can certainly blame her. She is, obviously, not an ethical, moral person—benefiting from the grief of others."

Allison felt the hair on her neck bristle, and she wanted to snap at the woman. Instead, she took in a calming breath, "Ms. Ross," she reached across and touched the Irene's hand to get her attention. "I am not sure if you are aware of my books, but all of them are written on behalf of the victims and their families. They are written to provide closure for the families, they aren't written for the perpetrator to glorify their crimes."

Her eyes narrowed and flicked from Allison's hand to her face. "Victims? Then shouldn't you be writing it on our behalf and not sitting at the jail day after day? I know how often you have been up there, I have friends associated with that prison and I keep tabs on who sees my daughter. You've been there over thirty times to discuss her story...how many times have you been here to speak with us? Don't bother answering that, because, before today, you haven't met with us even once."

Allison's eyes flicked to Hayley, who gave a small shake of her head. For whatever reason, Hayley hadn't told her mother about their initial meeting, but she wasn't sure why she'd keep it from her. *Probably because she knew how she would react.* Allison also wondered how Irene had known the number of times she'd been up to the prison. Lillian had talked about a lot of different things: her johns, memories both good and bad of Adam and her father, some of the girls she'd befriended over her life; some of the hours spent at the prison were useless for the book, but some were tantamount to explaining the reason behind the murders.

After she'd finally disclosed about the sexual abuse suffered at the hands of William Ross, more and more of their time had centered around those memories. No matter what lies Irene had told herself, the man had been extremely violent. Ten years of sexual abuse had shattered Lillian and while she didn't speak of everything he did, she'd shared enough to make Allison sick to her stomach. And then there was the emotional, mental and physical abuse he'd wrought on his family. They'd all suffered under him.

"The book for Lillian is slightly different than my other books," Allison replied calmly. She wanted to defend her visits, defend the fact that she had talked to Hayley, but she also didn't want to create an even bigger wedge through the pair. From the looks Hayley was giving her mother, it was clear the only relationship they had was the one that Hayley felt obligated to keep. "She approached me, but I assure you, I have a lot of experience speaking to the perpetrators and I take everything I am told with some skepticism. That is the reason why I am here today, to make sure everyone is represented properly."

Irene scoffed and rolled her eyes, "Really, is that why you are here or are you here to meet her bitch of a mother?"

"Momma!"

"Shut up, Hayley," her mother snapped, "I may not be a proper lady by using those words, but we are dealing with a woman who has no qualms about destroying us. I am sure that she has gone on about how cruel I was." She turned her angry gaze toward Allison, "Did she tell you I beat her? Is that her excuse?"

"No, she didn't," Allison said quietly.

"Then what? What was the big lie that spoiled brat would give you for...for killing her father?"

"I am not sure why she killed William. We haven't reached that part of her story and she has avoided speaking about the murders."

She smiled in triumph, "So she's avoiding the murder. Why? Hasn't figured out the lie yet for that night?"

Allison remained silent and Hayley touched her mother's arm. "Momma, please. This is not helping."

"I don't care if it is helping or not. I regret the day I gave birth to that child. She was such a moody thing. So dark, so much like her father in the way she looked and the way she acted. She made our life a living hell when she ran away." She turned toward me, "Can you imagine the hell of not knowing if your child is alive or dead? Do you even comprehend what she put her father through? What she put me through?"

Allison shook her head, "No, I am sorry. I can't imagine how hard it was for both of you...and for Hayley. To lose a daughter, a sister, in that way and to have to spend your life wondering...I can't imagine what you went through. And I'm here for you to tell me so the world can know how much you cared."

Irene went silent and just stared at her. It was like she was surprised by the lack of argument. Like she'd wanted to fight with Allison so she could finally say the things to her daughter...things she'd never said to her before. "What happened when she left?" Allison asked.

Irene shook her head and fiddled with the coffee spoon in front of her, "She was just gone. No warning, nothing. One minute she was here, being the usual moody teen, the next she was gone. It was like she'd been plucked off the face of the earth."

Allison nodded, "What did you or your husband do when she disappeared?"

"We called the police immediately. They looked into it, the conditions of the house when she left but since some items were gone, like her coat and shoes, they ruled it a run away. After that, we contacted as many agencies as we could in an effort to find her."

"Did you have any progress?"

She shook her head, "I thought I saw her one day when I was in the city shopping. I stepped out of a store and looked across the street and there was this girl. She was wearing expensive clothes and she looked just like Lillian. She glanced toward me and our eyes met for a few seconds but then I realized that the girl had blonde hair and blue eyes. And she didn't seem to recognize me, so I knew it wasn't her."

"How long after she'd run away did you see this girl?" Allison asked. She wondered if it had been Lillian since she'd dyed her hair and often wore colored contacts to hide her appearance.

"About five or six years after Lillian ran away."

"Did you tell anyone about this meeting?" Allison kept her voice calm since it seemed to be having the same effect on Irene. She seemed less angry, although she was answering the questions in an almost resigned manner.

"No, why would I? By the time I got home, I had forgotten the girl." Irene shook her head and stared down at her hands. Allison noticed she was still wearing her wedding ring—a large, square cut diamond in a bright gold.

Like you'd forgotten about your daughter? Allison wanted to ask it, but she didn't. "Did William ever say if he'd seen Lillian?"

She shook her head and grimaced, "No. Not even when he finally found her." She paused for a minute as though she was contemplating what she should say, "In all honesty, William and I were estranged for the most part by the time he went to see Lillian. We slept in different rooms and lived very separate lives, but we were trying to stay together. Despite the coldness that had grown into our lives after Lillian had run away, we still loved each other."

"When did you take separate rooms?" Allison asked.

"Not that long before he died," she said, "A few months maybe."

Allison grabbed her notepad and looked through a few of her notes, "Not before Lillian ran away?"

Irene's eyes narrowed and she glared at the pad in Allison's hand like she wanted it to catch on fire. She sucked in her cheeks as she thought about it. "Well, I always had my own bedroom," she said slowly. "But that was for when William was working late or I was feeling sick."

Hayley nodded in agreement and Allison said, "So then you slept with your husband while Lillian was still at home and he wasn't working?"

"Well, William did work a lot. I guess I was spending a lot of nights in my bedroom so I can understand why she would think that. Although, I'm not sure why that is so important for the book. It isn't that strange, lots of people sleep in separate rooms so they can get a good night's rest."

"Yes, I am sure they do," Allison agreed, "It was just something that she remembered so I made note of it. Even seemingly unimportant memories can be important. Were you close with Lillian?"

Irene nodded, "When she was younger, but she became such a willful child, it was better for William to take her in hand. She was always closer to her father than to me. Hayley," Irene clasped Hayley's hand, "was closer to me than Lillian."

"Was there strife between William and Lillian?"

Irene shook her head and said instantly, "No, they loved each other dearly, which is why it was so shocking...I can only blame drugs, but they didn't bring that up in the courtroom."

"Did he ever strike her?" Allison ignored the comment about the case.

"No!"

"That you saw or that you know for certain?"

Irene glanced toward Hayley as if to get reinforcement, and then said, "That I know of for certain. Lillian was a cherished daughter. Sure, we had to punish her when she was not behaving but we always did it out of love."

Allison stared Lillian's mother. Something in the way she sat, her eyes avoiding hers that it was clear she was lying about everything but, what wasn't clear was whether she lied knowingly or had simply tricked herself into believing it. Ending the debate going on inside her, she said, "Not all of Lillian's memories are bad. She did talk about the house...especially the garden. She loved the garden and the time she spent with you out there."

The worried frown was replaced with a genuine smile, the first one since Irene had walked into the room. It was breathtaking and Allison realized Irene was still a very beautiful woman. Even Hayley smiled at the mention of the garden and she said, "I remember how much Lillian loved that garden when we were little. She would take me outside to play when..." her voice trailed away.

Irene turned and gave Hayley a worried glance before she smiled at Allison. "Yes, we all love my garden. I have put a lot of work into it. You should see the grounds in the summer."

"She also spoke about the study a lot," Allison said. She didn't need to know about the garden or the time spent out there. That was the safe place, the few happy moments in a young Lillian's life.

The smile slipped and the anger flared back in Irene's eyes; but now it was mixed with worry. "The study? Why would she mention the study?"

"I think you know why she talked about the study," Allison said. She felt ashamed that she was doing this, but she wanted to rattle Irene and shake the truth free, "Probably for the same reason that Hayley wouldn't even step foot into the study when she showed it to me earlier."

Irene gasped and her cheeks went red, "I don't know what you are talking about."

"I'm talking about your husband and the things he did to the little girls in his care. The way he would bring them into his study for punishment. How any transgression would be severely punished? How often did your husband hit your daughters, Irene?"

"What? I..." Irene gaped at Allison, who ignored the emotions playing out on both of the women's faces.

"How often did he hit you? I know that it was frequently but I'm not sure what that equates to in your house. Every day? Week? Once a month?" Allison knew she was being cruel, but a rage had filled her that seemed so alien to her. She was angry at this woman who had left her daughters to the mercy of her husband.

"Allison," Hayley warned but Allison ignored her...just like Irene was.

"William didn't...he couldn't..." She choked on the words and cleared her throat, "Sometimes he hit me, but he never meant to, I just wasn't a good wife...I wasn't a good mother, but he never hit the girls."

"You have that right. You weren't a good mother. You abandoned your daughters for a reprieve from your husband. Didn't you?"

Irene glanced at Hayley before her eyes scanned the room...looking for an escape. The control that she'd had, the cold exterior, was melting away under the truths that she didn't want to hear. "No, I would never do that." Irene shook her head and Allison could see her hands shaking under the questions.

"That isn't what I have been told. I was told that you knew about the abuse and that you allowed it to happen."

"Enough Allison," Hayley said quietly as she stared at her mother.

"And you knew about other things that William was doing to Lillian...to Hayley," she waved towards Hayley, completely ignoring the anger radiating from the woman. "Didn't you?"

Tears sprung to Irene's eyes, but they didn't fall...too many years of practice to keep them inside so people wouldn't see. Tears meant life wasn't perfect and William had trained his wife exquisitely; she couldn't even admit there had been a problem.

"Allison, you need to stop, my mother is done." Hayley's tone was sharp, but Allison still ignored the warning. She wanted the confession, needed it.

"That's why Lillian ran away, wasn't it? Because her life was a living hell. Her mother didn't care about her and her father was a sadistic bastard who beat her. You knew about all of that didn't you?"

"No...no...no," she wailed.

"And you knew about the other things he did. You knew that your husband sexually abused Lillian and you did nothing about it."

She heard Hayley cry out the second she felt a slap across her face. She grabbed her stinging cheek and stared at Hayley, who had jumped up and slapped her. Irene was still shaking her head, still believing in the lie even when she was confronted with the truth.

Glaring at Hayley, Allison raised her chin in defiance and said slowly, "Lillian ran away because her father raped her repeatedly and you let her go..."

"Enough, dammit," Hayley snarled, "Get out of this fucking house!"

At the same instant, Irene moaned, "Lillian left because of the baby!"

Silence filled the room as Hayley and Allison turned surprised eyes on Irene. She was slouched in her chair, hands covering her face in shame as she continued, "She tried to tell me, but I slapped her. I slapped her and I hated her for saying those things. I blamed her for the man that William was, and I still do. Something inside her drove him to touch her like he did...something twisted...and it caused him to hurt Hayley. But what was I supposed to do? Lose everything, destroy my life...it couldn't have been as bad as I suspected...it couldn't be as bad as Lillian said it was when she finally told me."

Hayley's face drained of color and she sat, woodenly, in the chair she'd vacated. Tears filled her eyes and she swayed in her seat as she clutched her stomach. Allison didn't say anything—she was stunned, she didn't think Irene would have admitted anything.

Irene kept talking but she didn't look at them, "She got pregnant. I don't know who the father was...god, I pray I don't know who the father was, but she was fifteen and pregnant. She'd already been sexually active with some high school boys, so I thought one of them was the father. William said one of them was...Jason...Tim...I can't remember what his name was. I needed to believe," she looked up and her blue eyes burned with emotion, "I needed to believe, don't you understand."

She shook her head, desperation clear in her voice. "So we arranged for a private abortion...he came to the house. Lillian begged me but I didn't listen to her. She told me that the baby was the only hope she had left in the world. That she needed to keep it, or she would be dead before the year was over. She told me William had raped her and I slapped her over and over again until William had pulled me off of her. I didn't listen to anything she said after that," now the tears were finally falling down her face, "and then she was gone two months later, and I was happy. I thought William would become the kind, beautiful man I'd known when we were dating, and I didn't care what happened to Lillian. I felt guilty for years when she was growing up, guilty for not loving her...what type of mother feels hate for her child, but then I realized it was her, not me."

"She was twisted from the beginning, and I hated her since she was a little girl," Irene sighed in defeat, "That's why she did that to William, that's why she spent all those years as a whore. That's why I don't care if she burns in hell for everything she did."

Her words faded away and Allison stared at the woman on the chair. The amount of hate coming from her was palpable. She turned and glanced at Hayley, who was staring at her mother in horror. Tears streamed down her face, but she didn't move...she didn't speak. The three of them sat in the sounds of sobbing for what felt like an eternity before Hayley blinked and then stared at Allison.

She shook her head slowly, "I think you have done more than enough today," Hayley's voice was coarse. "You can find your way out."

Allison nodded and gathered up her things. As she walked through the doorway, she glanced back and regretted everything she'd just done; not just to Irene, who was still sobbing on the chair but also to Hayley. The grief on Hayley's face as she stared at her mother broke Allison's heart.

CHAPTER TWENTY

It is very important, people of the jury that we differentiate between William Ross and Adam Laurent when we are looking at reaching a verdict. On one hand, we can commiserate with Lillian Ross where Adam Laurent is concerned. He was her pimp and there is evidence that Adam Laurent was violent.

But William Ross was a good man. He was a philanthropist, dedicated to several charities, including one for missing and exploited children. He was a devoted husband of Irene Ross, who you heard in this courtroom. He was the loving father of two girls, Hayley Forester and Lillian Ross. He provided his family with a happy home. He was a pillar of the community; an affluent gentleman who helped his neighbors.

Life was perfect for the Ross family, except for that one shard of discontent in their midst. Lillian Ross was not a happy child. She was not a happy teen, and she was an angry woman. She hated the goodness that her family represented, and she ran away to get away from it.

Lillian Ross grew into a jaded, angry woman and that anger fed the cruel intentions of Adam Laurent. Was Adam a cruel man? Definitely, but that didn't mean he deserved to die. William Ross, however, was not a cruel man. He was a father and he didn't merit what his daughter did. He deserved to live and that is why, you need to strip away the lies that Lillian is trying to tell you and see the truth.

Lillian is an angry, hate-filled woman who carelessly killed her own father and for that reason alone, you should find her guilty of murder in the first degree.

~ Excerpt of the closing statement from Prosecutor Harold Deveins

Allison walked into the room and stopped when she found Kai sitting on the chair she usually sat on. She was reading a paper and didn't look up when the door opened. "Good morning, Allison," she drawled.

Closing her eyes to say a silent prayer, Allison said, "Good morning, Kai. I hope you are well."

Kai glanced up at her this time, a look of tired amusement on her face, "Well, that's the thing. I was doing well until I found this love letter from the Ross family on my desk. They are requesting that your visits be stopped or they will be seeking a court order to stop them. They are citing that you are harassing their family and they are concerned about what your book will do to the reputation of their family."

Allison had known it would happen. She'd spent the last few days feeling awful about what she'd done. Even now, she didn't know what had come over her. "Who is asking for the visits to be stopped?"

"It says it's from the attorney offices representing Irene Ross, the widow of a Mr. William Ross," Kai scanned the letter with an air of indifference, but Allison knew it was a ploy. "What have you been doing Allison?"

"My job," Allison said flippantly as Kai narrowed her eyes. Calming her nerves, she took a deep breath and continued, "I've been fact checking, Kai, that's it. Was it just Irene Ross or did it also come from Hayley Forester?"

"Hayley Forester?"

"Lillian's sister."

"Oh yes," Kai smiled, "No, just Irene Ross...no one with the name Hayley Forester or Hayley Ross was mentioned in the letter. But does that matter? You are causing some problems for me and my prison, Allison, and I remember telling you that if there were any problems you would be out."

Allison winced and sat down across from Kai. Allison needed to finish hearing Lillian's story so that it wasn't lost in a sea of lies. "I know Kai, but..."

"Save the excuses Allison," Kai said, "I gave you the warning and now I get to deal with an irate widow. Do you know how much harder you have made my job?"

"I could go and speak with her," Allison said quickly.

Kai laughed, "That might be a bit hard. From the sounds of it, Irene Ross is planning on getting a restraining order against you. I wouldn't be surprised if they have already started working on it. They are probably gearing up for a lawsuit against the prison and we really can't afford a lawsuit."

She leaned back in her chair and stared at Allison. "I just don't know what to do with you Allison. I ask you not to cause problems, and you cause problems. This isn't like your usual self. How many guests of my establishment have you interviewed?"

Allison shifted in her seat, "Three. Lillian would be the fourth."

"That's right, four women. Three to a completed book if I'm not mistaken."

"No, you're not."

"And I would imagine that you would really like to see this Ross book to completion as well," Kai said.

"Very much so."

"Hmm," Kai stared at Allison and then glanced down at the letter. She read quietly and Allison could hardly sit still as her nerves danced. Was this it? Would Kai tell her to leave and have her escorted out?

The sound of the door opening drew Allison's eyes to it, and she tried to give a reassuring smile as Lillian stepped into the room. "It's nice to see you Lillian," Kai said, "You look well."

Lillian returned a more hesitant version of Kai's smile and said, "Thank you. You look good as well."

"I always look well," Kai laughed as she stood up. "Well, it was nice catching up with you, Allison. I hope to see you before everything is all done with the interviews."

Allison nodded. She wasn't sure if she should say anything in case Kai changed her mind about letting the interviews continue. Kai walked by the guard, "Jayla, how are you today?"

The regular guard was back, "Good, ma'am."

"That's good...real good. Looks like we are all well." Kai paused at the door. Turning, she said, "Allison, do you think you can have these interviews wrapped up within two, maybe three, weeks?"

"Yes, I think we will be done in that time."

"Good...good," she drawled, "Well, I best be off so you can get to it."

When she was gone and Jayla had closed the door to lock them inside, Lillian asked, "What was that about?"

Allison grimaced, "We have a deadline now. Some people have threatened a lawsuit if Kai allows any more visitations. Obviously, she didn't take kindly to the threat, so she is giving us just enough time before she has to bar me from the prison."

Lillian shook her head in surprise. "Who would do that? And why now? We've been talking for a few months now...for over a year if you count the correspondence."

She sighed, "It's my fault," Allison said, and she felt a bone numbing fatigue wash over her. All she wanted to do was go home and sleep. This book was going to be too hard, too much for her to overcome. Even after the interviews, what would Irene do to stop the book from being published? "I spoke to your mother."

The color drained from Lillian's face and she looked like she was about to pass out. "My," she stopped and licked her lips. "My mother?"

"And Hayley."

"Why," she croaked. "What did you need to speak to my mother about?"

Allison shook her head, "I needed to hear what was happening in your house from more than one person. Hayley avoids it, the staff who worked for your family say nothing—that left your mother."

"But," Lillian paused again and swallowed. Allison wasn't sure what emotions she was trying to keep hidden, but it was clear she was struggling to stay reserved, "she would never admit to what he'd done to us."

"She did admit to the abuse."

The room went quiet as Lillian's eyes widened in surprise. She opened her mouth, closed it and opened it again. "Admitted to what?"

To hating you...to being an awful mother who didn't deserve the love you obviously still have for her. Concern for Irene shone on Lillian's face and Allison understood it so well. No matter how much you hate your mother, a part of you still loves her...still aches for her protection, her acceptance. "Everything. The physical abuse; the sexual abuse...all of it."

"No, I can't believe it. Why would she admit to it now?" Tears shone in Lillian's eyes, "Why wouldn't she admit to it when I was being tried for his murder?"

Guilt washed over Allison, and she said, "I don't know. Maybe because you are finally telling the truth and she feels she needs to do the same." She held her breath and prayed Lillian wouldn't end the interview when there was so much they needed to discuss, "She told me about the baby."

Lillian's eyes widened and her body tensed. A tear slipped down her cheek and Lillian swiped it away as if she regretted it falling. She drew in a shuddering gasp and then another as she slipped down to the floor. She looked lost...

Allison stood up in alarm and came around the table where she found Lillian curled up into a ball, hugging her knees. Tears flowed freely down her face and a sob finally escaped from her tense grimace.

She threw out Kai's warnings about touching the prisoner and fell to her knees a few feet from Lillian. She reached out, hesitantly but then her hand touched Lillian's back and she felt Lillian shudder under them. Without thinking, she pulled Lillian against her chest and laid down behind her. She spooned against

Lillian, her one hand wrapped around Lillian's frame and the other stroking her head. Lillian's sobs grew louder at the touch, but she moved closer against Allison.

Allison wasn't sure how long they'd laid there before her cries had, at first slowed and then, stopped, but her side was hurting from the hard floor. Lillian's voice was distant when she broke the silence and said, "I was fifteen when I got pregnant. At first, I thought I was just sick. I mean, I made myself sick all the time with not eating or getting drunk."

Lillian pulled away slightly and turned so she was looking up at the ceiling, although her eyes looked like they were seeing another time. "When I realized I was pregnant, I think I was about four months along. I didn't know what to do and I thought I should hide it."

"And did you?"

She shook her head and glanced at Allison when she sat up. Allison leaned against the wall and put a little distance between them, in case Kai or the guard looked in. "No, I was so scared about what would happen to the baby if I hid it. I knew I wanted it. Every night, I would lie in bed with my hand over the small lump and I swore I could feel it. I would talk to her, tell her of the beautiful life I would give her. I would tell her I wouldn't let anyone hurt her and it would just be the two of us."

Lillian's hand pressed against her stomach as though she could still feel the baby she'd lost. "I told my mother and she freaked out. She screamed and went straight to my father, although I begged her not to tell him. I knew what would happen if she did, but she didn't care."

She took in a deep breath, "Daddy lost it. He hit me pretty bad but then my mother stopped him." She laughed without humor, "One of the only times she did, and it wasn't for me, it was for the baby. She said, 'William, the baby, you'll hurt the baby.'"

Fresh tears rolled down the side of her face and into her hair, "He said that no daughter of his would ruin the family name and he would take care of things. I thought maybe he would send me away so I could have the baby in secret, but I was so stupid."

She shook her head, "He pulled a few favors, and had a doctor come to the home to perform the abortion."

Allison knew this part, but she didn't understand why the doctor came to the house, "Why didn't you go to a clinic?"

"Because he didn't want anyone to ask questions and because I fought it. If that had happened in public and not with a doctor he could pay off, the baby would have been born. That was the last thing he wanted."

She found herself dreading the next question, but she needed to know. "Was he the father?"

Lillian took in a shuddering breath as though she was stealing herself for the next words, "Yes, he was the father. I had slept with a few boys when I was thirteen and fourteen, but I never enjoyed it. I hated the way it felt, the way I wanted to scream during sex, so I stopped. My parents had found out about a few of the boys, but that had been about seven months before I got pregnant."

Allison's stomach ached at the raw emotion in Lillian's voice. She wanted to comfort her, but it was clear Lillian was somewhere else in her mind. "And you wanted to keep her?"

"Yes. I didn't care that it was his baby. I knew there could be health problems because he was my dad, but I didn't believe she would have them. I believed...I knew...in my heart that she would be perfect. We could lie about who her daddy was, and we would run away from him so he couldn't hurt her like he did me. She was the one hope that I had for the future."

Lillian wrapped her arms around her stomach, "About two weeks later. It took him a bit of time to find a doctor willing to perform the abortion. During those two weeks, he'd been so distant, rarely home, I actually thought life was going to get better. I started to look forward again, but I did as my mother asked and didn't tell anyone about the pregnancy. I didn't have many friends anyway and Hayley seemed too young to confide in. So I kept it to myself, but I whispered at night all my hopes and dreams for the baby."

"Then he came, and they gave me a sedative for the procedure. I didn't even know that I had taken it. 'Prenatal vitamins,' Momma had said, and I swallowed them. When the doctor arrived, the pills hadn't kicked in yet so I started fighting and screaming that I wouldn't let him kill my baby. I screamed that I wouldn't let Daddy do this to me and I begged Momma to stop it. Then I started to get dizzy and I don't remember anything after that."

Her voice trailed away on a sob and Allison watched her as she cried for a few minutes before she asked, "What happened when you woke up?"

Lillian chewed her lip as she stared up at the ceiling. "When I woke up, I knew what had happened. I felt empty and I couldn't stop screaming. They forced another sedative down my throat and kept doing it until I could sit and listen to them without screaming. By then, I knew that she was gone and there was nothing I could do to bring her back. I had lost her."

She stopped talking for a few minutes and Allison realized that she was probably grieving the child she'd lost. How hard it must have been after everything else that had happened to her. The sounds from outside the door seemed dulled, as if the prison sensed the mood in the room and was being quiet for her and her baby. "I gave up at that point," she said suddenly. "I wanted to die but I couldn't kill myself. I was scared of what would happen...even more than I was scared of him."

"What did he do?"

"He left me alone." She gave a sad laugh, "All those years I begged him to stop, and all it took was a baby being ripped from my womb. He didn't touch me, didn't go near me. My mother took care of me and it was easy to avoid taking the medication she gave me. I hid them under my pillow until she left the room and then I would flush them down the toilet. I ended up with an infection and I knew I was going to die from the pain in my stomach, but I hid it as best as I could."

"What happened after that?" It was clear they'd caught the infection or Lillian wouldn't have been here now.

"One day, I passed out from the infection and the pain. They found me and called our family doctor. He realized what had happened, but he didn't ask questions as to why the infection had gotten so bad. They told him I must have had an abortion on my own and been too scared to tell us. After that, they kept me on antibiotics through an intravenous and I had a nurse sitting with me non-stop. When I had recovered, the doctor told us that the infection had caused a lot of damage and scarring to my womb and I may never have children. I knew I was dead inside, I felt it and the doctor had been right."

She went silent. "When did you run away?"

"About two months after that...it was after I had told Momma who the father had been."

●————————————————————●

I stared at the dark window and wondered if tonight would be the end of it all. I wanted to die...wanted to climb up to the highest parking garage in the city and throw myself off of it. Nothing mattered anymore as I pressed my hands to my stomach...searching for some sign of life but there was nothing there...nothing but emptiness.

The creak of the door as it opened caused me to close my eyes, but she knew I wasn't sleeping. "Tomorrow Lillian," she said, and I wanted to scream...there was no tomorrow for my baby...there was no tomorrow for me. "Tomorrow you are going to stop moping and go back to school."

I turned and stared at her in disbelief. How could she act like everything was okay? How could she pretend to be so blind? She looked amazing with her stylish pantsuit and her perfectly styled hair. She was filled with life and beauty and I was a shell lying on the bed. I shook my head, "Not tomorrow Momma," I said, hating her more than I ever had.

She shook her head and clicked her teeth, a sure sign that she was frustrated, "You can't keep up this way. You need to go to school and we need to get back to being a family. Your actions have caused this family enough suffering."

"My actions?" I asked quietly before I repeated it louder, "My actions?" I started to shout, "My actions? What about his actions?"

"Lillian, shush," she said as she glanced toward the door, "I understand that you are upset but what's done is done and you need to accept that. Your father was only looking out for your future and having a baby at fifteen was not for your future."

"A baby at any time is not in my future," I screamed, "He took that from me when he allowed that bastard to cut her out of me. You took that from me."

She crossed the room and slapped me. My head whipped to the side and I clutched my cheek. My eyes burned with hatred when I looked back to her and then I started to cry. All my pain, all my heartache was there for her to see. I didn't hide any of it. All those years, the eleven years of abuse was there. All the times he hurt me shone in my eyes and I begged, silently, for her to see it. "Please Momma," I cried, "Please listen to me...see how much he has hurt me."

She took a step back and I saw revulsion in her eyes...and I saw something else as her eyes darted around the room...avoiding me...avoiding her daughter. "What are you talking about? I think you need to rest, and we'll talk about school in the morning."

"Momma, please listen to me," I moaned, "He took my baby. He killed her and he killed me when he did that. I have nothing left to live for...she was the only thing I had. The only thing that kept me from dying and he killed her."

"Lillian, stop," she snapped as she took a step back on her stylish heels. I hated those heels. I wanted the momma who wore running shoes in the garden. That momma had been warm and loving...the momma who wore heels was cold and uncaring.

"He killed me Momma," I couldn't stop the flow of words coming from my mouth. I wanted my momma to hold me and chase the bad men away. I wanted her to protect me from him like she should have done all those years before. "He killed a part of me every time he hit me," I sobbed the words, my chest aching, and I felt like I couldn't catch my breath.

Pinpricks of light filled my vision and I wanted to stop myself from saying the words bubbling out of me, but it was like someone else was talking to me. I saw the hate in my mother's eyes, but I couldn't believe the hate was towards me. It had to be towards Daddy. "He killed me every time..."

She crossed the room in two large strides and grasped my shoulders. "Stop it," she screamed, shaking my shoulders, "Stop it Lillian...Stop...it...right...Now!" She shook me violently with each word and my head snapped back and forth, forcing me to stop talking.

When she stopped shaking me, I looked into her eyes...ones that were so different than mine and said, "Every time he raped me Momma."

"Stop lying!" she screamed and threw me back against the headboard. Pain blossomed in the back of my skull and I saw black on the edge of my vision.

I shook my head to try to clear it, but the black was closing in and I knew I had to say something. She was standing beside the bed, babbling at me but I couldn't focus on her words, "Your father is a good man...a great man...he wouldn't do that. You're just confused and angry about your baby."

I pushed the hair from my face and glared at her, "My baby?" I laughed, a bitter sound even in my own ears, "It was his baby too, Momma, that's why he wanted the abortion so that no one would find out. So he won't go to jail where he belongs."

The air in the room filled with a deadly silence and I watched a strange transformation on my mother. Her anger fled and she seemed to cave in on herself. The pride was gone and all that was left was grief and guilt. She looked like a broken woman and I smiled at it. I needed someone else to be as broken as I was but then my smile slipped as I saw it shift to acceptance and I realized she wasn't surprised. "But you knew what he did to us, didn't you?" I spat the thought at her, "You fucking knew, and you didn't care that he raped me or Hayley."

She stared at me and loathing filled her face. She twisted her mouth as if she'd just smelled garbage and maybe she had, I knew, at that moment; my mother didn't care for me at all. Maybe she'd never cared about me. "You vindictive little bitch!" my mother snarled, "You are so bent on destroying our family you aren't willing to take responsibility for your actions. Being a slut and fucking every boy in your school. We all know about you Lillian...all our friends who have kids in that school know about you!"

Momma took a step closer to the bed, but I wasn't scared—I welcomed it and prayed she would beat me to death so I could be with my baby. "You are a little slut and your lies are not going to be used to destroy what your father and I have created together."

Fresh tears sprung to my eyes and I started to weep, "What have you created Momma? Daddy raped me and you let him."

My voice broke at the same instance she did, and I didn't have time to catch my breath or scream as her fists started to pummel my body. I felt them everywhere as I tried to curl into a ball to protect myself. She hit me on the head, my stomach, my back; she hit me and screamed and cursed me.

And I wept and begged for her to stop...not the blows but him. I begged for her to stop him and to save us. Then I heard his voice and the blows stopped. I knew that Daddy had pulled her off of me, but I didn't look up. Instead, I listened as he pushed her out of the room...I felt his gaze on my sore body, but he didn't check on me—we all knew he'd done worse damage to my body than Momma could ever do.

He walked to the door and said, "I think you need a few more days off of school," before he closed it behind him.

●————————————————————————————————●

"The next day, Momma was sporting a few bruises and I was glad she was. There was no love lost between us at that point and I didn't care what he did to her. For a few nights after, I could hear him beating her. I guess he had to gain control of her again, but I smiled every time I heard it. I hated her so much."

Lillian rolled over onto her stomach and then sat up, cross legged on the floor, "I was a horrible person even then, but I wanted her to hurt as much as she'd hurt me. I wanted her to feel the pain I was living with."

"How long after that did you run away?" Allison asked. She felt emotionally drained by the interview today.

"A few weeks. I hadn't planned it but one morning I was making breakfast for myself. The chef that worked in the house was away and I would cook small meals for myself and Hayley. I was making eggs and I cracked one open into the frying pan." She shuddered at the memory, "It was filled with blood and I just stared at that blood thinking it was a dead chick...I know now it wasn't but at fifteen, I didn't know."

"I stared at it and realized that Lillian was dead and all that was left was a husk. I picked up my coat and shoes, the only thing I allowed myself to bring of the dead girl. Then I walked out of the house and didn't even look back."

CHAPTER TWENTY-ONE

I was asked to write this victim impact statement but I'm not sure what I can say. I can tell you I love my sister. I have loved Lillian Ross for as long as I can remember. She was my hero when I was a little girl and she was the memory that I held myself up to.

Lillian was the girl who would sit in my closet with me and tell me stories about a garden and horses. Magical things little girls like to talk about. She was my best friend and I missed her so much when she ran away.

But the Lillian Ross I saw in this courtroom is not that girl. She is someone who is cold and uncaring. She listened to the evidence and she didn't show any emotion over what was said. She is nothing like she used to be, and I blame the life she's lived since she ran away. I can't see any other reason why she'd be this way.

I think that is the biggest impact on me. I had to give up a last hope that my sister was still alive. She wasn't. She was dead and it hurts me just as much as losing my father. In one day, I lost both my sister and my dad.

Lillian Ross has destroyed all the hope in my future. Her crimes were the mitigating circumstance around my divorce, and it has kept me from connecting with other people. I am left with the knowledge that my father will never meet my children and I am left with a great amount of fear of what the future holds. I worry Lillian will turn the blade against me if she was ever allowed free.

I don't know what the best sentence for her would be, but I do adhere to whatever sentence the court deems fitting for her crimes. I know that I have been served my own sentence and it is a lifetime of pain because of her actions.

~ Victim Impact Statement, People vs. Lillian Ross

Allison pulled up to her house and breathed a sigh of relief when she spotted the familiar car in the driveway. He'd gotten her message. Stepping out of the car, she watched as he got out before she said, "Roger," in greeting.

She hadn't expected him to come but she'd needed to see someone. The last thing she'd wanted to do was go home and sit in an empty house with her cat. She didn't want to be alone with her thoughts or with Lillian's story ringing in her ears. Allison didn't think she could stop thinking of how they'd destroyed that little girl. They'd murdered Lillian Ross even before she'd raised the knife to her father.

"Allison," he said, breaking into her thoughts. "I was surprised to get your call."

"I was surprised that I called you," she offered. She didn't smile, didn't moderate her tone. She let all the exhaustion she felt show. Something she couldn't do with her friends or with her mother. She couldn't let any of them know there were times when she hated her job; times when it was so exhausting she just wanted to lie down and never wake up. She couldn't tell them this because they would tell her to give up...to stop writing or to start writing books with happily ever afters.

Tears flooded her eyes, but what they didn't understand was that she couldn't. She didn't see the happily ever after in Lillian's story because there wasn't one. And she couldn't not write these stories because it helped so many people find the closure they needed. But Roger understood and that was why she'd called him. He'd seen the absolute worst in humanity and he still wanted to help them...just like her.

And that's why she'd called him. Not so he could tell her everything was okay but so he could help her find a few minutes of happiness in between the stories filled with so much unhappiness. She walked toward the door and unlocked it, glancing back only once to see if he followed her. He did, although he seemed to hesitate before he walked into the house.

"Do you want some wine?" she asked above the normal yowling that Mercutio greeted them with.

"Not really," he said, and Allison felt defeated until he added, "Do you have anything stronger?"

She nodded and motioned toward the kitchen. Reaching up into the cupboard above the fridge, she asked, "Whiskey or tequila?"

"Whiskey," he said.

Allison pulled out the bottle and wanted to cry. It had been her father's favorite when he'd been alive. Grabbing tumblers, and ice from the freezer, she poured two shots and passed one to Roger. "I'm sorry."

"For what?"

"For calling you to come over. I'm not sure why I did but I didn't want to be alone." Allison blushed at the confession and she covered it by taking a sip of her whiskey.

"She's," Allison struggled with the word, "different. Not the same woman I met in the first interview."

He nodded and studied her. Allison was suddenly aware of every wrinkle, every dark shadow on her face. She'd seen them in the mirror staring back at her in the morning. She looked like death and it was clear this book was taking its toll on her—and she hadn't even started the main writing yet!

"I think," he said slowly, "That you are taking this too close to heart. You need to distance yourself."

She shook her head and then motioned toward the living room. "I know. And I try not to but the things she is telling me...I just want to protect her from everything, and I can't because all those things are in the past."

Picking up the whiskey bottle and her glass, she walked into the living room and curled up in a corner of the sofa. She pressed the cold glass to her forehead and just enjoyed the feeling of warmth the liquid caused inside her belly. Roger sat down on the sofa beside her and stared at the liquid in his glass.

"She had a baby. Or rather, she was pregnant when she was fifteen."

Roger didn't say anything, just listened, which is exactly what Allison needed. "Her parents forced her to have an abortion and she lost everything after that. She got an infection and the scarring caused enough damage that they didn't think she could have children. She was lost, completely helpless and it was the final straw that made her run away."

"Did she say who the father was?" he asked, and Allison turned to stare at him. His eyes were hooded, and she couldn't really see what he was thinking. He studied his drink before he took a long swallow and then he turned toward her. He knew—she didn't know how he knew but he did.

"Her father," she whispered on numb lips, but she wasn't sure if it was the whiskey numbing them or her emotions. Her voice sounded dead and she could feel her body starting to shake as all the emotions started to unfreeze inside of her. She hadn't realized it until now, but it was no wonder she felt cold inside.

Roger continued to study her, and he stared down at her hands as they began to shake. "He'd been raping her for years. Beating her, her mother, and her sister. Doing who knows what to all three of them. She'd taken so much abuse at his hands, so much pain and humiliation. And then she found Adam and he did the same to her."

Allison pulled in a shuddering breath and fought the panic that was causing her heart to beat faster in her chest. She took another shaky sip, the ice cold on her lips as it tumbled into her mouth. "She seen so much shit and here I am, thinking I can save her when there is nothing that I can save her from. How am I supposed to write her book and how can I live with myself if I leave her there?"

She turned helpless eyes toward Roger and said, "She doesn't deserve to be there...not waiting for her death. She deserves to be free and loved by someone. After all she'd been through, she deserves some happiness, doesn't she?"

"Hey," Roger said, and he moved beside her. "Hey." He whispered again as he took the glass from her hand and set it on the dark wood coffee table. "It's okay. Just breathe and let it go. Let everything that you are feeling go."

Allison squeezed her eyes shut and tried to focus on his voice. She couldn't breathe, couldn't let go of the emotions gnawing at her mind. If Lillian couldn't have happiness, why should she be allowed it? Didn't they have similar stories? She closed her eyes and felt his hand on her body, she couldn't draw in a breath as the memory of his body crushing her small frame filled her mind. She wanted to escape, to run away and hide but she felt Roger holding her hands and heard him, "Allison, you need to breathe. You aren't in that place anymore and you aren't Lillian. Don't hold her pain as your own."

She focused on the words and then she tried to draw a breath again. The first one chewed at her throat and her lungs burned at the first touch of oxygen, but she ignored the pain—knowing, on some level, it was imagined. She drew in a second breath to Roger's words, "That's it, breathe and let go of everything when you exhale. Just focus on that breath and nothing else."

Allison shuddered and she blinked back the tears; her vision was blurry from them and she hadn't even realized she'd started crying in the first place. When she could finally see, she found Roger squatting in front of her, his hands wrapped around her own, a look of concern on his face. "Thank you," she managed.

He smiled and his eyes were filled with warmth as he said, "No problem. It has happened to me more than once. You have to learn not to take the work home with you and sometimes, you forget to do that."

Squeezing her hand, he sat on the sofa next to her...so close that his shoulders touched hers. "I always suspected that William Ross had been an asshole father but when I couldn't get a confession, even from Lillian, there was nothing I could do. It was easy to paint him as the quintessential family man when he had friends and family who spoke so highly of him. It was even easier to paint Lillian into the role of the villain with her past...and she was the only person left standing in that room at the end."

"I wouldn't call it standing," Allison said slowly, "I've read her medical reports in the case file; she was almost dead."

"I'm going to be pursuing the appeal for her," she said quietly.

Roger stiffened slightly before he relaxed again. "Did you talk to Lillian about it?"

"No, not yet, but I will." She just wasn't sure when. She only had a few more weeks to interview her and, until her story was finished, she didn't want anything messing up the book. She needed Lillian to finish her story and then they would discuss the appeal. But that didn't mean she couldn't get the ball rolling— really, she already had.

"Would you help me? Testify on her behalf?"

He leaned forward to grab the bottle and poured himself a double. Allison watched him, cursing herself for asking him. When he sat back, he took a long swallow and she wondered if he was trying to decide or trying to figure out how to say no. She figured it was probably the latter. Finally, he said, "I'm not sure if I can..."

"Oh." She pulled away and tried to stand but he grabbed her arm. She felt his heat immediately and the tears sprung to her eyes again.

Pulling her back, he said, "But I will help you as much as I can. I don't know if she deserves to be free, but I don't think she deserved the death penalty."

Allison turned and looked at him. His eyes held so much honesty in them she wanted to hug him. She could live with that. "Thank you," she murmured, "I think she deserves to be happy."

Roger's eyes turned sad and he touched her jaw, gently brushing away the stray hairs that had escaped her bun, "No one deserves to be happy," he said, "We have to work for it if we want it."

He pulled her into the crook of his shoulder. Allison sighed and placed her head on his chest. She closed her eyes as she listened to his steady heartbeat and used the sound to clear the memories clinging to her like spider webs. "Thank you," Allison murmured again.

"For what?" his voice was a rumble in her ear, and she smiled at the feel of it.

"For being here...there was no one else who would understand why I do this...or what it does to me."

"Don't mention it," he said, and Allison curled into his warmth and fell asleep.

CHAPTER TWENTY-TWO

Forensic Mental Health Assessment Report

Re: Lillian Ross

Page 6 of 12

VII. MENTAL STATE AT TIME OF THE ALLEGED OFFENSE: Records indicate that at the time of the offense, Ms. Ross was found unconscious with substantial injuries. There are no records of police speaking to her until she was alert in the hospital three days after the alleged attack. At that time, records have indicated that Ms. Ross was devoid of emotion and had a cold, almost calculated response to the details of the offense.

Ms. Ross did not have a history of mental illness, both as Ms. Lillian Jennifer Ross or her alias Lily Laurent. Furthermore, no one who has known Ms. Ross has spoken of any unusual behavior that may indicate a mental illness or distress. Records have shown that Ms. Ross does not have any criminal records under her birth name, however, as Lily Laurent, she has been arrested for prostitution on six separate occasions, dating back roughly six years before the offense.

As there is very little information on Ms. Ross's mental health history, determining her mental state at the time of the offense is based on interviews with the patient after she was referred to my assessment and reports from witnesses who knew the defendant at the time of the offense.

From these findings, I have found Ms. Ross to be an extremely intelligent woman with a high IQ. Furthermore, Ms. Ross is aware of the repercussions that her actions cause and was aware that the attacks on both William Ross and Adam Laurent would result in their death. She has shown little to no remorse for her actions and has been obstinate in discussing what happened on the night of the offense. Instead, she has reacted violently to any push towards exploring that night and has refused to speak.

From my findings with Ms. Ross, I feel that Ms. Ross was of sound mind and body on the night in question and not only knew what was happening but feels no remorse or guilt for her actions.

~ Excerpt from Psychological Assessment, Dr. Jessica Childers

●————————————————————————●

"I was supposed to be meeting Lewis that night," she said as she stared out the barred window where she'd been standing. It was a familiar position for her now. Lillian seemed to prefer the window...as though she couldn't get enough sunlight. The memories of their last meeting still clung in the air and Allison wondered how Lillian could be acting so distant today. For her part, she'd woken up on the couch with Roger. They didn't say much before he'd left but having him there had cleared a lot of the darkness from her thoughts. She'd found her way of coping and, maybe, the distance Lillian was putting between them was her way of coping. Allison had talked to Jayla on her way in and she mentioned that Lillian didn't seem to be sleeping at night.

Shaking the worry from her mind, Allison asked, "Lewis?" She hadn't heard the name before, but Lillian didn't mention names when she talked about her johns. Maybe Lewis was different though. She did know that the name hadn't been mentioned in any of the files concerning the case and subsequent trial.

She turned towards Allison and gave a weak smile, "Carlyle. He was one of my favorite clients. He could get a little rough in his play, but he didn't have that killer instinct. He just couldn't take it over the edge of violence, so he was safe. Really, he was harmless, but he was...is...into some kink. His favorite way to start the night was by fulfilling his rape fantasy."

Allison straightened and made note of the name. Lewis Carlyle was a powerful man and he wouldn't want Lillian's story to see the light of day. To his constituents, Lewis was the church-going family man who was their next best hope. He was making plans to run for president eventually and Lillian's story could kill any chance he had at that bid. Clearly the man had been one of the concerned citizens who had pushed for a speedy trial.

"He liked rape play?"

"Liked?" she laughed, "He loved it. Probably why he came to escorts for it. A few of my girls tried to please him but they couldn't handle the rough play. After everything ended between Eric and I...well..." her eyes grew dark with emotion and Allison knew she was fighting back the pain she kept buried deep inside her. It was strange but over the visits, Allison had come to know her as intimately as she knew herself. She could read Lillian even better than she could read her own mother. "It was easy to fill the role for him. He could get rough but most of the bruises were from me fighting back to keep him from raping me until the end."

She shrugged her shoulders and turned back to the window. "Anyway, I was expecting Lewis that night. I had gotten to the apartment around eight-thirty. Lewis liked to come up behind me as I performed some menial task. I decided to slip into a teddy and make a salad..."

The sounds of the radio filled the kitchen and I danced slowly to the B.B King song as I sliced the tomato for the salad. The large kitchen knife slid effortlessly through the tomato and I could almost pretend I was a normal woman enjoying her evening. For a moment, I forgot that Lewis was coming over to have sex.

Then I heard the door open and close as he slipped inside. As much as he wanted to play at this rape fantasy, he was a bumbling idiot. If he really got up the nerve to do it for real, and not just hire a whore to play the victim, he would be arrested before he even got two steps into the house. The man was as silent as a bull and he always hesitated before he began the game.

I shook my head and focused on the salad. Picking up a cucumber, I began peeling the skin from it, then washed it. I moved around the familiar kitchen as I half listened to the man hesitating in the hallway. I didn't look towards the hall. If I showed any sign that I knew he was there, Lewis would lose his erection and it was always a struggle to get him back to attention. The man was so meek, I had almost laughed the first time he told me what he wanted.

Of course, once he got into the struggle, he could be intentionally cruel, and his fists would rain down on me with a sexual urgency that scared me sometimes. I think it scared Lewis as well since he would always apologize after he was done, and he always gave me extra gifts besides payment. The gifts were for his guilt, but he still called and booked me every few weeks whenever the need overcame him.

I moved back to the cutting board, my mind on Lewis as I chopped the cucumber...my ears tuned in to the shuffling of Lewis hesitating on the threshold of the kitchen. I felt his eyes on the back of my neck and I wanted to squirm under his perusal, but I stayed focused on the salad—playing the unsuspecting victim he longed for in his sex play. The man was quite sick if I really stopped and thought about it.

"Lillian?"

The world pulled out from under my feet and I heard a whoosh of air in my ears. I dropped the knife and gripped the edge of the black, granite countertop to keep from tumbling to the white tiled floor. I squeezed my eyes shut as I begged for my ears to be wrong...begged for it not to be him.

"Lillian?" he said louder, and I knew it was him. A hard knot of fear choked me, and I grasped my throat in an effort to gain control of my emotions...it had been eighteen years since I had last seen him...eighteen years since I heard him call my name.

I turned slowly and took in his features. His green eyes were still hard and were filled with a strange mixture of grief and anger. He was as tall and handsome as he had been when I was younger, but his brown hair was obviously from dye and no longer natural. He had a few extra creases around his eyes and on his forehead, but he still looked young for his sixty years. And he still looked as terrifying as the last time I had seen him.

My eyes flashed down to his hands, which were by his side as he flexed them into fists. It was clear he was barely holding on to his emotions and I felt an all too familiar thrill of terror course through me. I was the little girl standing in front of him. It was clear that he was displeased with me and there was nothing I could say or do to fix it.

I swallowed back my fear and lifted my chin in defiance. My shoulders straightened without thought and my posture was the best it had been in years...Daddy didn't like a slouch. "A whore Lillian? You are nothing more than a fucking whore?"

I winced at the anger in his tone, but the words meant nothing to me now. I had always been a whore...he'd made sure of that when he took my innocence from me. "An escort Daddy. I needed to survive."

He shook his head and took a step forward. I immediately retreated but hit the edge of the counter with my back. "Do you know what we went through all these years? We thought you were dead...we prayed you were dead instead of living some horrible life. Your momma cried for you every night." He was speaking but it was as though he was speaking to himself or to the room. His eyes weren't focused on me, although he would occasionally look towards me as if he couldn't quite understand the image standing before him. "You should have come home Lillian. You shouldn't have become this."

I shook my head in reply as I felt tears of guilt brimming in my eyes. I had thought about going home...several times...hundreds of times but I couldn't spend my life with him. I couldn't stand the thought of him touching me again and I knew he would have touched me eventually. He couldn't help himself...he hid his monster deep inside, away from everyone, including himself. "I couldn't," I whispered.

His nostrils flared as if he could smell my guilt and fear. "You couldn't? Why not? Was there someone keeping you from calling? Could you never get to the phone?" His eyes focused on my cell phone resting on the counter.

"I didn't want to," I answered the question before he could ask it. "I never wanted to see any of you again...after...after everything that happened. After the baby..."

"You will not speak of that baby Lillian," he snapped and cut my words off. The tears fell freely now, and I swiped at them. I didn't want him to see me as the weak creature that had snuck away from his home. I had been broken when he'd last seen me and, if I was honest, I had run away to die.

And a part of me had died. Lillian had been murdered the moment her baby had been ripped from her body. Lily was what had grown on her grave and maybe I wasn't perfect, but most of the choices I had made to this point had been mine. I could have run from Adam just as easily as I had run from my father. "My name is Lily," I said, anger clear in my voice, "And I do not belong in your world anymore...I never did."

This time he looked at me and I realized this was the first time he had really looked at me since he'd entered the room. "You look like your momma," he said softly, "Your eyes are different and you're blonde now."

I wrapped my arms around my chest to hide my nakedness from him as I watched heat flare in his eyes. Sickness overtook me and I felt like collapsing to my knees to vomit. Even after all this time, I could see the lust in his eyes. I wanted to scream but I kept my voice cold as I said, "Smoke and mirrors. I still have green eyes and I dye my hair blonde. I needed to look like someone else..." *I needed to look like someone other than you*, I added silently before saying, "Besides, my clients prefer blondes."

It was as though I had slapped him. His mouth took on a sour twist as he looked around the room. "Are you expecting a client?" he asked, his tone filled with derision.

I almost said yes but then I knew that Lewis wasn't coming. I knew he was a friend of my father's, but he seemed almost eager to fuck me after realizing who I was. I wouldn't have expected him to give up his play toy by telling my father, but he must have needed a favor from him. Information was a commodity and my father traded in it freely. "I was expecting a client, but I know it was you who booked my time." I drew in a deep breath, "What do you want?"

"Want?" He smiled but it didn't reach his eyes, "I wanted to see my daughter...it has been almost twenty years without a sign she was alive. I needed to see for myself that she was."

I could feel my hands shaking but I clenched them to make them still. "Well, you saw and now you can go."

He shook his head again and moved up to the large island in the center of the room. His hands ran over the modern, white cabinets. I had designed this apartment with Adam when we'd first set it up. It had always been clean and modern, but it felt dirty now that my father was in it. I was quickly realizing I would never be able to come back here after this night. "I came, and I saw but I am not leaving without you, Lillian."

I flinched but held my ground, "Then you are going to be disappointed because I am not going anywhere with you. I am not going back to your house and I am not going with you. Lillian is dead."

He took another step towards me, but I straightened, my head high, my mouth a stubborn grimace. He was not going to cower me into doing what he wanted. I was not going back to that life and I was not going to do it for him or for Momma...or for Hayley. I winced as I thought of her. Of all my regrets in life, Hayley was my biggest, I should have brought her with me...should have saved her from him.

"Lillian, stop being childish. You are far from dead and you have a home with people who love you. Your momma needs you and Hayley does as well. She was destroyed when you ran away— she thought it was her fault." His tone was so soft...so gentle that I felt my resolve giving way. I wanted this daddy, the one who protected me...the one who cared about me. As though he felt my resolve slipping, he continued, "We love you, Lillian, and we don't want to live another day without you."

Another step closer and I realized he was standing right before me, "We have a room for you, sweetheart, and we will get you all the help you need to overcome these last few years." His hands reached out and I felt his thumbs sliding over my bare arms as he pulled me against him. His heat swallowed me, and I realized I was ice cold as his strong arms wrapped around my shoulders, and he held me in a hug.

His cheek brushed against mine before he placed his chin on the top of my head. Even though I was five-foot-eleven, my father still towered over me and made me feel small and fragile. I could smell his cloying cologne and I fought down the bile flooding my throat. My skin screamed where he touched me, but I couldn't struggle, couldn't break free of him. Tears slid down my cheeks as I realized Lily was as powerless against William Ross as Lillian had been. I was going to be taken back to that house and he would reshape me into what he wanted.

His lips pressed against my scalp before they moved to my forehead, "Oh Lillian. I missed this...I have missed us so much. Everything will be okay, baby girl. You're safe now that I've found you." He kissed my forehead again and his hands slid down my back, leaving a slimy feeling where they went. "Now get your stuff sweetheart, and we will go home."

I felt frozen by his words but when he said home, anger flashed in my blood and my cheeks reddened with heat. "No," I whispered.

He stiffened, "What did you say?" He pulled away slightly but kept me locked in his arms. I drew in a deep breath to steady my frantic heart and to stoke the fire of my anger. I needed this anger to finally be free of him. I needed this anger to stand up to my father like I should have done a thousand different times but couldn't.

"I said no," my voice was stronger, "I am not going home with you. I am not letting you rape me again." William winced at the words and I knew my strength had surprised him. "Take your hands off of me and get out of this apartment. I never want to see you again."

Pushing him away, his arms dropped from me as he stared at me in shock. It was clear he didn't recognize this creature before him, but I didn't care. This was Lily. This was the girl who had spent the last eighteen years playing the game. The woman who chose to be this. I didn't owe him or anyone an apology and I didn't deserve to be taken back into the life I had left. "Get out," I screamed, and it was like all the ties I had secretly held all these years were finally severed. I would never go back to that life.

"Lillian..."

"Lillian is dead," I screamed, as I pushed against his chest. He stood there unmoving. "Don't you get that? You murdered Lillian the first time you raped her. You kicked her corpse when you stole her baby and killed it. You buried her when she ran away. Lillian doesn't exist anymore, and her death is on your hands...not mine."

His eyes filled with horror at my words, but I didn't care. I wasn't going to protect him from the truth. He had killed that part of me when I was four. He killed that innocence. And then his eyes hardened as the words clicked into place. "You're right. Lillian is dead," his words were cold, and I felt my anger falter as fear tried to grab hold.

I nodded, "She is," I said quietly.

"And all that is left of her is a worthless whore," he snarled before he right fist shot out and connected with my jaw. I saw stars as tears of pain filled my eyes. It felt like my jaw was broken but before I could do anything, his left fist connected with my stomach.

I collapsed in half and groaned in pain as his fists began to pummel me. He moved with such speed, all I could do was curl up into a ball to shield my body. I crumpled to the floor he kicked me and cried out as each strike created a blossom of pain across my body. The anger that had filled me was gone and all I felt was terror as my father continued to hit me. *Please, just let him hit me and then leave...please...let this be over soon.* The words played over and over in my head and I felt like I wasn't in my body anymore.

And then he stopped, "Get up, you fucking whore!" He spat the words at me. My face ached from where he had hit me, and it felt like several of my ribs were broken. I pulled myself up into a kneeling position before I collapsed in pain. Fresh tears stung not only my eyes but the cut he had opened on my cheek. "Stand up!"

My fingers grasped the edge of the counter and I pulled myself up. Leaning against the edge of it, I focused on the butcher's knife still resting on the wooden cutting board—the assortment of cut vegetables in a neat pile next to it. The tomatoes flashed red like blood in my vision and I turned to look at my father.

His eyes were crazed, and I knew, without a single doubt, that he was finally going to kill me. This had been our destiny from the moment I'd been born.

I felt her inside of me, Lillian, as she gave up to the inevitable. I couldn't fight this destiny any more than I could fight my father. His hands slid over my shoulders again and then they were at my throat. "Oh Lillian," he whispered, "You have always been such a disappointment to me."

I nodded. I knew I was a disappointment. I could never be what he wanted me to be. There was something inherently broken in me...something so wrong that nothing he did could get rid of it. I closed my eyes as his fingers began to tighten around my neck. This was what Lillian deserved...what was supposed to be her end. "I tried so hard to be patient with you when you were a child, Lillian, but you kept disappointing me. And now...I can't have a whore for a daughter. I can't let you continue to defile the family reputation. I need to fix the mistakes I made."

...And I was that mistake. I knew it but still, my hands struggled with his as he squeezed. My eyes opened of their own accord and I stared into his. He looked sad...he looked disappointed as though he was putting a bad dog to sleep. Maybe that was all I had ever been to him...a bad dog that would eventually have to be put out of its misery.

My fingers fumbled against his hand, but he only clenched his fist harder. My throat felt raw on the outside and inside as I tried to draw in a breath. My other hand fumbled behind me and closed around the handle of the knife. I held on to it as he continued to squeeze and then, images of a little girl with large, green eyes flashed through my mind and I knew that Lily had to protect her.

The knife whipped around from behind me and I felt it slide into William's stomach. His eyes opened in surprise as I pulled the knife out. "Lillian!" he cried out, but Lillian was gone...fled to the space in my mind where I kept her safe.

"Lillian is dead, you son of a bitch!" I snarled as the knife plunged into him again. "You killed her, you bastard!" The knife flashed through the air, droplets of blood flying across the pristine kitchen and creating a macabre scene around us.

The knife fell over and over again...so often I lost count as the handle became slippery from the blood covering it. All the years of abuse that I had suffered flashed in my brain and that is all I saw. The room, my father, even my own body was gone and all that was left was the horrors that I had lived.

I slashed blindly up and watched in horror as the knife cut a wound across his throat. William grabbed his throat and struggled to scream but the slash had been so violent, I knew I had severed his vocal cords. I stepped back and slipped, the knife wrenched from my fingers as William sank to the floor. His body twitched for a few seconds before he went still but I could hear cries echoing around the room.

Then I realized they were my screams as I collapsed to the floor beside him. "Daddy?" I cried out as my tears fell like hot splashes against my cheeks. I glanced down at my hands and saw them covered in blood, my fingers were cut open where they had slipped on the handle and hit the blade. I gagged on the scream as I moaned, "Oh god! What have I done?"

My mind whirled around my crime — I had killed him. I had killed my own father! A part of me cried out at the horror of it and I glanced down at the knife on the floor. All I had to do was cut my wrists and this nightmare would end. I picked up the knife and pressed the blade against my wrist, leaving a smear of my father's blood on my skin.

The metal pushed against my skin as my hands shook and then I dropped the knife with a sob as I gave into the tears. No matter what, a part of me loved my father and I realized I was a monster just like him. I had no idea what to do as my eyes searched the kitchen for a way to hide my crime. My gaze fell onto my cell phone and I pulled myself up onto shaky legs. I held the counter as I walked toward the phone.

Reaching out, I stared at the blood on my hands before I tried to clean them on the white teddy I was wearing. I picked up the phone and punched in the only number I could think of. After two rings, a man answered and I said, "Adam, I need your help. I'm at the apartment, come quickly," before I hung up.

●━━━━━━━━━━━━━━━━━━━━━━━●

I sat in the living room as Adam waved his arms around him. "You stupid fucking bitch! What the fuck did you do and why the fuck did you call me?"

Rage flashed in his eyes and there was a small tick at the corner of one. He was clearly agitated, and I couldn't blame him. It had taken him an hour to get to me and I had spent that hour sitting in the kitchen as I watched my father. I spent the time expecting him to jump up and attack me again. I'm not sure why I called Adam, except that a part of me knew he could make bodies disappear and all I'd wanted was for William Ross to disappear.

I had grabbed the knife and held it in front of me as I waited. Adam had let himself in with his key and when he came into the kitchen, confusion and dismay had filled his eyes as he took in the sight. He'd pulled me from my crouch in the corner and dragged me into the living room. The last ten minutes had been him swearing at me for dragging him into this mess.

I understood why he was mad, but my eyes kept flashing toward the knife sitting on the glass coffee table. "I didn't know what to do...he tried to kill me, and I was defending myself."

Adam ran his hands through his short hair and glanced towards the kitchen again. "Who is he? I thought you had an appointment with Lewis?"

I nodded, "I did but he came instead."

"Did you know him?"

I nodded again as new tears filled my eyes, "He's my daddy," I whispered as I glanced up at Adam. He stopped dead in his tracks and horror filled his face.

"Your daddy. As in William Ross? What the fuck, Lily! I knew that there was no love lost between you two, but I didn't think you would kill him." I could see the plan clicking away in Adam's head. He was trying to figure out a way to make this work for him. He couldn't have a dead body...especially one as influential as William Ross...messing up his business. And despite everything I had done for him, I was just one of his whores...human garbage fit for nothing but the game. Adam had made sure all his girls knew this fact.

"Yes," I sobbed. "He tried to kill me, and, in the struggle, I ended up stabbing him."

Adam moved away from me and walked into the kitchen. I could see him over the island as he grabbed a towel and rolled William over. "Jesus!" he cried. "Lillian, you fucking butchered him. Fuck, I'm not a cop or anything but even I know this wasn't self-defense."

He stood up and tossed the towel into the sink before he moved toward me. His eyes were hard, and his lips were a tight line. He shook his head as he walked into the living room and I found myself glancing towards the knife. Anger radiated from him like a violent predator and I couldn't help but wonder what he would do to me. It was clear I had fucked up by phoning him. Adam wasn't going to save me...he was going to call the cops himself.

"You shouldn't have called me Lily," his words were cold. "But you were always a dumb bitch. You could have just gone home with your daddy or hell, killed the bastard and then took off. Sure, I would have had some problems with a dead body being in this apartment, but I know enough people to make it a small problem."

He stepped closer and I shook my head, "Please Adam. I didn't know what else to do. I need help."

"Jesus Lily! What happened to you? You were always such a little fighter. You didn't need anyone's help, remember?" he asked as he sat down on the couch with me.

His hand wrapped around the back of my neck and he squeezed. I shuddered under the pain. He hadn't touched me like this in years. This violence he saved for his street whores, not his escorts. It was clear he was upset with me. "Now we need to decide what we are going to do about this mess, Lily," he said.

"I don't know." I wracked my brain for some idea of what I could do but I couldn't think of anything. His fingers continued to squeeze and pinch the back of my neck as he thought as well. "I could turn myself in," I murmured finally. "You could leave and then I could turn myself in."

"But they would figure out I was here. That old woman across the way was at her peephole again when I walked in...nosy old bat. How would you explain that I was here but then I left without seeing the body?"

I shook my head. I knew what his mind was reaching for...what he was expecting from me. He wanted me to kill myself and then he could say that he came in and found a bloody mess. It would make it easy for him, but I wasn't ready to die. "I don't know," I mumbled.

He stood up and walked over to the table where he stared at the knife. "Really, I think the best thing for you to do is end things now Lily. No questions, no guilt...just the end." His voice took on the softness he used to get his way. Here was the beautiful man who would save the world. The man girls fell in love with. Hell, I had fallen in love with him when I had first run away but that girl was gone just like Lillian was.

"No," I said.

He turned towards me and cocked his eyebrow, "No?" He laughed, "What are you saying no to?"

"You know what. You want me to kill myself," I said as I nodded toward the knife. "Then you can say that you walked in to find me dead and my father murdered. It would make it easier for you."

He tilted his head to the side as though the idea was completely mine and not one he'd been thinking himself. "Lily...what can you gain from this?" he cooed, "This was your daddy and you murdered him. The police will be able to figure out what happened. They'll know you did this, and you will be getting the injection for it. They do have the death penalty in this state, you know. If you end things now, you don't have to drag others through hell with you. I mean, think about your mother and your sister...what was her name again?" He stopped as though he was trying to recall an old memory, "Hayley? That's it, Hayley. Do you want your little sister to suffer with you?"

I shook my head to remove his words, but it didn't work. Why should I live when my daddy lay dead not even twenty feet from me? Why should I continue breathing when my soul had been murdered so long ago? I stared at the tattoo on my wrist and thought about Eric. I had loved him and should have stayed with him but all he'd seen was a whore after he'd found out the truth.

Reaching out, I picked up the butcher knife in shaking hands. It was sticky with my father's blood and I had to fight the urge to put it down again. I stared at the bloodstained steel and positioned it in my hands so I could drive it into my stomach. I glanced up at Adam who was watching me with expectation. He smiled at me and nodded, encouraging me to do what we both knew was the right thing. "Do you need me to leave the room so you have some privacy?" he asked.

His words sliced through my guilt and I shook my head, "No," I screamed as I threw the knife toward him. It sliced through the air, but he stepped to the side and it slid past him, bouncing off the wall before it fell to the floor.

His face twisted into a mask of hatred as he snarled, "You stupid bitch," and then he lunged at me. I barely had time to get to my feet before his fist collided with my chin and sent me reeling backwards. He followed my descent onto the couch as his hands wrapped around my throat. I kicked out with my feet, feeling a wash of satisfaction as my heel made contact with his groin.

He gurgled in pain as his fingers loosened and I struggled to get out from under him. I rolled to the floor onto my hands and knees and began crawling towards the wall where the knife had landed. But Adam recovered too quickly, and he was on my back—his fists slamming down on me as I struggled toward the knife.

I collapsed to the floor as he scrambled to his feet. He swung his leg, his foot making contact with my stomach as he knocked the breath from my lungs. "You stupid bitch. All you had to do was make this easy for us. Now I have to deal with this mess and with you."

He pulled his leg back again and let it fly into my stomach again. I gagged on the pain that blossomed through my body. I screamed as his hand dug into my blonde hair and he wrenched me up onto my knees. His fist smashed into my face and I felt my nose break as a mushroom of blood sprayed through the air. I knew that he was killing me, but my mind was blank from the terror of it all. I had just survived one attack only to succumb to another.

My hands flayed out and I felt them dig into Adam's cheek. He shrieked in pain, "You fucking bitch!"

The back of his hand crashed against my cheek and I flew backwards, landing into the coffee table. The glass shattered around me and I felt hundreds of shards shred my teddy and my back. I laid in the glass, staring up at Adam, his face bloody from my scratches as it twisted with pure rage. He leaned down, his fingers wrapping around my neck again and I felt it breaking under his grip.

My fingers slid through the glass; I could feel the shards slicing my fingers as I searched for anything to defend myself with. Then my fingers closed on a large shard and with the last of my strength, I swung. The glass arched up and buried into Adam's eye. It popped like a ripe grape and sprayed me with his blood. Adam screamed, his hands falling away from my neck as he grabbed at his face.

I struggled to stand as glass sliced my feet and stumbled toward the knife, Adam screaming behind me. I fell on top of it, my hands bringing it towards my belly as I turned onto my back. I stared in horror as Adam launched himself at me.

The knife slid easily into his chest and I felt it hesitate briefly before it found its way between his ribs. Adam collapsed lifelessly on top of me.

Shaking, I pushed his body from mine and pulled myself up against the wall. A sob ripped through me and the room as I stared down at Adam. I had killed two men! I wanted to scream at the horror of it all. I wanted to collapse. I had felt something burst inside of me when Adam had kicked me, but I didn't have time to stop and look at my injuries. I needed help.

Stumbling to bedroom, I picked up the handset from the landline by the bed. I could barely see the numbers as I punched in 911. I listened to the phone ringing as I collapsed to the floor. The feminine voice filled the earpiece. "911, state your emergency?"

Tears filled my eyes and the sob tore at my throat as I looked around the room. I didn't know what I was doing but the words flowed out of me, "I need help..."

●━━━━━━━━━━━━━━━━━━━━━━━━●

Lillian's voice faded in the room and Allison could see tears shimmering in her eyes before she turned away from her. She went back to looking out the window, the sunshine, a complete opposite to the cold darkness of Lillian's memory.

They sat there like that for ten minutes as Allison tried to gather her thoughts. While Lillian had murdered both men, it was more a case of self-defense than premeditated murder. At the very least, she shouldn't have been sentenced to death. As she opened her mouth to say her thoughts, Lillian looked at her with such sadness that Allison couldn't speak.

Lillian looked so tired and Allison realized today's part of the story had been the most draining for her. Lillian said, "I'm done for today. I don't want to talk about anything anymore."

Pulling away from the wall, she walked towards the door and banged on it. "Jayla, I'm done for today!"

Jayla opened the door hesitantly and glanced towards Allison as she took in the haggard appearance of Lillian. "Everything okay in here?" she asked.

Allison nodded as Lillian said, "Just a hard day to relive."

Jayla restrained Lillian's arms as Allison stood up. Lillian glanced towards her when she did and Allison said, "I will be back in a few days."

Her frown created tiny wrinkles on her forehead, "Sure," she said before she allowed the guard to lead her out. The door closed with a deafening clang and Allison was alone in the room as the ghosts of the dead men echoed around her.

CHAPTER TWENTY-THREE

(Defendant Sworn)

The Court: Ms. Ross, do you understand that having been sworn, your answers to my questions will be subject to the penalties of the court if you make a false statement.

Defendant, Lillian Ross (LR): Yes, your honor.

The Court: How old are you, Ms. Ross?

LR: I am thirty-five years old.

The Court: How old were you when the murders occurred?

LR: Umm...thirty-three.

The Court: How far did you get in school?

LR: I started but did not finish the tenth grade.

The Court: Can you read and write the English language?

LR: Yes.

The Court: In the last twenty-four hours, have you taken any medications, drugs or alcohol?

LR: No.

The Court: Have you or are you being treated for mental illness or drug addiction?

LR: No, your Honor.

The Court: Do you understand what we are doing here today?

LR: Yes, I am giving my plea.

The Court: In the charge of Murder of the First Degree of Adam Laurent, how do you plead?

LR: Not guilty.

The Court: In the charge of Murder of the First Degree of William Ross, how do you plead?

LR: Not...guilty.

~ Excerpt from Plea Hearing, People vs. Lillian Ross

━━━━━━●━━━━━━━━━━━━━━━━━━━━━━━●━━━━━━

"Ira, you need to get me the name and contact information of the best criminal defense attorney you can think of," Allison said as she stormed into the office.

Ira glanced up and so did a client he was sitting with, a tall man with silver hair and a slightly oversized belly. He was dressed in a well-tailored black suit and a charcoal grey tie. Everything about him screamed money and privilege. Allison narrowed her eyes at him, and a blush covered her face when she realized how rude she had been.

The man gave her a withering glare and Ira stammered, "Al-Allison, I wasn't expecting you today. Is everything okay?"

"Yes, I'm sorry, I should have called but something has happened, and I needed to speak with you about it." She wanted to say she was sorry about the last time they'd seen each other.

After she'd thought about it, she realized she didn't have a right to be upset the way she had been. What Ira did was his own choice and he had to live with it. She couldn't be angry with him for the rest of her life because he was the last link to her father. That he wasn't honest with her still stung but she needed to work through it, especially since she needed his support with this.

Ira's eyes opened in alarm and Allison shook her head, "No, nothing about me or Mom." She addressed the man sitting across from Ira, "I'm sorry. I'm being rude. I will wait outside until you are both finished."

Ira held up his hand, "Allison, wait. This concerns you, so please stay."

Ira motioned toward the man sitting opposite and said, "Allison, this is Mr. Charles Tanner. Mr. Tanner, this is Allison McKinnon. Mr. Tanner is here as a professional courtesy to let me know that his client has decided to pursue legal action toward you if you continue writing your book. He thought it would be best to come to me first as a favor to your father and to allow me to tell you."

Allison took the vacant chair near Ira's desk. Trying to draw her thoughts, all she could think about was that this was Irene's doing. This must be her lawyer. "Irene send you?" she asked.

"No," Mr. Tanner replied instantly, his voice was smooth and deep. A lovely voice for a snake, which this man surely was. "I represent a different client who prefers to remain anonymous. All that I am at liberty to say is that he knew Lily Laurent...intimately...before she was charged with murder and he is hoping to stop any risk of his relationship from becoming a public matter."

Allison stared at him in disbelief. It wasn't the first time in her career she'd met some obstacles and she wasn't worried about the legal battle. Her publisher would support her. She looked at Ira, whose eyes were filled with worry. "I'm sorry Mr. Tanner, but I am not sure why you are here."

"I'm here," he said as though he was speaking to a simpleton, "to encourage your lawyer to talk some sense into you."

"Sense," she cocked her head at him and thought about what he was saying. "Wouldn't it be the sensible thing to just let the book be written instead of drawing national attention with a lawsuit? I mean, your client obviously doesn't want his name associated with this book or this case."

Ira interjected, "Allison, please see a little reason with this. I know you don't want to put your publisher at risk of a lawsuit and Mr. Tanner's client is more than willing to sue both of you."

Allison turned her angry eyes towards Ira and said, "Yes, well, you know as well as I do that my publisher will look out for me. They have stood by me for several books and this isn't the first threat of a lawsuit. I think that they would be more than willing to stand by this book as well."

"Ms. McKinnon, I assure you this lawsuit will be different," Mr. Tanner said, his face getting redder with every second they sat together. She smiled at him but there was no warmth in it as she thought about her options. In all honesty, she didn't want to start a battle. While she had every faith in her book getting published, she didn't want the delay a lawsuit would cause. In addition, she didn't want to put that type of problem on her publisher simply because she pissed off this man and his client.

Deciding to use tact, Allison said, "Mr. Tanner, I understand that your client may be concerned about Lillian giving names, but I assure you, she has only mentioned a few of her clients and none of them by a full name." Except for Lewis Carlyle but she wasn't going to mention that right now.

"Yes," he said dryly, "I am sure she hasn't but that doesn't meant people won't put two and two together. There could be intimate details that could help to identify my client and we want to end any chance of that happening."

Allison nodded, she did see his point but since most of the stories involved Lillian's client's sexual tastes, she didn't think anyone would really know who the person was...and that was if someone who knew the man read the book. She just couldn't see it happening, which made her think that maybe something else was pushing this lawsuit forward.

"I can offer one option," Ira suggested, and they turned in unison to stare at him. "Why don't you agree for Allison to send a copy of the book before it is sent to her publisher? If there is some identifying marker in the book, you can flag the chapters and Allison can remove it or alter it."

Allison's cheeks felt like they were stained red, but she nodded. It wasn't unusual to make changes, but she really didn't want to make changes simply because an old pervert was scared of getting caught. Mr. Tanner said, "No, that won't work. We are busy people and don't have time to read the book and send you our edits. We still stand with our original option. The book should be cancelled."

She stared at him in disbelief and was ready to scream. She narrowed her eyes and said in a very tight voice, "Then I guess we will be seeing you in court, Mr. Tanner."

"I suppose we will Ms. McKinnon," he sneered at her as he studied her. "You know, I knew your father. He was a great man."

"Thank you. He was a great man." She wondered how they'd known each other as this man was someone her father would have hated.

"It's a pity his daughter didn't inherit any of his traits."

She felt the sting of the words, but she couldn't help the laughter that spurted out of her. Ira looked at her in shock and so did Mr. Tanner. He glared at her as she said, "Yes, I am often told I take after my mother and she can be a bitch at times."

His mouth opened in surprise and she continued, "But since you have nothing else to say, I guess our meeting is over." She glanced at Ira, "Do you want me to leave or are you finished with Mr. Tanner as well?"

Ira sputtered and turned toward the obstinate man, "As far as I can see, there is nothing left to say, unless you have something to add."

Mr. Tanner's eyes turned thoughtful and, after a few minutes, he said, "Actually, there is one alternative that my client is open to. After all, lawsuits can be exhausting for everyone and he doesn't want to keep this going forever."

"I'm listening," she said.

"You sign a waiver stating that you will only be using pseudonyms for Lillian Ross's clients in the book..."

"Done," she said quickly.

He raised an eyebrow and leaned forward, "And you drop any idea of pursuing an appeal for Lillian."

If he'd hit her, she wouldn't have been as surprised as she was at that moment. She hadn't expected him to ask for that and she wasn't sure what to say. She glanced at Ira, who looked as shocked as she was, and then back to Mr. Tanner, who sat smugly in the oversized chair.

"How did you know I was pursuing an appeal?" she asked.

He waved his hands in the air as if to indicate the space between them, "Here and there. Word travels quickly and after you told Harold Deveins of you plans, it travelled even faster."

She closed her eyes to fight the headache that was forming, "Why does it matter if we go forward with the appeal?"

"Honestly?" he asked, and she nodded. "It doesn't matter on some levels. My client is not a cruel man and he would love to see Lillian freed, however, he worries that the appeal may finally pull him into the spotlight. You see, he worked hard to stay hidden from the public eye when she went through her trial. Now you are talking about bringing forward new evidence and that could turn the spotlight on my client. He may not be able to keep out of the public notice this time."

Allison stared at him in shock. How far did this go? "I don't think that it would do anything like that."

"Hmm, perhaps not," he mused, "But it is always better to be pre-emptive when you think there aren't going to be problems. Don't you agree?"

She nodded and ignored the hidden insult. She hadn't been pre-emptive. She'd bumbled along and went with her gut instead of watching what she said and to whom. She shouldn't have approached Harold Deveins. It was clear Mr. Tanner had little respect for her. He watched her and waited as she gathered her thoughts. "So what is your decision?" he asked.

Allison had several options, but she took the first one that came to mind. "I don't think I have a choice," she said slowly, "I guess I will agree to drop the appeal." She shrugged, "At this point, I don't even know if there are grounds for one."

The grin he gave her was wolfish and she felt sick to her stomach. She hated that she gave in to him so easily. "Wonderful." He looked between her and Ira, "Well, I think that concludes our business. I will draw up that waiver and send it to you in a few days, Ira."

He stood up and smoothed his suit before he picked up the briefcase that had been sitting beside his chair. "Ms. McKinnon, it was a pleasure to meet you finally."

Holding out his hand, he waited for Allison to take it. She did, hesitantly, and her skin crawled under his touch. "I wish I could say the same, Mr. Tanner."

Laughing, he walked to the door. Allison watched the closed door for several minutes and she could hear Ira shuffling papers behind her. She closed her eyes and drew in a steadying breath. She wasn't going to allow this bastard and his client to change things.

Without looking back at Ira, she said, "Ira, it still stands what I said. Please help me find a criminal defense lawyer who can handle this appeal."

"But, you said?" Ira's voice was filled with worry and she closed her ears to it. She didn't want to hear all his reasons to not do this.

"I know what I said," Allison turned toward him, her eyes blazing with resolve, "But I wouldn't be able to live with myself if I didn't try to help her."

CHAPTER TWENTY-FOUR

Forensic Mental Health Assessment Report

Re: Lillian Ross

Page 8 of 12

IX. MENTAL ASSESSMENT TO REOFFEND: I had the opportunity to sit with Lillian Ross and observe her. The meetings took place over the course of two weeks and were done five times over that time period. At first, Lillian Ross appeared to find the interviews annoying and would often say that they were no longer necessary.

She showed no guilt during discussions of her alleged crimes and she made three jokes at the expense of the deceased. She appeared almost proud of what she had done. She spoke openly of Adam Laurent but not about her life or the alleged prostitution through the escort services where she was employed.

Lillian Ross did show avoidance techniques when speaking of her father, William Ross, and grew violently angry when pressed on the subject. She reacted physically by throwing items in the office during one intense questioning session.

Through the observations, I find Lillian Ross to be suffering from several anxiety disorders, which are not identified due to lack of time with the client. She definitely suffers from avoidance disorders and has violent tendencies. Her moods shift frequently and without warning, leading me to wonder if she is exhibiting bipolar disorder, more sessions are recommended for diagnosis. She exhibits high levels of anxiety and she has no evidence of remorse.

For those reasons, I feel that Lillian Ross is at high risk to reoffend if she is ever placed in a position where there is a man or men disagreeing with her. I feel that it is important for Ms. Ross to be cared for by a psychologist during her incarceration to prevent further aggravating the mental illness she clearly exhibits.

~ Excerpt from Psychological Assessment, Dr. Jessica Childers

●————————————————————————●

She was like a caged animal the way that she paced behind the table and Allison wasn't sure what had set her off. She'd thought they'd come to an understanding with each other and they were done with this battle. But from the moment Lillian had walked into the room, she'd been on edge. Not talking, smoking cigarette after cigarette.

Twenty minutes had passed since she'd entered the room and they'd sat with an angry energy around them. It was clear something was bothering Lillian, but it was like she didn't know where to begin.

Lillian finally turned toward Allison. The anger was clear in the hard slash of her mouth when she said, "Who do you think you are?"

Shaking her head, Allison tried to think of what she'd done but nothing came to mind. She stared at Lillian and the woman glared back—her entire body was tense and seemed to hum as though a barely contained energy coursed through her. "I don't understand," Allison said carefully, "What happened?"

Lillian smiled and there was no warmth in it. "Do I really need to spell it out?" she asked, her voice filled with cold fury. "I received a lovely letter from my defense attorney."

Then Allison understood the reason for Lillian's anger, but she found it even more confusing than before. Why wouldn't she want the help Allison was offering? What could she gain by staying in prison? Why would she choose execution over a lesser sentence or even freedom? It was then that she realized that despite all the time they'd spent together over the last few months, Lillian really was a stranger. She kept a lot of things inside, even when they were sharing the darkest moments in her life. "I don't understand," she said truthfully, "I thought I was helping you."

"Did I ask for your fucking help?" she snapped, "I asked you to write a fucking book, so my story was finally told instead of all those lies that have been published already. Don't you get that? I asked one thing of you."

Allison felt like she'd been slapped. She stared at Lillian as tears filled her eyes, but she swallowed the lump in her throat and fought the emotion raging inside her. "I am doing my job." Her voice was as harsh as Lillian's and she wondered just how much the woman had become a part of her. She felt like she was fighting with a piece of her own heart, "But I saw something more than you did, obviously. I saw self-defense, Lillian!"

"Bah," Lillian threw her hands out like she was washing the idea from the room now that it had been said, "I told you one thing when we first started all of this and it was that I killed those men. I did. I was in full control when I chose to fight and kill them and a part of me was happy I did it. They couldn't hurt anyone else."

"But don't you see," Allison pleaded, "that is exactly why it was self-defense. They both tried to kill you and you chose to live. Why are you throwing it all away by not defending yourself and not admitting the truth about that night? You didn't kill them...you defended yourself from being killed."

"What difference does it make?" Lillian sounded exhausted. "There are still two men dead," tears brimmed her angry eyes as she continued, "Two men I said I loved at one time or another and despite everything, a small part of me still loves them. He was my father; don't you understand that? I should have let him finish what he'd started all those years ago. Lillian Ross had been murdered over and over again, her innocence, her baby, her wonder, her belief that there was good in the world. It was all murdered by my father first and Adam second. All that is left is this empty vessel that remembers every moment like some sick monument to her."

"That's not true. Lillian is still in there," Allison whispered, "I saw her when you spoke. I saw the fire that survived."

"And that fire is nothing. It is twisted and cruel."

She shook her head before Allison said, "No, it isn't. It is soft and filled with warmth. It cares for others and you can see that in the way Eric remembers you. It can be felt in your memories and your stories. You are still alive, Lillian, and there is a chance that you could have more of a life than what you have."

Lillian sank into her chair as she started laughing. It was a shrill, cold sound and Allison shivered when she heard it. "You are so naive, Allison," she spit out when she was done laughing. "What life is there? What do you see in that writer's head of yours? Do you see this perfect little world where I will walk out of the courthouse after an appeal and I will have a full life with children and a husband?"

Allison would be lying if she said that she hadn't dreamt of that for Lillian. But she wasn't naive. Lillian would still have to serve time, there was no way around it, but she might be able to get a lighter sentence, one that would see her on the outside one day. Life wasn't a fairytale and she hadn't expected a fairytale ending for Lillian, but she'd thought that maybe she could taste freedom for the first time in her life. Something Lillian had never experienced.

"No," she said slowly, "But I thought you deserved more than what you have been living with throughout your life. I saw some hope in the future for you, but it means having to fight and coming forward about everything like you did with this book."

For a second, Allison thought she saw some hint of hope in Lillian's eyes and then it was like a window closed and all that was left was the cold. Lillian shook her head and the side of her mouth quirked into a twisted smile. "There is no hope for the future, Allison. I am not the person you think you know. I told you the memories of a dead girl because I was sick of holding onto them myself."

Allison shook her head and opened her mouth to argue when Lillian raised up her hand to stop her. "You would be wise to realize your first impression of me was the correct one. I am nothing but a psychopath and you played easily into my little game."

It was like being punched but despite how cold Lillian's words were, Allison couldn't believe them. She felt the bond between them over the last few months. It was faint but every day, she'd felt it growing strong...two survivors who could be healed together. *Maybe it was the monster inside you that felt the bond*; a thought whispered across her mind, slithering from the darkest parts of her—the parts that wished she'd been as strong as Lillian and murdered her rapist.

Shaking the thoughts out of her head, Allison said, "No, I don't believe it. Maybe there are parts of you like that but most of you is better than even you know. I saw you. Lillian. I saw a girl who survived so much and who still had things to hope for...to dream about. I saw a girl who wasn't destroyed despite everything she'd lived through and everything she'd been forced to do."

"Did you see me?" Lillian asked, her thin eyebrow arching to perfection.

"Yes," Allison nodded, "I did."

"Are you sure you didn't see yourself? Maybe you're saving me is all about saving yourself from your own monsters."

Her voice was cold, but it spoke volumes about how much she knew. Despite the fact that the court documents were locked, Lillian knew.

Allison felt the blood drain from her face as a wave of nausea washed over her. She gagged at the thought.

"Surprised, aren't you?" Lillian asked.

Allison nodded but she couldn't say anything. Her words had turned to ash in her mouth.

"I don't know the details, if that is what you are worried about, but I saw it in your books; in everything you write. The fact that you are always writing from the victim's side. The fact that you pursue the darker stories but aren't going for the sensationalism. Did you think I just chose you because I liked your writing?"

Allison hadn't thought about it and had assumed Lillian had been telling the truth at their first meeting. But why had she really asked for Allison? After all the memories she'd shared, Allison had assumed that it was because Lillian was the victim of the story...not those two men. "I thought it was because you wanted to share your story," she said lamely.

Lillian sat back and crossed her arms. Propping her leg up on her other knee, she continued to glare at Allison with barely suppressed anger. "I wanted to share my story," she said flatly, "What I didn't want was for you to go and get a savior complex."

"What I wanted," she stood up, "Was for you to feel ever so sad that another victim, just like you, had to suffer through so much abuse."

Lillian leaned against the table and glared at her, "I wanted to just tell my side of things and be done with it. I don't want to think about it, worrying about no one knowing the truth and that is what you were supposed to do. I'm serving the sentence I deserve, and you can't fix that."

Her mouth twisted into a sardonic smile, "You can't make your own abuse go away because you saved me, especially when I didn't ask or want to be saved."

"That isn't the reason," Allison whispered as her mind whirled around all the ways Lillian could have found out. She had never publicly talked about it.

"Yes, it was, and you damn well know it." Her eyes glittered with hate and Allison felt every bond they'd created before now being stripped away with each word she said. "So tell me, Allison, how did he do it? Was it one rape; was it over several months...years? How violent did it get? Come on, I shared the details of my pain; let's see the details of yours. I think it is only fair."

Allison stared at her as the shadows of memories blurred in her mind. She was there, standing in the room while his fists

~ 299 ~

pummeled into her mother...screaming for him to stop but unable to pick herself up from the floor where she lay. The shadows clung to her the way her torn clothes had clung to her broken body.

Tears began streaming down her face, but she didn't think she was crying. No sobs came out, just the pain she'd spent years discussing with therapist after therapist until there was nothing else they could do about it. "What happened Allison? Did someone save you like you wanted to save me? Do you have some false sense of obligation?"

Allison shook her head but maybe Lillian was speaking the truth. Maybe she'd had some false sense of obligation, but she didn't think that was it. She wanted to believe that that much suffering had something better after it. She needed to know that no matter how far the abuse took a person, they were still able to come back from it...to not be consumed by it. She wanted to believe her own story didn't have an inevitable end with the monster inside her...the one that would have gladly killed Lillian's monsters...Adam and William, being destroyed.

She shook her head again. "No, I wanted to help you. I didn't know that you didn't want the appeal. I thought you'd just decided you wouldn't win so why bother trying but you could win it."

"No, I can't," Lillian shouted, "I am nothing but a fucking whore...didn't you see that; didn't you hear it in the words. I don't want to fight for an appeal, I don't want to do anything except tell the goddamn story and be left alone."

"But..."

"Fuck you!" she screamed. "Fuck you and your help and all the dumb thoughts you are fucking having. Do your job, Allison! Feel like you beat your attacker because you are the strong Allison, the survivor, who helps others survive by jotting down their secrets. Live your fake life of believing you are healed because you aren't...you're just as fucked up as the rest of us and no amount of writing, no amount of saving, is going to change that."

"So just write the goddamn story and stay the fuck out of the rest of my life," Lillian finished. She took in a deep breath as though she was about to say something else but, instead, turned toward the door and crossed the room. She paused at the door and turned back to her, "A part of me wants to know what the sick asshole did to you but most of me just doesn't care. I don't care about you...your past, your present, your future, all that I care about is that you do the job I asked you to do. All I care about is that my story is told so if you can't do that, let me know right now and I will find someone else."

Allison swallowed in an effort to force the words out and then she said, "Yes, I can do my job." She felt numb, felt like she had just lost something important, but she couldn't understand why.

"Then do it and leave me alone. I will be asking Kai to limit your visits from this point on." Lillian closed her eyes but not before Allison thought she saw tears in them. "I don't want to see you until the book is written, and maybe not even then."

"Why are you doing this?" Allison whispered.

Her eyes hardened, "Because I am sick of you staring at me in pity. I didn't ask for your pity, I asked for your ability as a writer. So do everyone a favor and go home, write and try to figure out how you're going to survive your own abuse instead of worrying about me."

She whirled toward the door and began banging on it, "Guard, let me out! We're done here today!"

CHAPTER TWENTY-FIVE

Jessica Hunt (JH): Lillian worked a lot that last year with Adam. She was taking every client and not just the regular five. Some of the girls got a bit upset because she was cutting into their money.

Prosecutor Deveins (PD): Do you know who she was supposed to be seeing the night of the murder?

JH: No, but I think it was one of the regulars. It was set up at the apartment Adam kept for his escorts. You know, more discreet than a hotel.

PD: I see. Did you use the apartment?

JH: Yes, several times. We had a schedule for the apartment and girls would book it. Adam charged a fee, but it was cheaper than a hotel or taking someone home with you.

PD: How often did Lillian book it?

JH: Not often. She was the girlfriend experience.

PD: The girlfriend experience?

JH: Yeah, she was the one guys called to take out and see the town. She'd travel with them, attend functions, that kind of stuff. But Lillian was cool. She didn't rub it in your face and she'd often let other girls take the jobs from her. She'd hide it from Adam, you know...so he wouldn't pocket the lion's share. And instead, she'd give her pay to the girls. She made the most at the escort service and I was always happy when she offered a client to me because I knew I was going to make a lot of money that week.

~ Official Court Transcripts: People vs. Lillian Ross

She stared at her hands as they squeezed the steering wheel and willed them to stop shaking. Her entire body thrummed with nervous energy and no matter how she tried to stop, she couldn't. She tried to focus on the highway before her and prayed that she could get home before the panic attack took full control.

Allison cursed as a man cut her off, barely missing her front bumper and she felt the stream of tears when she did. Only five more minutes and she could collapse in her driveway.

Lillian's words echoed in her head, *So tell me, Allison, how did he do it? Was it one rape; was it over several months...years? How violent did it get? Come on, I shared the details of my pain; let's see the details of yours. I think it is only fair.*

"Does it matter?" she said to no one.

All that mattered was that it had happened to her and it had taken years for her to get through it. First, it had been the trial, then it had been learning to trust and move forward with her life. "I'm a survivor," she said to herself and it was like a mantra to her. She'd survived.

But have you? a new voice whispered in her head. It sounded so much like Lillian's. She fought back the panic. She'd survived. That's what countless therapists and support groups had said. She'd survived. She was successful, and she controlled her life.

Taking the off ramp toward her house, Allison knew she only had a few more minutes before she was home and safe. But would she be safe? It had been almost eight years since her last panic attack. Eight years where she'd thought of herself as mostly healed. Sure, there were moments when she was scared, but that was normal.

Taking a deep breath, she turned the corner to her house and then her hands started shaking even harder as she saw Roger's car in the driveway. She had forgotten they were supposed to meet up tonight. Sliding into her driveway, she cut the engine and then clawed at the handle of the door.

Tears blurred her vision and she struggled to get out as her breath came in shorter and shorter pants. The world around her sped up and slowed down at exactly the same time and echoes of her screams filled her ears, but she couldn't tell if they were screams from memories long ago or if she was really yelling right now as she fumbled with the door.

She beat against the glass as the tears burned her eyes and the panic clawed up her chest. She felt him behind her—felt him reaching for her like he did when she was fourteen. Felt his hand on her shoulder, squeezing it as he threw her across the room and onto the couch. She struggled for the breath as the ghost of the memory crushed the air out of her lungs...just like he had done to her.

The door flung open and she screamed...she knew it was her screaming this time and punched out toward the face swimming in her vision. She heard him curse as strong hands wrapped around her, but she struggled against them. "Let...me...go," she cried as sobs wracked her body and she slid to the ground beside the car.

Roger leaned down toward her, but she put out her hands, "Don't touch me, let me breathe...God! Let me breathe."

Roger stood up and took a step back. She could see the worry and pain in his eyes, but she ignored them. Instead, she crawled away from the car and collapsed onto the grass, which was coated in a light snow. She ignored the cold as she tried to focus on her breathing, a technique she'd learned years ago but the memories still pressed down on her.

Looking over at Roger, she said, "Phone my mom, please. Her number is in the house."

Roger nodded but he didn't turn toward the house. Instead, he grabbed her keys from where she'd dropped them on the ground, closed the car door and then walked over to Allison. He knelt and carefully slipped his hands behind her shoulders and under her legs. "Please," she cried, "Don't...not like this."

She felt the panic, but she could tell that it was loosening its grip on her...and that was even worse since she could feel the pain in her heart. The memories would come now, and she would have nothing left in her to fight. Lillian had shattered her. All these meetings had worn away at her own defenses.

"I'm just going to take you inside to call your mom. After that, you can go and lie down while you wait."

He picked her up as though she weighed nothing and carried her into the house. And for the first time since she was a little girl, she buried her head into the chest of a man and just allowed herself to cry.

She could hear them outside her door, whispering about her health. She wasn't sure who'd come but she recognized Roger's voice and a bittersweet smile crossed her lips at how protective he sounded. She also recognized the sound of her mother's voice and felt the familiar frustration that always seemed to surface with her.

Closing her eyes, she ignored the fact that she'd been sleeping for about two hours. Roger had carried her into the house and placed her on her bed and before he'd disappeared. Allison hadn't stayed awake for much longer after that. She'd needed to avoid the memories that were swallowing her alive and sleep afforded her that escape.

Tears pricked her eyelids and she buried her face into her pillow when she heard the bedroom door open. She knew who it was, she heard her breathing as she fidgeted in her spot. Something about that seemed like a sick twist...her mother never fidgeted, it wasn't lady like.

"Allison," her mother's voice was strained as though she wasn't sure how to approach this. Allison ignored her and listened as her mother crossed the room. Feeling her hand on her shoulder, Allison tried to shrug it off, but her mom held fast. "Allison?" she said again. "You need to talk to me, baby."

And that was all it took. Her mother never called her baby anymore. She stopped doing that years ago when she'd decided she was too old...too grown up. Allison had always suspected it was because she'd chosen her dad over her mom, but they never talked about it.

She felt her mother sit on the edge of the bed seconds before she felt her gathering her into her arms. She heard her whispered shushes as she brushed her hand up and down Allison's back. "It's okay baby, everything will be okay. You're safe."

Allison buried her face against her mother's chest and cried as all the hurt spilled out of her. She didn't understand where it was coming from, but she felt like a new wound had opened in her heart. She knew she'd allowed Lillian to get inside her.

She needed Lillian to be okay because she needed to feel okay. Allison let the tears roll freely and sobbed against her mother as every bad memory surfaced in her mind. She knew that some of the memories were colored by her heartbreak...and that was what it was. She was heartbroken that she'd been used when she'd felt a bond with Lillian. She'd felt like they were the same in some ways...enough ways for it to matter to both of them.

When she stopped crying, she stared at her dark room and said, "I've hated you for a long time."

Her mother went still, and Allison felt her withdraw slightly, although there was no movement from her. Instead, just her words filled the space, "I know," she said flatly. "You were always your daddy's girl, but it was worse after everything had happened. I hated your father for that."

"Why?" she asked and pulled away slightly so she could see her mother's face. She looked tired and, for the first time, more her age than ever.

"Because he could give you the kindness I couldn't, and I hated that he made me feel weak as well."

"He let you move in with us after the attack and you were out of the hospital," Allison stared at her in disbelief. "You hate a man who put his life aside for his ex-wife so she could heal?"

"Allison," her mother said, and she pushed her away so that there was a space between them. "He didn't do it out of any sense of duty toward me. He helped me because you needed that. If he'd said what he wanted to, about how it was all my fault that Brian...hurt you. After all, I'd had the affair, hadn't I? I was the one who invited Brian into our lives, and I moved in with him after the divorce."

Allison didn't say anything, simply stared at her mother, who continued. "I was a lonely woman and I made a mistake. It cost me my marriage...or what was left of it. You don't remember your dad before everything. Maybe you remember little things about him, but he wasn't there for us. He was always working and when he was home, he was always thinking about a case. He ignored you most of the time and he ignored me all of the time. That is why you moved in with me instead of him when we got divorced because he didn't have time for you."

Ruth stood up and shook her head, "Brian showed interest and I thought that interest was in me, not my daughter."

Tears filled her eyes and threatened the perfectly applied makeup. "So yes, I chose Brian over my marriage because I didn't love your father anymore. But, Jesus, there hasn't been a day that has gone by where I didn't wish that I had chosen my marriage...or, at least, chosen to live on my own without another man in my life. I wish I had chosen for it to be the two of us against the world."

Allison didn't know what to say. She hadn't known any of this. Ruth didn't talk about things...she never did, even before the attack. But she remembered the early days with Brian. Allison had hated him at first. He'd been the man who'd broken up her parents' marriage but then he'd slowly gained her trust and her friendship. He became the guy who said funny things and made her mother laugh. He'd been the guy who brought home gifts and distracted Ruth when her daughter was misbehaving.

Then things had turned strange when she hit puberty. He'd grown darker, always watching Allison as though he was waiting for something. She'd catch him staring at her when she was out in the pool and she'd started locking her door because he always seemed to walk into her room.

After that, he'd become more insistent. The way he would touch her body when they passed one another or were doing something together became bolder as the weeks progressed but she didn't tell her mother. She'd been terrified to tell Ruth that he'd grabbed her breast or walked in on her in the shower, although she'd been positive, she'd locked the door. She thought it was something she was misreading because he would joke and laugh at her discomfort. Like he was just playing another gag.

But he wasn't laughing that afternoon in the spring. Allison had been sitting on the couch while she did her math homework. Brian had walked into the room and stared at her. His eyes had searched her body as he asked, "Where's your mother?"

Allison had said, "Went to run errands. She'll be home in a few hours."

The words had been her mistake because as soon as she'd said them, and he rushed her. Trying to stop the memories from coming back, Allison said, "Didn't you sense that something was wrong?"

"No, I didn't," Ruth said from her spot across the room. She sat down in the reading chair Allison had set up in the corner. "I thought you guys were friends. I didn't think he thought of you as anything other than my daughter. If I had, I would have left him."

Ruth placed her forehead in her hands and curled up on herself. Ruth's voice sounded like it was coming from a million miles away when she said, "But I knew something was wrong when I was out. I had this feeling you were hurt or scared and I turned toward the house, instead of making that last stop at the grocery store. If I had stopped there, he would have finished up and it might have continued for months or even years."

Allison didn't want to relive the story, but she needed to hear what her mother had to say. If she didn't, she knew they would just keep going on the way that they were—Allison hating her and Ruth trying to forgive herself. "I found his car in the driveway and when I walked into the house, I heard you crying. It was such a broken sound that I wanted to run out of the house. And then I heard him grunting and I knew what was happening. Something broke inside of me and I ran into the living room and found him on top of you. Your mouth was bleeding, and you were staring at the doorway with dead eyes. I don't even think you saw me, even though you were staring right at me. And he..." Her voice cracked and she cleared it before she started again, "He was raping you. I didn't see anything else, just him and this red washed over my vision. I threw myself at him and started beating him with my fists. I wanted to kill him for what he did to you...for what he did to my baby."

She stopped and looked at Allison. Her makeup was a mess, which was something Allison had never seen before. "I was screaming and digging my nails into his face as I pulled him off of you. And then he started fighting back and I knew he was going to kill us. I knew there was nothing I could do to stop him."

Allison stood up and took a step toward Ruth, but she stopped...she wasn't sure if she should. The memory of the rape still filled her mind and she could only think of her own pain. "I remember you screaming," Allison said, "That's when I realized you were in the room being beaten by him. I didn't know how you got there or why'd he'd stopped. All I knew was that I had to help you."

She laughed and it was a bitter sound, "I know. I know that you crawled away, in your ripped clothes and aching body. I know that you grabbed the phone and dialed emergency. Then the police were there, and we were safe. Your dad came and moved us both into his house as soon as we were released by the hospital. Then he'd become a saint of a father. Always there for you, always making sure I was okay, but it hurt. It hurt that I couldn't save my own daughter from that man. It stung that I was the cause of that pain. I was angry because you were the one to save us when you called the police. It broke my heart when I heard you crying out at night in fear and it was your father you called for. I hated him for it, and I was so angry with you that you didn't want me. I knew you hated me, and you had every right."

Allison closed the distance between them and collapsed to her knees in front of her mother. "It wasn't your fault," she said as she stared up at her, "I hated you because I saw you heal. I saw you move on to Frank after I graduated from school. I saw you moving forward, and I couldn't."

She took in a deep breath and said, "And I still don't know if I can. I thought I had. I thought that writing what I did, pursuing the career I wanted, was the end result of my healing. But after this, I don't think I've healed fully. I mean, I don't even date...that's how much I have been bothered by this book. It's shattered me completely and I just don't know how I am going to keep going."

Ruth looked at her and her eyes were wide with worry before they hardened into resolve. "You are going to keep going. You're going to write this book and you are going to write your next book. And we," she said, "are going to work on talking to each other."

She sighed and caught Allison's chin in her hand, "I know I didn't protect you back then. I know that I let my own hurt and pain keep me from being a mother to you."

"No..." Allison started but Ruth cut her off.

"I wasn't there, I admit that, and I will never overcome my guilt about that," she said, "But I have never not loved you. I have never blamed you for what happened. That blame belongs to Brian and you have healed...you've just stumbled a little and we are all allowed that from time to time."

Allison could hear the truth in her mother's words, and she could feel them in herself. Despite the stumble, she had a plan for her future. She could see her happiness and it all started with finishing Lillian's book.

"But we need to work on us," her mother's voice broke into her thoughts and Allison searched her eyes before she nodded. "I mean it Allison, I know that we have drifted apart because of everything and your father was there to see you through the tough times, until he passed away, but you have to start trusting me again. I only want what's best for you."

She nodded, "I know, Mom, and my career is what's best for me."

Ruth grimaced before she sighed, "As much as I wish you'd write something else, I know that this is where your passion lies. I will," she paused as though she was having a hard time forcing the words out, "show a bit more support for your career."

Allison smiled at her and felt the memories fading back into their proper places. She couldn't forget completely, but she was able to force them behind thick invisible scars so she could go days without thinking of them.

"That's all I can ask for."

Ruth studied her for a few minutes and Allison realized she was mentally checking a list to make sure she really was okay. "I'm okay now ,Mom," she said, "Honest. I was shaken by the day with Lillian and I was hurting, which made things worse."

"What did she say?"

Allison pulled away and stood up. "I don't want to talk about it, but I know what I'm going to do."

"And what is that?"

"I'm going to do exactly what she asked me to do and write the book. I was going to try to get an appeal for her but if she wants it, she needs to go for it herself. My job is to write the book."

"That's good," Ruth didn't seem surprised about the appeal information so she must have been talking to Ira again.

Taking a deep breath, she said, "Well, just look at me. I'm a mess. I think I should go freshen up and then we'll order something in and stay to eat dinner and watch a movie."

She stood up and Allison felt like she was finally on even ground with her mother. Despite how much they'd been through together, they'd never really talked about that afternoon or what had happened. It had always been hinted at, but they didn't dare talk about it. "Besides," her mother added, "I want to get to know this Roger man. He seems...nice."

Allison felt a blush rise up in her face, "He's still here after all of this?"

"Yes, and he seems quite concerned about you." Ruth grabbed the doorknob and smiled at Allison, "But we'll talk about that later, for now, come out and get something to eat."

CHAPTER TWENTY-SIX

Lillian Ross, pursuant to the verdict as given by the jury, finding you guilty on all counts of the indictment, the defendant is adjudged guilty of two counts of murder in the first degree. I would like to stop for a moment and say that I have watched the defendant throughout this hearing. I have seen a girl who lacks common decency and is not remorseful in any shape or form regarding her heinous crimes.

I see a woman who doesn't care about the hurt that she gave to her own family or the family of Adam Laurent and that alone has affected the recommendations of the jury and the judgment of the court.

Pursuant to the Federal Death Penalty Act, with the jury's unanimous vote, it is the judgment of this court that the defendant, Lillian Ross, be sentenced to death.

May God have mercy on your soul.

~ Sentencing Hearing: People vs. Lillian Ross

It had been two long months since Allison had been in the prison and she'd been working hard on the book. It was coming along but there was still work to get done. Facts had to be checked and cross checked but the long process was coming to an end. Soon it would be in the hands of her publisher.

During those two months, Allison thought about Lillian on a daily basis. She'd called the prison and asked if Lillian was accepting visitors but each time, she'd been told no. It had stung. After everything, to be cut off so easily for one mistake hurt her to the bone. She'd stopped the process of the appeal completely so that Lillian would be happy.

She'd done everything Lillian had asked her and nothing more where she was concerned. But then, out of nowhere, Kai had phoned her and told her Lillian would like to see her. It was surprising and terrifying all at once.

Smoothing down her blue silk blouse, Allison second guessed the casual way she was dressed. Her dark jeans matched the blouse perfectly and she'd allowed her curls to fall naturally down her back instead of keeping them in a bun. Waiting for Lillian, she couldn't help but think of how many things had changed for her since that first meeting.

As if it was perfectly timed with her thoughts, the door clanged open and Lillian stepped through it; as beautiful as ever. She seemed tired but when she looked up at Allison, emotion filled her eyes. She looked...remorseful.

She didn't say anything, simply waited for the guard to be done. Allison looked at Officer Jenkins and said, "How have you been?"

"Good. You?"

"Good. Anything new?"

The woman shook her head. "No same as usual."

She took the shackles off of Lillian and gave her a pat on the shoulder before she stepped out of the room. Lillian had been silent during this whole exchange and had followed Officer Jenkins with her eyes. When the door closed behind the guard, she turned and stared at Allison, her green eyes dark with emotion. "Hi," she whispered.

"Hi," Allison answered and stared down at her hands. "I'm glad you asked to see me."

She dared a glance at Lillian, but she couldn't read the emotion on her face. That she'd gone as far as she could go. Allison felt a thrill of worry, but she stamped it down. Worry for this woman was what had caused it to go bad in the first place. She wasn't going to be worried anymore. "How have you been?" she asked when Lillian didn't answer.

"As well as I can; considering," Lillian waved around her to indicate the prison. "You look well."

Allison couldn't help but smile at that. She felt well. After her breakdown, she'd started back at therapy. Some days were better than others, but she was finally working through a few things she'd never addressed. She'd even started inviting her mom to a few sessions to work through issues they'd had.

"I am well," she sighed, "I've been busy with your book. I'm almost finished it."

Lillian raised an eyebrow and smiled sadly. "I'm glad but that isn't why I asked for you to come."

"It isn't?"

Lillian shook her head and the long locks fanned out around her face. She was still as beautiful as when they'd first met, but there was a vulnerability to her now that hadn't been there before. "No," her voice faded away and she looked around the room, "I wanted to say I was sorry for what I said."

Allison hadn't expected that, and she wasn't sure if she trusted it. "You don't have to apologize. I overstepped my role and I'm sorry."

Tears pooled in Lillian's eyes. "No, don't be. I shouldn't have reacted like that. I just..." Her voice cracked on a sob, "I don't trust when people are trying to help me. There has to be some reason why they are doing it and I don't trust that those intentions are good. I should have trusted you and I'm sorry I didn't."

"It's okay," Allison whispered. Her heart ached for Lillian and she wanted to cross the room and hug her. Despite everything, she still felt that bond to Lillian...she'd pushed it down as much as she could but the moment their eyes had met, she'd felt it again. The world that Lillian had shared was etched across Allison's mind and she would never forget it...no matter how Lillian's story ended.

"I'm sorry that I left without trying to explain things." Allison began but stopped when Lillian held out her hand.

"Don't rehash it. Let's just agree that we are both sorry...for everything."

Allison nodded in agreement and the two women fell into a comfortable silence. Allison wasn't sure what else there was to say. She was still struggling with her ending for the book. It didn't seem right that Lillian would be in prison for the rest of her life until the execution. That could be another ten to twenty years with the way everything moved in this state.

"So what now?" she asked Lillian.

The woman looked at her and gave a watery smile. "I don't know. What do you plan on doing?"

Allison shook her head, "Finish the book and get through publishing. After that, I'm sure there will be another book to start researching but I was thinking about taking half a year off to work through some things."

Lillian didn't ask her what things. They both knew what demons were in their pasts. There was no reason to share and they simply sat together and enjoyed the silence. "Will you find someone to spend that half a year with? Maybe fall in love," Lillian asked wistfully, and Allison wondered if she was thinking of Eric.

"Maybe," she said carefully. Part of her wanted to tell her that she had already found him. Over the last few months, she and Roger had started to grow closer and they were often together when work wasn't calling the other away. She'd never thought she'd become involved with a cop, especially a homicide detective, but they connected so well. They were each other's grounding rod and they knew that the other understood what they were dealing with.

They didn't talk about Lillian anymore, although she was the reason they'd found each other. Allison wanted to tell Lillian that, to thank her, but she wasn't sure how she'd react to the news.

She closed her eyes, steeling herself for the reaction, before she asked, "Have you thought about an appeal?"

Lillian grimaced, "Yes, I've thought about it and sometimes, I think I should go for it. I mean, they couldn't give me a harsher sentence, right?" She laughed but it was without mirth and it echoed sadly around the room.

"I think you should," Allison said quietly and smiled. She reached across the table and placed her hand, palm up towards Lillian.

Lillian stared at the palm and then she reached forward and slid her hand over Allison's. The strange heat that was Lillian radiated through Allison and her blue eyes met Lillian's green ones as they held hands. Allison smiled, tears sliding silently down her cheeks as Lillian gave her a sad smile and squeezed her hand once more. "I'm going to miss you," she whispered.

"I can come and visit you if you want me to," Allison offered, and she meant it. She wanted to stay connected with Lillian. She wanted to help her through her appeal, and she knew she could talk her into it eventually.

"I might not be here when you do," Lillian said, and a fresh tear slid down her cheek.

"You will be here," Allison said with certainty, "You have your appeals, and everything moves slowly. You don't have to worry."

Lillian cocked her head to the side and thought about it. "You're right, everything moves so slowly."

She drew in a shuddering breath, "You know, when I killed my father, I wanted to slice my wrists right then and there. I couldn't imagine living one more minute, but something stopped me. Then, when Adam was finished with me, I chose life again. I called 911 and I shouldn't have. I should have let myself die in the apartment with them. I know that now."

Allison's smile slipped and she glanced at the door with worry. Lillian's voice was flat and hopeless. "But you made it," Allison said, "You survived, and I know you are going to survive this."

"Did I?" Lillian asked her as more tears ran down her cheeks. "I don't think I ever left that apartment. I think they breathed life into a corpse, and she has been walking through the world without any joy...without anything but pain. That's why I didn't fight the charges...at least, not really. I knew I deserved death and I owed it to my father to let him be the hero. I'd killed him, after all."

She tried to pull her hand away, but Allison held it tight. Lillian stared down at the hand and then back at Allison but there was no surprise there, no anger, just a subdued sadness that seeped into Allison as she watched her. "But I had to tell my story. I know that now. It's why I survived, why the execution hasn't come yet. I have been fighting it for so long, but it needed to come out."

Allison shook her head, "There's more to you than just a story. I know. I've seen who you really are. You are beautiful inside and there are no monsters in you. You can still have a life if you go for the appeal."

Lillian smiled at her and it was the saddest smile Allison had ever seen in her life. "I knew from the start how my book was going to end," she whispered, "But then I found out about the appeal and a part of me felt hopeful. It scared me so much and that was why I was so angry with you. How could you make me feel so much hope when there is nothing but death in my world?"

The sob that broke from her was shattering. There was no accusation in her eyes and that was when Allison knew she'd given up. Lillian wasn't going to fight. She was just going to allow the state to execute her because she hadn't expected any other ending for herself. "Lillian, please don't give in to this," Allison cried, and she didn't care that she was. She would get on her knees to plead with her if she could.

"I already have," she said bluntly and then snatched her hand away from Allison. In a fluid motion, she stood up and was pressed against the wall. Her hand clutched something white and she pushed it against her throat. A bead of red flashed on her ivory skin and Allison cried out softly as she realized it was some type of shiv in Lillian's hand.

"Don't," she cried out. She stood up and took a step around the table, but Lillian held the crude razor towards her.

"Don't Allison," she cried, "Don't you understand. This is all that is left of my story. My end...the one choice I can make freely. Don't take that from me, please."

"I can't let you do this," Allison said, and she glanced toward the door, praying that someone was watching through the camera and was alerting Officer Jenkins of what was happening.

"You don't get that choice, Allison," she said sadly, "I can't live with the memories in my head any longer. When I close my eyes, he is there. And I dream of killing him over and over again. I dream of my father killing me. And I can't stop. I try to forget but I can't. He destroyed me and I was never able to glue those pieces back together and I never will."

She sobbed, "But I want you to glue the pieces together for me. I want you to finish the book with the proper end. I want you to learn from my demons and face your own. I want you to live for me, Allison."

Lillian turned the razor against her skin. "I fell in love with you, like a sister and I thank you for giving me a little happiness in the end. I'm just sorry that I couldn't offer that to you."

"NO!" Allison screamed and she lunged toward Lillian as the door flew open. Lillian moved like a serpent, quick and precise, and the sharp, thin metal sliced into her neck; deep and unforgiving as it severed her carotid artery.

Allison caught her as she was sliding to the floor, her weight bearing them both down on the ground. Blood coated her hands, warm and sticky, as she tried to press down on the gaping wound. "No, oh, God! No!" Allison screamed and she turned her eyes toward the door, "Get help! Get help!"

She turned back to Lillian and she could see the light in her eyes. "Stay with me, Lillian," she whispered to her as she pressed her lips to her forehead, "Stay with me and show me that this doesn't have to be the end. Give me that happily ever after. Don't leave me."

Lillian lay still below her, and Allison watched as the light began to fade and then it was gone. Allison sobbed loudly and her chest constricted with grief. She felt, rather than saw, the guards pulling her away from Lillian and she could look at nothing but the beautiful woman who was no longer in this world.

EPILOGUE

Lillian was a good person. I know she was because she helped me escape from a cruel world. I met her when I was thirteen after I'd run away from home. There wasn't a big reason why I ran away but a dozen little reasons. I felt like my parents didn't understand me and that life would be easier if I didn't have the responsibilities, they were giving me.

If I hadn't met Adam Laurent, I probably would have gone home but I met him, and I thought I was special. I thought that he had picked me, out of all these girls, to love. He had me tied up in knots by the end of the first week, let alone the first month when I finally met Lillian Ross, although I knew her as Lily Laurent.

I knew the moment that I met her that she was the one. She was the one Adam loved and I hated her at first, but she cared so much for me. She would sit and talk about my home. She would ask me why I had run away and who was looking for me. She would talk about what the future held for me if I stayed and she didn't sugar-coat it. I knew I would be a whore. They: Adam, her and the other girls, called it the Game. The prostitutes nothing more than human garbage they sold. But Lillian told me I was different, I didn't have to be like her.

Then she started standing up for me to Adam. He'd wanted me to start making him money and I would hear them fighting about it. She would say I wasn't ready and that she didn't think I would ever be ready. And she took so many beatings because of that. I could hear him hitting her repeatedly, but she never mentioned it to me. She hid the bruises, but I saw them sometimes.

During that time, she talked to me about going home and I started to want that more than anything. I knew Adam didn't love me, I knew I was just money to him, but my parents didn't have any money. The amount they'd raised to find me was only ten thousand and he wanted at least fifty to let me go.

Lillian did that for me. She contacted my family. Told them about the reward and gave them the remaining forty thousand for Adam. I didn't know that when she'd told me I was going home. All that I knew was that Adam was getting more money than he should have. I don't really know where she got that type of money but if it was money, she'd saved...somehow...I think she used every penny to send me home.

I found out what she did after I got home, and I knew I couldn't mess up what she'd given me. I went back to school. I straightened out and I went to college to obtain a doctorate in medicine. She did that for me.

I don't know what happened in that apartment, I don't know if she killed those men like the press is saying, but I wanted to write this letter to you to let you know that the Lillian I knew wasn't a cold murderer. She was kind, empathetic and she cared about all the girls who suffered under Adam. She was the person who we went to for everything and she tried to save as many of us as she could.

For that, I will always be grateful to Lillian Ross.

--Anonymous Letter: People vs. Lillian Ross--

The funeral was a held on a beautiful day. The cool air as winter begins to fade into spring was just warm enough for everyone to stand outside as the pastor talked about Lillian in life. Allison smiled at him, but she knew he didn't know who she was. Lillian was just a name he'd been given.

Allison looked around at the people standing in the sunshine and realized that there were a lot of people in attendance. Many were here out of morbid curiosity, but there were some who were here because they had loved the complicated woman. Allison wiped away a tear and rubbed it between her fingertips. It felt like the blood that had covered her hands after Lillian had died.

There'd been a suicide letter in her cell that had talked about how she needed to decide the how and when she would die. She had told Allison she was sorry for doing it with her there, but she wasn't brave enough to die alone. She wanted to die with someone who loved her, and she knew a part of Allison had.

Allison couldn't blame her. She'd wanted to but she couldn't. She'd felt a sisterhood with Lillian, and she felt her loss completely. Roger squeezed her hand and strength flowed from him to her. He'd been there, he'd held her while she'd cried out her heart. He'd listened to her as she worried over whether she'd do what Lillian had done. She knew she wouldn't. She would grant Lillian her final wish and she would live. She would thrive despite the scars that the abuse had left on her.

She glanced across the space and watched Eric as he placed a single lily on her casket. His eyes were red with unshed tears and, when he looked up at Allison, he nodded. She knew what Lillian had meant to him and she knew a part of his heart had died with her.

Looking around, she spotted Hayley, sitting several seats away from her mother. She didn't glance at Irene as she sobbed softly in her seat. Allison stared at the woman who was perfectly made up in her designer clothes. She looked every part the grieving mother, but Allison knew it was an act. She'd wanted Lillian dead a long time ago.

As the service wound down and came to an end, Allison watched as the mourners broke off from the crowd, slowly, one by one. Roger squeezed her hand and when she looked at him, he said, "I'll meet you by the car."

She nodded but she didn't follow, instead, she watched the crowd dwindle down until it was just her, Hayley and Irene. They stood together—the three women who had known Lillian the best. Hayley's eyes were filled with tears as she said, "I heard you were there with her at the end."

Allison nodded, "I was."

"Did she say anything about me?" her voice was wistful, and Allison wished she could say she had.

"No, I'm sorry," she said, and Hayley's eyes filled with tears, "But I know she loved you. I know her biggest regret was that she couldn't come and get you after she'd run away."

Hayley nodded and then she burst into hard sobs. They stood silently as Hayley sobbed and Allison wanted to comfort her, but she knew it wasn't her place. "I loved her," she said, "Even after the murders. I loved her."

"I know."

Hayley nodded and turned to leave but Irene's words stopped her, "Hayley, we need to talk."

Allison stared at the woman and noticed the years had crept up on her. She looked tired and old. No longer filled with youthful beauty that money bought. "There is nothing to say Momma," Hayley said. "After today, I don't want to ever see you again."

Hayley turned toward her mother and her eyes blazed with anger, "You did this to Lillian. You didn't want to see what was happening to us and you let him do all of those things to us. You need to accept what you did for yourself, not for me. There is nothing between us anymore."

She turned on her heel and quickly fled down the hill toward the cars. Irene watched her with cold, dry eyes and Allison marveled at the lack of emotion in this woman. "This is your fault," Irene said to the air.

"No, it's not. I wrote the story. Lillian chose the end," Allison said, and she knew that was the truth. She wondered if Lillian had planned it from the beginning. If she'd known she was going to end her life even before the first memory was shared. "Hayley is choosing to live something other than the control and abuse she's grown up with."

Irene turned her cold eyes on Allison, but she didn't back down. "Hayley was right," Allison said, "Lillian's death could have been prevented if you'd only listened to her. She told you that she was being abused. She told you the baby was William's and you ignored her. Every time William touched her, you were to blame for it because you didn't stop him."

She took a step away from the casket before she turned back, "But your guilt is something you will have to live with yourself. Hayley deserves the happiness Lillian couldn't have. I hope she takes it and never looks back at you."

Irene stared at her in disbelief as she opened her mouth to say something. Then she closed it and, for the first time since they arrived, a real tear slid down her cheek followed by another. Allison nodded, turned back toward the cars and walked down the hill. She walked towards life, just as she'd, silently, promised Lillian she would.

LETTER FROM THE AUTHOR

Thank you for reading The Murders of Lillian Ross.

During the writing of Lillian Ross, I was presented with the problem of Lillian's final outcome. It became clear to me, at a very early stage, that Lillian would choose the path she did.

When faced with this dilemma, I took the time to consider if this was the only option for the character. In the end, I ultimately decided that Lillian's fate was as depicted in the final pages of her story.

However, as a survivor of childhood sexual abuse myself, I wanted to emphasis that I strongly advocate for survival over suicide. While Lillian's story is tragic with a tragic end, survivors do not have to live their own tragic endings.

For that reason, I wanted to take the time to encourage anyone who has suffered abuse, sexual assault or childhood trauma to seek help.

There is a path to not only surviving your trauma but thriving. You are not alone and even in the darkest periods of recovery, there are people who love and cherish you. There are people, such as me, who want you to succeed and value the fact that you are here with us.

But I understand that the path is not an easy one and I wanted to share valuable help lines for you to turn to.

If you are a survivor of abuse, please contact a local support center to help you through the healing process. There are thousands around the world, although I have only been able to list a few.

Canada

- Canadian Association for Sexual Assault Centres: http://www.casac.ca/content/anti-violence-centres

- Assaulted Women's Helpline: http://www.awhl.org/home

- Ending Violence Association of Canada: http://endingviolencecanada.org/getting-help/

USA

- RAIIN: https://www.rainn.org/about-national-sexual-assault-telephone-hotline

- National Center for Victims of Crime: http://victimsofcrime.org/help-for-crime-victims/national-hotlines-and-helpful-links

- National Center on Domestic and Sexual Violence: http://ncdsv.org/ncd_linkshotlines.html

UK and Europe

- The Survivor's Trust: https://www.thesurvivorstrust.org/

- The National Association for People Abused in Childhood: https://napac.org.uk/

- Rape Crisis Network Europe: https://www.rcne.com/links/sources-of-help-for-survivors/

Australia and New Zealand

- Reach Out: https://au.reachout.com/articles/sexual-assault-support

- Safe to Talk: https://www.safetotalk.nz/

South America

- National Association of Adult Survivors of Sexual Abuse: http://www.naasca.org/Groups-Services/SOUTHAMERICA.pdf

For anyone who is suffering from depression, PTSD, anxiety and other mental health crisises, please know that you are not alone. Again, there are many support lines around the world with a multitude of services geared not only for depression but trauma-related depression and PTSD.

Please, if you or anyone you know is suffering from depression or considering ending their life, seek help. There are many trained professionals who will help you through this dark time.

Canada

- Canadian Association for Suicide Prevention: https://suicideprevention.ca/need-help/

- Crisis Services Canada: http://www.crisisservicescanada.ca/

- The LifeLine Canada: https://thelifelinecanada.ca/help/call/

USA

- National Suicide Prevention Lifeline: https://suicidepreventionlifeline.org/

- 2-1-1: http://211.org/

- Crisis Text Line: https://www.crisistextline.org/

UK and Europe

- Samaritans: https://www.samaritans.org/
- Support Line: https://www.supportline.org.uk/problems/suicide.php
- International Association for Suicide Prevention: https://www.iasp.info/resources/Crisis_Centres/Europe/

Australia and New Zealand

- Go Gentle Australia: https://www.gogentleaustralia.org.au/suicide_help
- National Mental Health Commission: http://www.mentalhealthcommission.gov.au/get-help.aspx
- Lifeline New Zealand: https://www.lifeline.org.nz/
- Suicide.org: http://www.suicide.org/hotlines/international/new-zealand-suicide-hotlines.html

South America

- IASP South America: https://www.iasp.info/resources/Crisis_Centres/South_America/

World Wide Hotlines

- Cocoonais Mental Health Hotlines Worldwide: http://www.cocoonais.com/mental-health-hotlines-worldwide/
- Suicide Stop: http://www.suicidestop.com/call_a_hotline.html

I hope that you are able to not only survive the tragedies of the past but to move along the path to truly thriving.

If you have any questions or comments, please contact me at authorsirenavanschaik@gmail.com

Thank you and know that together, we can not only survive but thrive.

ABOUT THE AUTHOR

Sirena Van Schaik was born in British Columbia, Canada, the youngest of four with two older brothers and an older sister. She spent much of her childhood in the wilds of her home province, escaping from a troubled family life.

When she wasn't outdoors, Sirena could be found escaping to the written word. She lost herself in hours upon hours at the local library: researching and reading, before launching into her own stories.

At the age of 18, Sirena moved to Ontario, Canada where she earned her honors degree in early childhood education and later her post-graduate certificate in creative writing. She recently finished her MA in creative and critical writing.

Today, you can find her in London, Ontario, still enjoying both the outdoors and the written world. She resides with her husband, two children and several pets, including her English Mastiff.

You can find out more about her at www.authorsirenavanschaik.ca or on social media:

Twitter: https://twitter.com/sirenavanschaik

Facebook: https://www.facebook.com/Sirenavs

Email: authorsirenavanschaik@gmail.com